Family Matters

Laurinda Wallace

3-Mice Productions

Sierra Vista, AZ

FAMILY MATTERS

Cover Design by Annie Moril

Author Photo by Reign Photography

ALL RIGHTS RESERVED

ISBN: 0985432853
ISBN-13: 978-0-9854328-5-0

DEDICATION

For my husband David, who has encouraged and supported
my writing adventure every step of the way.

CONTENTS

Chapter 1

It was over. Reverend Minders had pronounced the final "amen," and the mourners drifted away from the artificial grass carpet draped against the sides of the open grave, an oak casket suspended above it. White roses, already wilting lay across the top of the casket. Gracie, more than eager to leave the cemetery, hurried over the thick, spongy grass toward her SUV. The rain shower that had pummeled the stained glass windows of the church during the funeral had cleared, but the trees still dripped, the light breeze spattering leftover raindrops on her face. She kept her eyes down, determined not to look in the direction of the gravestone that had her husband's name carved deep into the granite. The small stone next to it with the white lamb on top only doubled her determination. Gracie had parked under the shade of an ancient maple tree at the edge of the cemetery. Now that the sun had finally burnt away the remnants of storm clouds, it was a perfect July day. Punching the unlock button on the key ring, the familiar click was silenced by the unmistakable grating voice of her cousin Isabelle.

"Gracie, wait. Aren't you coming back to the house?" Isabelle's tone indicated it was more of an imperative than a question.

"I don't think so, Isabelle. I need to get back to work. It's pretty busy right now." She pulled on the door handle of the red RAV4.

"What are you talking about? Of course you're coming back to the house for the meal. The family should be together. Mother would have wanted all of us to be together. Your mother's not here, so..."

Gracie saw the look in her cousin's eyes and knew she wasn't getting out of town any time soon. She had no valid reason to skip out anyway. Work was merely an excuse.

"Well, I guess I could come for a few minutes."

Family duty is a powerful force. It makes one do the most uncomfortable and inconvenient things. But she was her family's official representative today, and she needed to hold it together no matter how she felt.

"Good. I'll meet you at the house in a few minutes. I must catch up with Reverend Minders and make sure Tim gave him a check." Isabelle, in her tailored navy blue silk suit and perfectly coifed blond hair, walked quickly to where her husband was talking to the silver-haired, slightly paunchy Reverend Minders.

The rest of the funeral group straggled toward their respective vehicles. She saw Greg and Anna, Isabelle's teenage children, shuffling toward the family Lexus with their heads down. They looked as uncomfortable as she felt.

"At least I'm not the only one," Gracie muttered to herself, turning the key in the ignition. She began to ease the car back onto the street. A pile of papers slid from the passenger seat onto floor and she noticed dog hair clinging to her skirt and a small run in her pantyhose inching over her right knee. Gracie's eyes went back to the street, just in time to jam on the brakes. Mrs. Youngers had blithely backed out into the street without looking. At 80-something, her license renewal should be in question after that maneuver, although she was usually a careful driver around town. Gracie judiciously refrained from laying on the horn and gripped the steering wheel while the elderly woman took an eternity to put the car in gear. Even with the meandering sedan in front of her, it took just minutes to arrive at her cousin's house on Crescent Lane. The church ladies were setting out huge amounts of food on the picnic tables lined up family-style in the front yard. Fortunately, the canopy of sugar maples kept it all in the shade. Isabelle's flower gardens were lush and well-tended—like everything in Isabelle's house. Foxglove, iris in a rainbow of colors, red roses, and delphiniums were only a few of the flowers banked against a fieldstone retaining wall on the side lawn. The grass was cut to perfection, and no dandelions invaded the golf course-like turf. It looked like Tim had set up a putting green at the back of the property. That must be new. She hadn't noticed it when she'd stopped by a couple of weeks ago.

Helen Smith, one of the blue-haired church ladies, smiled and waved to Gracie as she parked on the street.

"Come and get it, honey," she called, as Gracie came up the walk. "We've got lots today."

"It all looks great."

"It is, so help yourself."

Gracie decided she'd just load a plate and stand. If she sat at a table, she'd never get away. Cousins, along with a raft of great aunts and uncles, were descending on the house, chattering and eyeing the food with anticipation.

She piled potato salad, a thick slice of cold ham, and a warm roll on her plate. The crowd was finding places to sit and getting down to the business of life after a funeral. Todd Graham, a distant cousin and the local investment guy, grabbed her elbow to steer her toward a table. She sighed and readied herself for his usual sales pitch. He was fit and dressed in an expensive suit. Todd's thin mustache and darting eyes always made her uneasy.

"Gracie, it's good to see you."

"You too, Todd, but I don't have much time. I've got to get back to the kennels."

"Come on, Gracie, what's the hurry? I don't see you much around town. You're always working."

Gritting her teeth, she pasted on an insincere smile.

"Well, running a new business is pretty demanding; you know that. It's vacation time, so we've got a steady stream of dogs. Plus we've got some new kennel helpers, and someone has to keep an eye on them."

"They'll be fine for a couple of hours. We need to talk since you don't ever return phone calls."

She absently nodded while Todd droned on about how he could improve her investments, and how she needed a man to look after her interests now that Michael was gone. A claustrophobic moment passed over her as she saw that she was completely surrounded by relatives with more headed toward her. A few stopped to pat her shoulder or give her an awkward hug. A few comments made her cringe. "How are you holding up, dear? This must be hard for you." Her pantyhose were suddenly very hot, the run was creeping up her thigh, and she felt sweat trickle down her back. She needed to get back into jeans and a T-shirt.

Gracie caught a glimpse of her Uncle Stan, Isabelle's father, picking up another longneck bottle. He'd been conspicuously absent at the committal service in the cemetery. Gracie noticed two brown bottles unsuccessfully hidden in the perfectly trimmed yew hedge. There were probably several more stashed in there. Isabelle must be steamed about his absence, and now she could be upset by his choice of beverage in front of the church crowd.

"I should talk to Uncle Stan. You'll have to excuse me, Todd. Nice to see you." Gracie blurted out, patting his arm. Todd stopped mid-sentence, nodded, and shrugged. Before she made it to the porch, he'd already latched onto the church organist. Isabelle was talking to the Minders, plus the few dignitaries from the village, and hadn't yet noticed her father.

Gracie admired the furniture on the huge wrap-around porch of the Craftsman-style house. The dark wicker had deep cushions in a tropical green and brown print. It looked much more inviting than the flagstone steps Uncle Stan was sitting on, but Gracie joined him there.

"Uncle Stan, how are you doing?" She sat down gingerly, trying not to snag her hose in any more places.

"I'm OK," he mumbled, looking down at the half empty beer bottle. He twirled it between his fingers. "Shirley and I had a lot of years. I hope she's better off today. She was awfully sick the last few months." He sniffed and wiped his eyes with his shirt sleeve. "Life's been pretty hard."

"I know, and I'm so sorry. It's been tough on everybody and especially Aunt Shirley. She was always busy, and being in the hospital or stuck in bed wasn't for her."

Gracie was trying to think of anything else kind she could say about her Aunt Shirley. Aunt Shirley had been a difficult woman on her best day. Life with her had always been tough, but she had made everyone's life a true misery these final months of her battle with cancer. Nurse after nurse had quit or been fired in three months' time before she'd ended up in the hospital the last few weeks. Gracie guessed there was probably a great deal of relief in this day for her uncle...in a lot of ways.

"Wouldn't you like a little something to eat? You probably haven't eaten all day. Gotta get something in your system that's...uh, well, solid."

"Isabelle will give me what for, so I'd better." His voice trailed off.

"Let me get you some potato salad, ham, and that great three bean salad."

He waved her off, staring at his feet. Gracie quickly made a plate for him and hurried back, relieved to see that Isabelle and Tim were still engaged with the cousins from Castile and the mayor. Stan picked at the carb-laden funeral food and made an attempt to eat.

"Come on, Uncle Stan, let's keep Isabelle happy today, and you'll feel better too." She smiled at her weary and well-worn uncle. His greasy gray hair was slicked back, and the creases in his face told the story of an unhappy life. He managed a lopsided smile as potato salad slid off his fork and onto his white shirt. Gracie grabbed a napkin and handed it to him.

"Thanks, Gracie. I think you're the only one left who'll even talk to me anymore. Isabelle just yells. Tim never says a word, but gives me that look. I don't think Isabelle wants the kids to talk to me. Guess I've made a mess pretty much of my whole life, well at least since..." He cleared his throat. "You've had it pretty tough, too, with Michael and all."

Hot tears sprang to her eyes and she blinked furiously to stop them. Gracie didn't want to talk about Michael today. The cemetery and the service were hard enough. The ache of missing her husband of 16 years, 2 months and 4 days wasn't over yet.

"I'm...well, I've gotta go. If you need anything, just give me a call." The perfunctory farewell to the bereaved rolled easily off her tongue. She couldn't believe she was saying it. People had said it to her, but she'd bet the farm they hoped with all their might she wouldn't call. And she hadn't.

"Thanks, Gracie." He finished the potato salad and washed it down with the last of his beer.

"I'll say goodbye to Isabelle and then head back to the kennels. It's really crazy right now."

She patted her uncle's shoulder and saw that Isabelle and Tim were headed toward the food tables. She started down the sidewalk, but Uncle Stan grabbed her arm. His beery breath hit her face; his watery brown eyes suddenly intense.

"Listen, Gracie, I've got some things I want you to have. Some books for your collection and some things that are family stuff. I want you to have it now. You know, before Izzy gets in a tizzy."

Gracie grinned. Isabelle hated being called Izzy. Isabelle hadn't ever handled teasing well, and it was entertaining to rile her.

"Sure, Uncle Stan. I can pick them up sometime. Maybe tomorrow or Saturday."

"No, I've got 'em here in my car. I want you to take them now. I don't want her trying to stop me. You know how she is."

She patted his stringy, darkly tanned arm.

"OK, sure. Well, let's put them in my car, and I'll tell Izzy goodbye." She winked and smiled reassuringly at him. He headed for his ancient blue New Yorker just a touch unsteadily.

Gracie waved to Isabelle and Tim, and started walking toward their table to keep attention away from her well-marinated uncle. It looked like an official head table with the mayor and his wife and some distant cousins, whose names Gracie couldn't remember, along with Albert and Gloria Minders. Greg and Anna were standing under a nearby tree in an attempt to be inconspicuous. When Gracie surveyed the tables that were filled to capacity, she wondered, how did I end up with so many relatives? Her mother's side of the family must have multiplied like rabbits. She steeled herself for the closing remarks with Isabelle.

"Isabelle, I'm headed back to the kennel. Let me know if there's anything you need help with. Mom and Dad are so sorry they couldn't be here. There was just no way to get them back in time from the cruise. And Tom couldn't get leave to come back from Afghanistan."

Isabelle ignored Gracie as she continued picking at her plate. She wiped her mouth carefully with a white paper napkin and glared at Gracie.

"I understand about Tom, but it's unbelievable that Mother's own sister couldn't be here today. It's not right, but we couldn't put off the funeral for another week. I just hope Aunt Theresa can still enjoy the cruise." The sarcasm and stinging judgment were all too apparent in her voice. Tim placed his hand over his wife's, which she quickly shrugged off. A wisp of the perfect blond hair blew out of place; Isabelle dabbed one eye with a tissue, avoiding Gracie's gaze.

Gracie sighed. "Of course you couldn't put it off. Mom didn't want you to wait, and I'm sure she's having a difficult time dealing with..."

Isabelle cut her off.

"Well, she'll have to carry that burden for a long time. I can't understand such selfishness. Why would they go on this cruise when mother was so ill?" Her voice was sharper yet.

Gracie bit her tongue. Tim put his hand on Isabelle's shoulder and looked at Gracie with silent pleading. Everyone shifted uncomfortably at the table, concentrating on their plates of food. Isabelle pulled away from her husband's touch. Gracie felt anger flush across her face.

"Well, it's their 45th anniversary, and it's been planned for over a year. They couldn't have known your mother would die three days after they left."

The low hum of conversation at the surrounding tables ceased. Isabelle's smoldering eyes shot Gracie a look that could peel paint. Gracie pressed clenched fists against her legs. Resisting an urge to slug her cousin, she spoke evenly.

"I'm headed back to work. Bye, everyone. Isabelle, I hope you'll forgive my parents."

She prayed that she wouldn't break a heel or fall as she walked away with what she hoped was a somewhat dignified exit. Her mother would be proud she hadn't given Izzy the tongue lashing she so richly deserved. If she had, it would surely be all over town by this afternoon. This was enough family drama for one day.

Uncle Stan was struggling with a large brown paper grocery bag that was full of books, sitting on the backseat of his car.

"Let me help you with that," she offered, thankful that she could feel the color draining from her cheeks.

"Uh, thanks. I guess it's heavier than when I put it in here this morning."

Gracie quickly lifted the bag from the backseat. "Thanks, Uncle Stan. I'm sure these will be a great addition to my dog library."

A 1953 AKC breed book was on top. It was actually a year that she was missing in her collection. He was always finding old dog books for her in yard sales and musty used bookstores. Maybe this gift was a good one after all.

Stan opened the left rear door of her small SUV.

"Don't you dare," she grumbled at the precariously overfull bag and dumped it on the seat. She gave Uncle Stan a quick hug. He immediately blew his nose on a rumpled white handkerchief. Sliding into the driver's seat, she waved to him and drove with eyes focused on the street and not on the tables of relatives who watched her departure with interest.

Chapter 2

Things at the kennel were frantic, and Gracie was greeted by dogs barking furiously. Beth, one of the new kennel helpers, chased a yipping Scotty through the corridors. Gracie had known things would be dicey with this new teenage help, but it was much worse than she'd anticipated.

"He took off when I tried to put him on the grooming table," Beth tried to explain, continuing the chase.

"Never chase a dog, Beth. It only makes it worse. Come on back and let's do this right."

Gracie grabbed her treat bucket and gave a couple of biscuits to Beth. She took a handful herself and sat down on the cement.

"Angus, sweetie—treat!" she called.

Angus turned to her familiar voice. He stopped running and sat panting, looking obstinate.

"Come on, Angus. Treat!" Gracie sweetly coaxed him.

The independent Scotty cocked his head to one side and decided that it was time for a treat break. He trotted over to where Gracie had laid the liver-flavored biscuits next to her. He greedily chomped one and began wagging his tail.

"You little tyrant, let's get you bathed and back home before you think up something new."

Gracie stroked his head and scooped him into her lap. After scratching Angus' ears and giving him a kiss, Gracie lifted the stocky Scottie up to Beth.

"Give him the treats and get him back on the bath table, just like I showed you. This time, make sure he's leashed."

"Right, uh, I'm sorry, Mrs. Andersen. He's really quick, and he just took off." She looked miserable.

"Well, no harm done. Just get him bathed, dried, and brushed out. His mom is going to be here in an hour. I really need to change."

"OK." She held the dog tightly and headed back to the grooming room.

Gracie looked down at her once white blouse and black skirt. Angus had covered her with his inky hair, and paw prints were evident on her pantyhose and shirt.

"Ugh. I hate dressing up, and here's another reason not to," she complained to herself.

Her business partner Jim Taylor came around the corner as she got up from the cement floor, which had also left its mark on her skirt. He grabbed her hand as she struggled to balance on the uncomfortable high heels.

"Glad you're back," he laughed, obviously enjoying her disheveled appearance. "The phone's ringing off the hook, Alison lacks customer service skills, Beth seems to be afraid of dogs, and our shipment of dog food hasn't been delivered yet."

"Great. I'll be right back, as soon as I get out of these clothes. Oh, and you'd better check on Beth. She's bathing Angus."

"Right, Chief. You really need to get the phone situation with Alison figured out when you're changed."

Gracie scowled, mentally berating herself for hiring Alison. That's what happened when you were desperate for a kennel helper. Whining and a bark from the backyard came from Haley, her black Labrador. Opening the gate, she stooped to scratch behind the dog's silky ears. The dog raced to the kitchen door. She trotted inside and slurped water from the dish by the door while Gracie quickly stripped off the ruined shirt and skirt on the way to the bedroom. Haley with dripping jowls stood in front of the French doors to the patio.

"All right. You can go back out."

The dog loped to the back of the fenced yard, sniffing the base of a white birch. Gracie shook her head, smiling. Continuing to the bedroom, she tossed the clothes into the wicker hamper, and ripped the shredded pantyhose off and tossed it into the wastebasket.

The shower felt good, washing away the stress of dang-it-all family togetherness. Isabelle was at the top of her list for frustrating relatives. She could push Gracie's buttons like no one else. However, she should cut her some slack. Her mother had died after all and they'd been really close, maybe closer than she was with her own mother. But Izzy was a perennial problem. It had been that way since they were small, playing in the sandbox. Somehow the grit had always ended up in Gracie's underwear.

Within minutes, she was zipping up her jeans and pulling on a T-shirt. The jeans were a bit tighter than she preferred, but it seemed that it was harder to lose any pounds lately. She wound her long curly red hair into a manageable damp twist and clipped it in place. She dabbed on a little green eye shadow and some mascara. Her reflection in the mirror looked fairly presentable. Attaching a small walkie-talkie to her jeans, she opened the French doors, calling for Haley. The big Lab bounded in, tail wagging dangerously close to a floor lamp.

"Come on, let's go back to work, girl."

Alison held the phone away from her ear, tossing brown bangs from her eyes, sighing as she absently thumbed through the reservation book. She finally put the phone back to her ear.

"Mrs. Greene, I said we don't have anything today. We're really busy today and can't..."

The girl looked up as Gracie came through the doorway. Gracie motioned for the phone and grabbed the book.

"Well, uh, I can have you talk with Mrs. Andersen. Here she is," Alison said sullenly. She sat with arms folded in the black task chair while Gracie leaned over the desk studying the grooming schedule.

"Sylvia, what can we do for you? Uh huh...a shampoo and nails clipped. No problem. We've had a cancellation at 4:00 today, so bring her on in. OK then, see you in a bit." Sylvia Greene had four Silky Terriers and was already one of Milky Way's best customers. One or two of Sylvia's dogs always needed grooming.

She handed the phone back to the teenager. "Alison, you forgot to cancel the Dunbar appointment at four. I told you about that before I left, didn't I?"

"Yeah, I guess so. It's been so crazy here, I can't remember everything. Mrs. Greene was pretty mean. I shouldn't have to take that." She sported an unattractive pout for emphasis.

"Well, could it be something you said?"

"I don't know." Alison's voice became whiny.

"We're here to accommodate our customers. We also need to be accurate with the appointment book. If you have a problem or a question, you ask. Understood?"

"Yeah, I guess so. She talked like she was better than me and... "

"It doesn't matter what she said. It matters what *you* said. Take a break from the phone and go help Jim clean out runs. I'll handle the phone for a while." Gracie's jaw tightened to control her temper.

"OK."

Alison stalked away, her jeans riding a little too low for Gracie's taste. Alison also had flip flops again instead of sneakers. How had she missed that this morning? It was one more thing to take up with her later. Gracie sat down at the desk to scan the rest of the day's appointments. Three more dogs were coming in, and two dogs were being picked up. Business was really beginning to...well, get busy.

She was dialing the number of Hillside Feeds when she heard the growl of their old truck pull into the driveway.

Another problem solved. She grabbed the portable phone as she headed out the door. Harry jumped down from his truck with his usual grumpy look and handed her the invoice.

"I know I'm late. Your order's all here," he snapped. "Unload in the barn?"

"Thanks, Harry. In the barn is fine. I'll get Jim to help."

She heard Harry mumble something about Jim, but couldn't quite make it out. Oh, well. Harry was always griping about something. He was cantankerous and knew all the farm gossip. He was glad to share it with anyone, so Gracie had learned years ago to be circumspect in what she said to him. The truck backed around to the storage barn, a 20 by 20 red metal building, with the façade of an old-fashioned barn, complete with white cross buckles on the doors. She slid the walkie-talkie off her waistband to call Jim.

"Harry's here."

"All right, I'm on my way."

"Thanks."

The gravel crunched under her sneakers on the way back to the reception area. Three cars were turning into the entrance. She recognized Angus' mom, Susan Whitford, in her black Ford Taurus in the lead. She hoped that Beth had finished the bath in time. The phone rang as she waved to the cars and opened the Dutch door to reception. She was greeted with the stressed voice of Bill Stephens. He was freshly divorced and now the single dad of Bob and Buster. Canine parenting was a whole new experience for him.

"Do you have room for the boys for a couple of days? I've got a business trip that just came up. Have to take red-eye to Chicago tonight."

"Tonight and tomorrow night?"

"Yeah. I'll pick them up on Friday morning."

"Let me check to make sure. Same run or separate?"

"Same run is fine."

Gracie moved the mouse to get the screensaver off the monitor. She scanned the availability.

"You're in luck. We have one run left. Just be here before five."

"Thanks. I'm on my way right now."

Susan practically filled the doorway. Wearing a khaki blouse that strained against her girth, she buttoned the bottom button and then unbuttoned it again. Her short hair was slate gray, and she had a surprising bird-like voice.

"Is Angus ready?" she chirped.

"Let me check."

Gracie hurried to the grooming area to see how Beth and Angus had fared. Although Beth was soaking wet, Angus was clean, slightly damp, and smelled un-doggy for the moment.

"Good job, Beth." Gracie grinned at her. "His mom is here. I'll take him up."

Angus acted like a perfect gentleman as he danced on his tiny terrier feet on the way to the front.

"Here he is, ready to dig more holes."

"Don't you know it! I can't keep him clean for more than a day or two. I'm sure we'll be back next week. Here's the check."

Gracie tucked it in the cash drawer, while two other customers came in with their dogs, a Boxer and a Collie mix. She grabbed the walkie-talkie and called Alison to take the dogs to their runs.

"Cody and Barney are looking good," she said, glancing away from the computer screen.

"Cody's doing pretty well for an old guy," Sharon Dean, mom of Cody, replied with a smile. Cody was a regular already since Sharon and her husband often traveled on business.

"I wish Barney would just get calmer," said Chris Bingel through gritted teeth, hauling the strong Boxer away from Cody.

Barney was always anxious to make new friends, and his greetings were a little too enthusiastic. He was all boy and had to sniff everything in sight. At least he wasn't lifting his leg, so far.

Gracie finished checking out their vaccination records and declared them both legal.

"Any changes in feeding, or do either one of them need medication?"

Both women shook their heads.

"How about a playtime?"

"Cody could use one exercise time a day."

"OK, we can do that. What about Barney?"

"He needs at least two a day. He'll be bouncing off the walls without it."

"Got it." Gracie entered the feeding and instructions into each dog's record. "We'll keep him occupied. I wonder where Alison is. Well, let me take them one at time."

Gracie took off Cody's collar and slipped the light lasso lead over his head. Sharon handed her a plastic bag with chew toys and gave Cody a quick hug.

"See ya, Gracie. We'll pick him up Monday morning."

"Will do. Come on old guy, let's get you settled. I'll be right back, Chris."

Alison was still nowhere in sight. Where could that girl have gone to?

She walked Cody, who was slightly arthritic, but a cheerful soul with a constantly wagging tail, past the line of barking and excited kennelmates.

"Here's the new guy," she said as she opened the run near the back door. She slipped off the lead, locked the run, and headed back to get Buster. She looked through the window of the back door and saw that Jim and Harry had finished unloading the food and were now shooting the breeze. Alison wasn't with them either. The girl was probably going to have to find a new career path. She didn't have time for irresponsibility. Gracie prided herself on great customer service, and Alison wasn't catching on to the corporate culture. Beth appeared from the grooming room as Gracie walked quickly back to get Barney.

"Beth, I can't find Alison. Help me get the next dog to run 22."

"Sure, Mrs. Andersen. Is it a big dog?"

"He's a nice big Boxer, very friendly."

"I don't want him to get away. Maybe I should watch you take him." A look of fear flashed over her young pretty face.

"You'll be fine. Just get him leashed properly. He's pretty strong. Builds upper body strength."

"Well..."

"You'll be fine. You need to get used to handling all kinds and sizes of dogs. Barney's a friendly guy, just strong and energetic." Gracie was trying with all her might to be patient and encouraging. She was kicking herself for being so anxious to hire extra help when business had gotten hectic three weeks before.

Barney sat panting with hind legs splayed out. Drool was running down both sides of his jowls from all the excitement of kennel smells. Gracie grabbed a more substantial leash from the desk drawer and handed it to Beth.

"He's a handful," said Chris as she unclipped Barney's collar, and Beth quickly slipped the thicker leash over his broad, fawn-colored head. Barney gave Beth's hand a slobbery lick.

"I've got him, run 22, right?" Beth said as Barney pulled her through the doorway.

"That's right. Thanks, Beth."

"New girl?"

"Yeah. That's Beth Simmons, Frank and Evie's daughter."

"Wow, she's all grown up now. Hard to believe. Well, I've gotta run. We'll pick up Barney on Tuesday."

"See you then. Have a good trip."

"Thanks." Chris waved as she closed the door and walked toward her shiny red Mustang convertible. Gracie remembered Chris saying that it was her mid-life crisis car, and she was enjoying every minute in it. She was surprised that Barney was an approved passenger. Maybe the thrill was past, as was her own enthusiasm about Alison. Now that the customer traffic had slowed down, she needed to find the girl. Gracie strode down the hallway on the office side of the kennel. She paged her again on the walkie-talkie.

"Alison, my office right now."

Static crackled in reply. Gracie peered through the wooden blinds on her office window to check the back parking lot. No car. Great, she thought. Where had she gone?

Jim was now standing in her doorway.

"Looking for this?" He held up a walkie-talkie by the antenna.

"Is that Alison's?"

"Sure is. She handed this to me about five minutes ago and said she couldn't work in such an awful place. I wished her good luck in life." His grin was infectious, and Gracie had to smile.

"Well, this isn't the place for her then. We're pretty mean, but we've had all our shots. Her leaving saves me from having to fire her."

"She's got a lot to learn about the real world."

"Don't we all. I guess we had our moments." Gracie's dark brown eyes flashed with humor. "Especially in high school. What were we thinking?"

"We were lucky we didn't get thrown out of school. I still have a few deep dark secrets about pranks though."

"Whaddaya mean? I thought I was in on all those."

"Not the Limburger in the typewriter in Jarvis' class. No one ever found out it was Michael and me. We were pretty lucky on that one."

"You're kidding. Michael never said a word. That room reeked for a week. The janitor couldn't even get the smell out with that awful disinfectant he used in the bathrooms. I think they ended up throwing out the typewriter."

"Yeah, we didn't think they'd have to do that. Mr. Jarvis tried to scoop it out with his hands and ended up trashing his suit. It was great." Jim's eyes twinkled with fond remembrance.

"Mr. Jarvis was a strange man. I think he developed a tic while I was in his class." She smiled, momentarily lost in a high school daydream. "I guess we'll be looking for another kennel helper. Any ideas?"

"Nope. Well, wait a minute. What about your cousin's son, Greg? Is he working this summer?"

"I don't know. He's a pretty good kid. I'm not sure I want family around though. Isabelle will be pumping him for information every day. I don't need that right now. I'll ask Beth and see if she knows anyone. I'd better get back up front." She sighed and shoved her hands into the tight pockets of her jeans. "We'll talk about this after we close, OK?"

He nodded and said, "Sure thing. We'll get it figured out. I'm off to feed the inmates," he teased.

Gracie walked quickly to the reception area, where Beth was waiting for her.

"I got the big dog in OK. He's really strong."

"I knew you could. Just be confident. You're the one with the leash. Let them know you're in charge."

"Right. I think I'm getting the hang of it." Her cheeks were flushed with exertion, but her eyes shone with new confidence. "Did you find Alison?"

"Alison decided she wasn't cut out to work here after all, so I guess it's just us to finish up today. Do you have any friends looking for work?"

"Gosh, I think everybody's working now. Hmm, maybe Casey needs a job. She adjusted the limp ponytail still damp from the bathing adventure with Angus. She attempted to brush the dog hair stuck to her jeans and white T-shirt. "Let me check, I might know somebody."

"Have them call me or stop in. I'll interview them right away. Same pay as you're getting and every other Saturday."

"OK. I'll ask around."

"Thanks."

Gracie looked up to see Bill Stephens pulling in with his two Cocker Spaniels. He was true to his word. Two other customers followed right behind him to pick up their canine children.

"Get ready for some more transporting here. We've got a bunch at once. Let's get the Cockers settled and then get the dogs from runs 1 and 6."

"Sure. Are they big dogs?"

"Nope. These are all small guys."

The rest of the afternoon went without incident. It seemed that Beth was probably going to work out, maybe. Gracie locked the front door at exactly 5:30 and pulled the cash drawer out from the desk. She methodically rubber-banded credit card receipts, checks, and bills separately to count in her office. Jim came in the backdoor, whistling some unknown tune in a minor key.

"Hey, Jim, I'm closing up here. Let's talk, if you've got time."

"OK, I'll meet you in the office."

Gracie put the cash drawer back in the desk and took the day's receipts. Jim had put the coffeemaker on, and the aroma of her favorite coffee filled the small space. Haley opened one eye from her bed in the corner, scratched half-heartedly, and stood. She shook, jangling tags. Jim gave her a scratch under the chin.

"You read my mind. I need some serious caffeine." Gracie gratefully sank down into her high back swivel chair and threw the bank bag in the half-opened bottom drawer.

"So do I. It's been an interesting day."

"No kidding. First the family funeral and that stress, and then the Alison incident."

Jim poured two mugs of coffee, handed one to her, and sank down on the recliner and pulled the lever. Gracie noticed the weariness in Jim's handsome, chiseled face as he closed his eyes and let out a sigh. She took a sip of the strong coffee, leaned back in her chair, and put her legs up on the desk. Haley found a rawhide chip from a basket and settled next to the desk, chewing intently.

"Was the funeral that bad?"

"No. Not really. Nice service and everything, but Isabelle and I got into it, as usual, at the dinner. She's pretty mad at my parents for going on that cruise." Gracie massaged her forehead, trying to still the dull ache that threatened to become a full-blown migraine. She rummaged in the top desk drawer for some ibuprofen. "Mom and Dad knew there was a good chance Aunt Shirley wouldn't be around when they got back. They had said their good-byes. Aunt Shirley had even told them to keep their plans, which was surprising too." She washed three pills down with a swig of coffee.

"So, what's Izzy's problem?" Jim's strong fingers tapped the white ceramic mug.

"You know how Isabelle thinks. The world revolves around her, and we're all supposed to toe the line when it comes to family obligations."

"Well, let your mother take it up with her when she gets home. You shouldn't have to defend your parents; they can talk to Izzy." Jim finished his coffee and brought the recliner upright. "Are you OK? You know, dealing with the funeral and all?"

"I think so, but it was harder than I thought. I miss Michael so much, Jim." Her voice caught, and tears began to slide down her cheeks. She quickly grabbed a Kleenex and blew her nose. "Sorry. I guess…"

Before she could finish, Jim had jumped from the recliner and pulled her from her chair. His arms were wrapped around her, crushing her with one of his famous bear hugs.

"Hey, Chief, we all do, but you're gonna be fine. You *are* fine."

When he released her, Gracie took a deep gulping breath. No matter how busy she kept herself or how hard she tried to forget, the tears still came.

"Maybe. Thanks for putting up with me."

"No problem. But we need more responsible help in here. Any ideas?" Jim was all business again and settled himself back in his painfully ugly plaid-upholstered recliner.

"Beth's going to ask around to see if any of her friends need a job. I should have anticipated summer vacations and that we'd need extra kennel helpers."

"I guess your research was on the money, literally, with this business. I'll check at the restaurant in the morning when I'm having breakfast. The kids working there usually know who's looking. Midge'll know for sure. She knows all."

Gracie rose from her chair and refilled her mug. "Great. Well, I'm beat. Are you going to check on everybody and set the alarm?"

"Sure thing, Chief. I'm beat too." Jim set his mug by the coffeemaker, and headed down the long kennel corridor. The yips and barks of greeting were constant as he made sure everyone was settled for the night.

Gracie turned off the light, shut the office door, and headed for the house. She passed the RAV4 and suddenly remembered the bag of books. The books wouldn't unload themselves. She might as well do it now. With shopping tomorrow, she needed the back seat space anyway. Grabbing the tattered brown paper bag, she carefully balanced it in her arms without spilling the coffee. She made it up the steps to the kitchen and into the house. She set her mug on the counter and the bag onto the floor.

Haley, in her usual exuberant manner, bounded in ahead, already at the French doors.

"Hey, girl, ready to take a run?"

As she opened the doors, she saw Jim's Explorer pull out of the rear parking lot and head down the road toward Route 39. The sun was just beginning to lower in the sky. The long summer days were welcome after the endless darkness of the Western New York winters. Gracie sucked in a deep breath of early evening air filled with the heavy smell of corn tassels in the distance. Sweet corn would be ready soon. That meant the church's annual chicken barbecue and corn roast were just around the corner. Summer was a wonderful time of year in the Genesee Valley. The third cutting of alfalfa was underway, the corn was high, tomatoes were beginning to ripen, and the rolling hills were lush with green. The brown heads of several does popped up from the tall grass in the field beyond her lawn. Crickets were warming up to chirp their evening song, and Gracie took another deep breath of the cooling night air. Thankfully, the headache was beginning to relent.

Grabbing Haley's mostly shredded squeaky toy, she threw it to the back of the large fenced backyard. Haley joyfully charged after the beloved toy and brought it back in seconds, her thick tail waving wildly. After a few more minutes of retrieving, Gracie called it quits. The dog went directly to the water bowl in the kitchen and slurped down most of it. She lay panting on the cool tile floor, water dripping off her shiny black jowls.

"I'm going to get the mail. I'll be right back." Haley looked up with sad eyes as Gracie made a quick exit out the kitchen door to the mailbox. When she returned with the armful of mail, the trail of brown paper bag pieces went all the way through the kitchen to the living room. Books were scattered in another trail leading to the patio doors. Haley was nowhere to be seen.

"Haley," Gracie growled with hands on her hips.

Haley innocently appeared from the bedroom with her pathetic sock monkey squeaky toy, looking with mild interest at the path of destruction.

"When are you ever going to grow up?"

Haley merely wagged her tail and lowered herself into the plush dog bed in front of the fireplace. Gracie bent over, picking up the trail of dog books and romance novels, and spotted it. It was one of those diaries you poured your heart out into while you endured high school. It had a worthless clasp that supposedly locked. The cover was pink striped. The clasp wasn't locked; it was broken. She opened it quickly, burning with curiosity. Maybe it was Aunt Shirley's or Isabelle's diary. It was not. It was Charlotte's. Gracie felt her heart jump and sink all at once. Uncle Stan had given her Charlotte's diary.

Chapter 3

Charlotte. The cousin, who had been like a sister. The beautiful, sweet, but rebellious cousin, who was the exact opposite of her sister Isabelle. Her life was cut short on a rainy October night. Run down by an unknown and supposedly drunk driver. Gracie's stomach churned in the remembering. She had answered the phone in her dorm room at SUNY Geneseo and listened in disbelief as her father told her that her cousin was gone. Gracie had driven home that night without remembering how she got to Deer Creek.

She turned back the cover again and looked at the neat feminine script that read: "Charlotte Browne, Private." The first date in the diary was three months before her death. Charlotte had been just 18, two years younger than Gracie. Could it be more than 20 years ago? The freshness of the pain stung and surprised her. Too many memories had come back today. She couldn't look at the diary tonight. She slammed the cover shut. An unwelcome emptiness and sadness crept over her. Haley's wet nose on her hand snapped her back to the present.

"OK, Haley, I know it's supper time." She laid the small book on the coffee table and went to the kitchen to scoop out Haley's kibble.

Gracie shoved a plate of leftover casserole in the microwave, hoping that it was less than a week old. She picked at the chicken and pasta, while Haley happily crunched. She turned on the floor fan to move the humid air in the living room. Haley strolled over and flopped in front of it, panting and looking expectantly at her mistress.

Gracie bent over the oak coffee table and fingered the striped cover once again. Tears began rolling down her face.

"Why do the ones you love the most get taken? Why doesn't the hurt go away? Why am I the one who has to keep going?"

Her heart was pounding, and the tightness in her chest took her breath away. Gracie took slow, deep breaths, attempting to slow her racing heart. Haley got up, whined, and circled her solicitously. The medicine cabinet was not far away. The prescription bottles stood in a neat row. The pills slid down easily with the glass of water. It had been a horrible day, and she wanted to find the painlessness and nothingness of sleep. Gracie waited for the familiar warmth of the pills to relax her. Collapsing on the bed with two pillows propping her head, she could only hope the pills would work long enough for her to get a few hours of sleep. Haley jumped up next to her and stretched out comfortably.

Chapter 4

Haley's barking woke a disoriented Gracie. The heaviness of prescription-aided sleep clouded her reactions. She suddenly realized that the kennel's security alarm was going off, and frantic barking competed with the piercing sound. Haley ran back and forth to the kitchen door while Gracie struggled to get her bearings. She slipped on worn leather huaraches and managed to clip a leash on Haley. The attempt to control the 80 pounds of excited dog and the adrenaline rush quickly cleared her foggy brain. She grabbed the phone and punched in 9-1-1.

The dispatcher told her the security company had already called in the alarm and to wait for a deputy to arrive, but that wasn't going to happen. The dogs' safety was her priority. She held Haley's leash tightly and stepped out into the steamy and raucous night. The motion lights were on in the yard, and the lights on the backside of the kennels shone starkly against the darkness. Haley's hackles were raised, a steady growl rumbled from her throat. The alarm continued its ear-splitting tone.

"Good girl. Everything is all right. Let's check it out." Gracie was trying to convince herself and Haley. The window of the front door to the reception area was broken, and dagger-like pieces of glass were scattered on the floor inside. She didn't want Haley to cut her feet. Giving a quick jerk on the leash, she firmly told her to sit and stay. Haley, amazingly enough, did both. Shoving the door open, she kicked back some glass, and stumbled to the wall behind the reception desk to the security keypad. She punched in the code, and immediate relief hit the night air. Barking decrescendoed, and Haley was whining and poking her face into the reception area. The quiet was quickly shattered by the sound of sirens. The sheriff's department was certainly speedy tonight. Like most law enforcement agencies, the Wyoming County Sheriff's Department was chronically undermanned. There must have been a deputy just down the road to respond this fast. Gracie grabbed Haley's leash as she turned to exit the reception area. The dogs began howling again as the wailing got closer. The Lab pulled at the leash, then sat to offer a sympathetic howl, her head raised skyward.

Two sheriff's cars pulled into the driveway, scattering gravel as they came to a stop by the entrance. The sirens were cut, but the lights in the grills pulsated in the darkness. The barking once again began to subside.

"Mrs. Andersen?"

"Yes, deputy..."

"Stevens, ma'am."

"Thanks for coming. I haven't checked on the dogs yet. I need to make sure they're OK."

"Hold on. Before you go any further, let Deputy Williams and me check out the premises. We want to make sure it's safe."

"OK. I need to call my partner anyway." Gracie stuck her free hand in her back pocket, realizing her cell phone was in the house.

"Who'd that be, ma'am?"

"Jim Taylor. He's just up the road a couple of miles. Near the old Taylor farm on Valley View Road."

"Yeah, I know the place. We'll need you to go through the building with us after we check it out." He pulled out a long flashlight from his Crown Vic, and the other deputy joined him. Gracie nodded and watched them go into the reception area. She pulled Haley back into the house, grabbed the kitchen phone, and dialed Jim's number with shaking hands. She looked at her watch: 3:30. It had been a short night. The phone rang three times before he mumbled into the receiver.

"Jim, I need you over here. We've had a break-in."

"What? Are you OK, Gracie?" His sleepy voice was suddenly crisp and alert.

"Yes, I'm fine. The sheriff's department is here."

"On my way." The phone line went dead.

Gracie watched the inside lights go on in the corridors, and the barking once again took on a frenetic tone. She couldn't wait; the dogs needed her. She quickly made her way back to the runs. Haley heeled perfectly as Gracie carefully picked her way through the reception area. The dog stepped gingerly, as if watching for glass. Her tail thumped against the doorway.

"I need to get these dogs calmed down," she called through the corridor.

"Looks like whoever broke in is gone. You can go through," Deputy Stevens shouted over the din.

She let go of Haley's leash, allowing her to wander up and down the corridors, reassuring her canine buddies. The long training as a therapy dog was coming in handy tonight. Gracie began checking each run to make sure the dogs were all accounted for and OK. With Haley's calming presence and Gracie's confident voice, the kennel began to settle. Satisfied that everyone was fine, she quickly walked back to the reception area. The deputies stood surveying the mess. Papers were scattered everywhere, and the desk drawers were opened.

"Oh, no, they took the money." A sick feeling swept over her. "No, wait a minute. I put it in my office. I need to check."

Deputy Stevens followed Gracie to her office door.

"We didn't see any damage in here, but you need to make sure." The door was unlocked and Gracie anxiously hurried to open the bottom desk drawer. The bank bag was still there. She unzipped the bag. The cash and checks appeared to be intact. All were still rubber-banded as she had left them. Gracie let out a grateful sigh.

"Is it all there?" asked Deputy Williams. He had his clipboard and was scribbling quickly.

"I'm not sure, but I think so." She felt like throwing up with relief.

"You usually leave all that money in an unlocked desk drawer?" Deputy Williams scowled officiously.

Before Gracie could answer Jim appeared in the doorway slightly out of breath. His shirttail was half in and half out of his jeans. His black hair was sticking out at various angles.

"Everything OK? Did they take anything?"

"We're checking that out right now, uh Mr. Taylor, right?" Deputy Williams said glancing up from jotting on a thick leather-covered notepad.

"Right."

"They didn't get as far as the office. I forgot to put the bank bag in the safe. So we're pretty lucky, even though I was stupid."

"I guess the alarm must have scared them off. Are the dogs all right?"

"They're fine. Haley helped get them settled down. Where is she anyway?"

At the sound of her name, Haley came out of the bathroom with a wet face.

"Not again. Why do you drink out of the toilet?" Gracie was embarrassed and disgusted all at once.

"I had a dog that did the same thing, Mrs. Andersen." Deputy Stevens was obviously amused at Haley's bad behavior. He had removed his hat to smooth back his blond military cut, which didn't need smoothing. He was tall, extremely fit, and had that quarterback look. He looked to be in the 40ish age range. Deputy Williams was just the opposite; he was short with a bubble of a stomach that threatened to pop out of his tightly buttoned uniform. He'd removed his hat and was wiping sweat off a shining wide forehead with his white handkerchief.

Gracie sat down in her desk chair with a heavy weariness, her head in her hands. Haley pushed her wet muzzle into Gracie's lap.

"Looks like you were pretty lucky tonight. We've had quite a rash of these robberies. They usually get some cash or electronics." Deputy Williams scowled at her and finished writing on the metal clipboard.

"Ma'am, I'd recommend you remember to put your money in the safe," Deputy Stevens gently rebuked Gracie.

"I agree, Deputy. It isn't my usual practice. Kind of a tough day. That's my only excuse."

"Well, mistakes happen. I guess, except for a little damage, it's not too bad." Deputy Stevens adjusted his hat and put his flashlight back in his belt.

"The dogs are OK. That's the important part," Jim put in. "Do you have any leads on who's involved in these break-ins?"

"We're still investigating. They've cleaned out some businesses in Perry and houses at Silver Lake. Hey, Jack, I'll walk around the property one more time with Mr. Taylor. Why don't you check out around the house with Mrs. Andersen and make sure she's all set. We'll get back to you in the next day or two if we have any developments."

"Thanks." Gracie involuntarily shuddered at the thought the thieves might be in the shadow of her house.

Deputy Williams pulled out a long flashlight and swept his arm signaling Gracie to go ahead. Gracie grabbed Haley's dragging leash and carefully led her back through the trashed reception area.

"I guess I've got my work cut out for me tomorrow."

"Yes, ma'am." Deputy Williams was all business as he began walking the perimeter of the house, peering into bushes and checking windows.

Gracie waited with Haley near the kitchen door for the deputy to finish. Her T-shirt was damp, but her throat was dry. Haley sniffed the night air and growled softly. Her hackles were raised.

"It's OK girl. We're all right." Gracie was not convinced, but she tried to sound sincere.

"Looks like you're clear to go in. Don't see any signs of entry or footprints around windows." The deputy was mopping his forehead again.

"Thanks. I really appreciate your help. You'll get me a copy of the report, won't you?" She hoped her voice was steady, unlike her hands, which were still shaking. She needed to regain some control over her emotions and the sick fear roiling in her stomach.

"Just call and request it from Administration tomorrow, ma'am. It should be ready. You're pretty lucky tonight. Take care now and lock your doors." He headed for the flashing lights of his cruiser.

The night sounds were back to normal. The peepers were singing with enthusiasm. Her shoes were squishy from the heavy dew on the grass. The three men continued talking in low tones near the police cars as she unclipped the leash and stepped back into the bright kitchen. It looked like Jim could handle the rest. Haley immediately drank deeply from her water dish. With all the commotion, Gracie was glad the nearest neighbor was a half mile away. She didn't feel like fielding any noise complaints. Lightning flashed in the distance. It looked like a healthy thunderstorm was brewing. Maybe the rain would clear some of the humidity. She filled a small water glass at the kitchen sink and downed four ibuprofen tablets.

Curling up on the sofa, she watched the storm move in from the west. Haley maneuvered onto the sofa and put her head on Gracie's feet. A light knock on the kitchen door roused her. Jim stuck his head through the door.

"Want me to sleep on the couch? Won't be a problem."

"Go on home, Jim. I'm not going to sleep anyway. Haley's on guard."

"OK, if you're sure Chief. I boarded up the window and reset the alarm."

"Thanks, Jim. You're the best."

Gracie heard the door shut and the Explorer's disintegrating muffler start up. There was no more sleep for tonight. Dawn was just around the corner, and the workday would start. Lightning cut across the sky again, and the rumble of thunder followed as Gracie and Haley stared out the window.

Chapter 5

A bleary-eyed Jim sat at the restaurant counter contemplating the stack of pancakes and three sausage patties that had just been put in front of him. It was exactly what he needed. Well, that and a gallon of coffee. He drained a second cup of coffee and then went to work on Midge's famous buckwheat pancakes with real maple syrup. The village DPW workers were lined up on red vinyl stools for their early coffee break. Several dairy farmers were also among them with varying degrees of cow fragrance. Between the manure, coffee, bacon, and hot sweet roll smells, Midge's was a veritable buffet for the nose.

"Hey, Jim. What's this about the kennel getting broken into last night?" Jason, one of the village guys asked.

"It's true," Jim answered, taking a bite of sausage. "Didn't get anything that we know of. Made a mess of the front office though."

"There's been a rash of break-ins. Especially around Silver Lake," Corky Lockwood added. Corky was the manager of Raven Ridge Dairies. He was short with flaming red hair that swept around his forehead in an attempt to cover a balding head. "Saw it in the paper this morning. They've been takin' computer stuff and TVs."

"Lots of the cottages over there are empty quite a bit of the time, so it's probably easy pickings," Jim replied.

The rest of the crowd on the stools put in their two cents of how the sheriff's department should be tracking down the crooks, while Jim finished off the pancakes. When he looked up again, Midge was filling his coffee cup. He gave her a grin.

"Pancakes are top notch as usual."

Midge grinned back. "Of course. Why wouldn't they be? Did I hear you got robbed last night?"

"Well, they broke in. Didn't get anything that we could see. Broke the window in the door, messed up the desk. It's a good thing we've got the alarm system. Scared 'em off before they got to the back office where the money was."

"That's good then. Gracie holdin' up OK?"

"I guess so. It was a pretty tough day with her Aunt Shirley's funeral and then that. We'll see how it goes."

"Looks like Isabelle's doing all right." Midge nodded her head toward the dining room. "She's already working on some fundraiser with Gloria."

Jim groaned inwardly. "I'm sure she is. She's probably heard everything out here too."

"Probably," Midge quipped. The woman of indeterminate age put the coffee pot on the counter. She was scrawny with a smoker's gravelly voice.

"Sheesh. I'd better get out of here before she sees me." Jim slapped down a $10 bill. "Keep the change."

He never made it off the stool. Isabelle in a cloud of sweet perfume was on him like a duck on a June bug. Why women thought it was necessary to douse themselves in bug spray was beyond him.

"Jim! Is it true? You and Gracie were robbed last night?"

He sighed. "Yup. They didn't get anything though. Made some mess, but we're in business today."

"How absolutely awful! The kennel is so isolated. You're a perfect target for something like that. You'd better get some sort of security."

"Well, we do have..." Jim wasn't allowed to finish.

"I'd better check on Gracie. She wasn't herself yesterday anyway. She really upset my father. Plus we have some family business to discuss." Isabelle drew herself up, her blue eyes determined.

"I don't think that's necessary. She's got her hands full with work. Gracie's fine. We're looking for some more kennel helpers, so..."

"You need more people at the kennel?" Gloria Minders joined Isabelle at the counter.

"Well, yeah. Business is growing pretty fast and one of our summer helpers quit yesterday. We need a couple of people, maybe more."

"That's good to know, Jim. I might be able to help. You may not have heard, but I'm heading up a new organization called Second Chances. We're working with parolees and probationers to find them jobs to get back into the work force and be productive again."

"Uh, that's great," Jim was unsure of how to extricate himself gracefully from two determined women. He edged nearer the door.

"Maybe I could call Gracie later about it," Gloria offered.

"Maybe. You know, I really need to get going. I'd call before you come, Isabelle. Like I said, Gracie's pretty busy."

Isabelle brushed some stray crumbs from her pink jacket. "Family doesn't need to call, Jim."

His cellphone sang out "Jeremiah was a Bullfrog," which got a chuckle from Corky and a glare from Isabelle. Grabbing the cell from his belt, Jim almost ran out the door. He sat in his truck and watched Isabelle drive away. He held the phone to his ear, even though the caller had apologized as a wrong number and hung up. Gloria gave him a wave as she walked across the street to the parsonage that was behind the church. The brick church with the gray steeple sat on the corner of Main and Park. Lydia Wheeler, the organist was just getting out of her car in the church parking, carrying an armload of music. Gloria stopped and chatted with the rotund Lydia before crossing the driveway into her yard. Jim started the truck and eased out onto Main Street. He thought he caught a glimpse of a man darting through the bushes that separated the church and the parsonage. That was a little strange, but maybe it was the Reverend. He didn't think so though.

Chapter 6

The phone jangled incessantly, dogs were barking, people were picking up and dropping off their dogs. Gracie determined that she absolutely needed help today. There were only so many things she and Jim could do. They had certainly miscalculated at how the business would grow in three months. It was great, but it was also a disaster. Another kennel helper and a groomer were necessities. She finally made it into the office to call Marian Majewski, a retired groomer. She'd run into her a couple of weeks ago in the grocery store. When she'd asked Marian about working again, there had been some interest. She'd beg Marian on her hands and knees to help them for at least a couple of weeks until a more permanent arrangement could be made. The phone was ringing. She crossed her fingers that Marian would answer.

"Hi, Marian. This is Gracie Andersen at Milky Way. I'm wondering if you're still interested in working. We could sure use you here even if it's temporary. We're swamped, and I know you could get the grooming schedule under control."

"I've been thinking about calling you," Marian laughed. "Honestly, I've been bored out of my mind, Gracie. I don't think I'm settling into retirement like I thought. I'd love to help out. I miss those fur balls and their sloppy kisses."

"Any chance you could start today?"

"You bet. Let me tell my husband and I'll be there in about an hour or so."

"Wow! Great! Thanks!" Gracie breathed a sigh of relief.

Some real help was on the way and so easily too. Marian's reputation with the dog community was impeccable. She could shampoo a dog and clip his toenails before he knew what hit him. She could put the most hyper or distressed dog at ease in minutes. She had a reputation for being the same way with people. Marian would certainly get the grooming organized.

Gracie was turning people away because there just weren't enough hours in the day. Having Marian around would give her some breathing room which meant she wouldn't be doing the books late at night—maybe.

Beth informed her she hadn't been able to locate a friend, so the search for a kennel helper continued. Gracie had a call in to the security company to get them out to check the system. She had also spent a lot of time soothing the fears of customers who were concerned about the safety of their dogs. Word of the break-in traveled at lightning speed—in town and out of town. Her head stilled ached, but was manageable. Gracie had just finished another call, calming an anxious dog owner, when she saw Isabelle's Lexus pull in. At least Jim had been able to give her a heads up when he'd arrived a few minutes ago.

"OK. Here we go," she said to a sleeping Haley. The dog opened one eye, groaned, and went back to sleep. "Thanks for the support, girl."

She met Isabelle in the parking lot to discourage sitting or lingering of any sort.

"Hi, Isabelle. What brings you out so early?"

"I heard about the break-in. I just had to see if you were all right."

"I'm fine, except for lack of sleep. The sheriff's department is working on it."

"I don't have a lot of confidence in them. They're not known for their investigative skills. You should have a security system or something, you know." Isabelle was impeccably dressed, as usual in a cropped pink jacket with delicate cream piping and black capris. Her hair and makeup were perfect. Only the hardness in her eyes belied her appearance.

"We have a security system. That's why they took off so fast. There have been several burglaries lately and the deputies are working on it—like I said."

"We'll see. But I do need to talk to about the things Father gave you yesterday. Can we go inside?"

Gracie's stomach began to churn. There was no way Isabelle was getting anything from her, at least right now.

"I really don't have time Isabelle. I'm short staffed and..."

"Well, this is family business. Father didn't consult me before he gave you that bag of books and whatever else."

"Isabelle, it was just some old dog books...nothing exciting. I haven't even had a chance to go through it yet." She felt a twinge of conscience, but she wasn't going to mention the diary.

"I'd be glad to do that for you and then pass along the appropriate books to you."

"I'm sure Uncle Stan..."

"Father is not himself and hasn't been for years. I—"

"Listen, Isabelle, I'll go through them soon, and let you know. I really don't have time to deal with this right now. I can't believe you're concerned about some old books. Don't you have more important things to do, like your mother's probate?"

Isabelle was not mollified, but Gracie could see a hint of defeat in her cousin's face. "You're right, Gracie. I do have an appointment with Mother's attorney today. There's so much to do. I'll call you tomorrow."

Gracie knew Isabelle wouldn't let this little tug-of-war go. She'd just regroup. But Gracie wasn't in the mood to be pushed around. Two could play this game.

"I'll look forward to it." Gracie stood with arms folded across her chest and saw with satisfaction the flicker of uncertainty in Isabelle's eyes.

As the Lexus spun its way onto the highway, Jim called to Gracie from the front door of the reception area. He had just finished replacing the broken panes of glass.

"Hey, Chief, way to handle the extremely difficult cousin."

"Well, maybe, but it's not over. Isabelle won't let this go, especially after what I found in that bag."

"Some dark family secret?"

"Something interesting, but I haven't had a chance to look at it yet. I'll show you later."

"It's a date." He picked up his toolbox and headed toward the storage barn. "Hey, I'm headed to Midge's for a coffee break. With any luck I'll snag a kennel helper. Maybe Gloria Minders can help us out."

"I'm not so sure about that avenue, but I hope you can find someone. I do have Marian Majewski coming today. She'll whip the grooming into shape. Bring me back a sweet roll, if you can remember. I need a sugar boost."

"Not to worry, Chief. Sweet roll and a warm body. No problem."

His noisy Explorer headed back out to the highway.

Chapter 7

Gracie was navigating a sparkling Westie named Jasper in the holding area, when Jim strode in with a thin gray-haired man, in worn jeans and a gray T-shirt. He slouched a little and kept his eyes on the ground.

"You'll never guess who I ran into, Chief." Jim was grinning from ear to ear and looking pleased with himself.

"I have no idea, but I'm sure you'll tell me." Gracie's first impression of Jim's companion didn't warrant a smile.

"This is Joe Youngers. You know, from high school. He was a year ahead of us. You remember him on the wrestling team."

Gracie looked closely at the man. He did look vaguely familiar.

"Joe. Really? How are you?" From what she could remember, Joe had been a troublemaker in high school and had continued his bad behavior into adulthood.

"Hey, I'm doin' OK. I've had some tough times, but I'm gettin' myself straightened around."

"Glad to hear that. So where are you living these days?"

"I'm staying with my grandmother, Bea Youngers. She's helpin' me get back on my feet."

"Mrs. Youngers. Oh, right. She was at my Aunt Shirley's funeral. She's such a nice lady." Her near collision with the white-haired matron ran through Gracie's mind.

"Yeah, well..." he looked down at the ground again, shifting his feet and looking more uncomfortable.

"Joe's looking for work and he can start today. He's willing to do whatever we need. I ran into Gloria Minders and she got me hooked up with her new program, Second

48

Chances. Joe, here, was at the top of the list for employment when she called over to Warsaw."

"I thought you were..." Gracie caught herself; the stubborn look on Jim's face warned her that he'd already made up his mind about Joe. Clearing her throat and attempting to adjust her attitude, she said, "Well, why don't we let him fill out the paperwork first? I've got a couple of things to talk to you about and then we can see."

They needed help, but Gracie's gut told her that Joe wasn't the kind of help they needed. Jim avoided her eyes and put his arm around Joe's shoulder, steering him to Gracie's office.

"Sure. Hey, Joe, come into the office, and I'll get you set up. Regulations, you know."

"No problem. I know all about 'em."

Jim pulled the employment packet out of the second file drawer and got Joe settled at the Gracie's desk. Joe began studying the application.

"Take your time, Joe. I'll be right back."

"Hey, thanks Jim. I don't think it'll take too long." Joe began to scribble in his information.

Jim stepped around the corner to the grooming room, where Gracie stood with her hands on her hips.

"What are you doing?" she hissed, trying to be quiet enough so Joe wouldn't hear. "He's been in a lot of trouble hasn't he? He was always in trouble in school. He got kicked off the wrestling team if you remember."

"Yeah, well, some, but he's trying to get his life on track. He needs a break. He's been picking up odd jobs at dairy farms. This would give him a real second chance. You know, like this program is all about. Your pastor's wife recommended him. What more do you want?" She wasn't sure what more she did want, if Gloria was sure of him.

"Do you know what kind of trouble he was in?"

"Yes. He said something about a couple of burglaries and reckless driving. DWI, I think. Gracie, sometimes you've gotta take a chance on somebody. My opinion counts here too. We're partners, 50-50. Remember?"

"Yeah, well we were just robbed. I'm not feeling too generous toward thieves." Her volume was steadily going up.

"Calm down, Chief. Your red hair is showing. As I remember, you hired the last two."

Gracie frowned, but slowly nodded her head. He was right. She'd made a bad hiring decision on Alison.

"I'll watch him like a hawk. We'll give him a week. If you still feel the same way, I'll tell him it's not working out. Remember, we need the help."

"All right. I'm not in favor of this, but..." Gracie saw Joe round the corner into the grooming room.

"Hey, I don't want to cause any trouble. If you don't think..."

"No problem, Joe," Jim reassured him. "Gracie and I've got it worked out."

"Thanks. I really need the job and I won't disappoint you. I love dogs, so I think this will work."

Gracie bit her tongue savagely and managed a smile.

"I sincerely hope so, Joe. Let's take a look at your paperwork."

She felt a flush of anger creep up her neck as she struggled to maintain a modicum of professionalism and some Christian charity. She could hear her mother's voice about being kind to those less fortunate. Jim smiled in his maddening way with blue eyes twinkling, and strode down the corridor.

"There's a sweet roll for you in reception," he called over his shoulder without looking back. "Sweet roll, warm body, mission accomplished."

It's not quite that simple, Gracie thought as she glanced over Joe's application and withholding forms.

"I hate to ask, but are you on probation or something?" She was sure her tone was sharp, even though she was trying to soften her voice.

"Yeah, I've got three months left. I'm not going back for another round of prison. I want to get on with my life. I've screwed up enough. I can give you my probation officer's number. I have to go counseling with Second Chances every week, so I'll need to make those appointments. I hope that won't be a problem." Joe's voice had a tone of sincerity that Gracie hesitantly began to believe.

"That shouldn't be a problem. We'll give this a shot. Jim will show you the ropes. Can you start at 7:00 during the week? We open at 7:30."

"Sure. That's good with me. We always had to get up early to milk when I was a kid. 'Course, prison...' His voice trailed off.

"Great. Can you work Saturdays and some Sundays?" Gracie quickly filled in the silence.

"I've got nothing else going on. I want to keep busy."

"OK. We'll find Jim and get you started." Gracie adjusted her ponytail and made another attempt with her attitude while she led Joe down the hallway to the runs. When she glanced out the window, she noticed an old pickup driving slowly by the Milky Way entrance. The driver was craning his neck to look at the kennels.

Chapter 8

It was late when Gracie began to go through the books. She was freshly showered, with her damp auburn hair clamped securely off her neck. A few stray curls fell around her tanned and lightly freckled face. She was tired, but felt relaxed for the first time that day in the comfortable knit black shorts and green tank top. She sat cross-legged on the living room floor in front of the fan, with Haley snoring softly next to her. There were a few interesting old dog books. Along with the 1953 AKC book, there were two books on retrieving and field work. Where did Uncle Stan find these? She flipped through the musty pages. Old newspaper clippings were tucked here and there through each book. She carefully unfolded the well-creased paper. All of the clippings were reports on the hit-and-run accident that killed Charlotte. The final rectangle she unfolded was the obituary.

Charlotte Browne—age 18, died from injuries received in a tragic accident on October 24, 1992. She is survived by her parents, Stanley and Shirley Browne of Deer Creek, New York, along with her sister, Isabelle. She is also survived by an aunt, Theresa Clark (Robert), and cousins, Thomas and Grace Clark. Charlotte was a senior at Letchworth High School. She was active in cheerleading, drama, and the band. She had been accepted to the University of Buffalo for the 1993 fall semester. Friends may call at the Harwood Funeral Home on Friday, October 28th, from 2:00 – 4:00 p.m. and 7:00 – 9:00 p.m. Funeral services will be held at the Deer Creek Community Church on Saturday, October 29th, at

10:00 a.m. The Rev. Albert Minders will officiate. Burial is in Hope Cemetery.

The rest of the books were romance novels from her aunt's library. Aunt Shirley was known for her voracious reading of romance novels. Uncle Stan knew that Gracie had no use for the genre. He must have used them to hide the good stuff. She carefully checked through the pages to see if any other clippings were hidden away. A half page letter dropped from the last novel. It was written in neat, slightly slanted script. There was no signature, and Gracie quickly scanned the contents.

It's over, so you'd better deal with it. Don't call me again or you'll be sorry.

It wasn't Charlotte's writing; it looked like a masculine hand. She grabbed the diary that was close at hand and compared the handwriting. She was correct. The writers were different. The note certainly sounded ominous. Who would have threatened Charlotte? She kept looking through the thick novel for any more hidden treasures. Sure enough, there were two more: Charlotte's death certificate and a bad photocopy of a police report. The weariness that Gracie felt earlier was erased as she began to lay out the pieces of paper on the floor to try and make sense of Uncle Stan's disturbing gift.

She put the tea kettle on, set out a large white ceramic mug, and tossed a teabag in it. While the water was heating, she double-checked each book for any other papers that might be tucked inside. Nothing. The kettle whistle sounded, and she quickly shut off the burner and filled the mug. Carefully picking up the fragile papers, she placed them on the dining room table to take a closer look. Haley began to growl and was on her feet. Headlights flashed through the front windows. A car was turning into the driveway. She pulled the curtains back on the kitchen door. It was Isabelle.

"Of all the nerve," Gracie said to Haley. She swept up the clippings and other papers and dumped them in a kitchen drawer. Isabelle was already ringing her doorbell.

Gracie answered the door with her hands on her hips.

"What's the problem, Isabelle?"

"I know it's late, Gracie, but I must have a look at the books Father gave you."

"You've got to be kidding. What are you so worried about? He didn't give me anything that affects the value of the estate."

Somehow Isabelle was now fully in her kitchen, scanning her counters.

"Well, there were books that Mother promised to me that had great sentimental value, and I need to know if he gave them to you."

Isabelle had now seen the books lying on the living room floor. Gracie stood in her way as Isabelle attempted to step around her.

"Wait a minute. Your dad gave these to me. He's the next of kin, not you. I'll go through them first. I'll let you have what I don't want."

"I'm the executor of the will. I'm in charge."

Charlotte's diary was on the coffee table, and Gracie could see that Isabelle's eyes had locked onto the distinctive cover.

"What's that? That looks like..." She strained to peer over Gracie's shoulder. You have no right to have it."

Gracie thought frantically. "Sorry, Izzy. That's my diary from high school. I've been looking over old pranks that I pulled with Michael and Jim."

"You're lying."

"How dare you! You need to leave—now."

"You'll hear from my attorney tomorrow."

"Great. You know the number."

Both of them were breathing heavily and glared at each other with stormy looks. Isabelle turned abruptly and slammed the door. Haley's hackles were still raised as the Lexus sped out of the driveway. Hands shaking, Gracie grasped the mug and watched the taillights disappear in the darkness. Haley thrust her cold nose on Gracie's leg and whined. "It's OK, girl. The extremely difficult cousin is gone."

What was going on? Uncle Stan had done her no favors with this gift. It was proving to be upsetting and really putting Isabelle over the edge. What was so important in the papers and the diary? Gracie locked the kitchen door and threw the deadbolt. She checked all the other doors before she settled onto the sofa with the papers. An unknown drunk driver had taken the life of a beautiful girl. There was no satisfactory ending to the story. What was the point in revisiting it?

She read through each clipping. The newspaper reports were standard. They seemed to be of no value. There was a paragraph though that caught Gracie's attention.

Police continue to investigate the hit-and-run death of Charlotte Browne. A witness to the accident has given authorities a partial plate number. The vehicle is believed to be a late model sedan, dark blue or green with a plate number beginning with WY. Anyone with information is encouraged to contact the Wyoming County Sheriff's department.

Why hadn't the police found the car? Who was the witness? Gracie remembered vaguely that a teenager out past his curfew said he saw someone driving erratically on Mill Street that night. He hadn't been named, though. Charlotte had been walking home from a babysitting job on that windy and rainy October night. She'd stepped out to cross Main Street at the corner of Mill Street and was hit by a car that came swerving around the corner of Mill. Charlotte had been left in the street, with broken bones and internal bleeding. Either a car passing by or the witness had found her and called for an ambulance. Gracie couldn't remember. There hadn't been much else to go on from what she recalled. It had all been so shocking. Maybe her parents knew more. They'd be home in another three days. A family pow-wow was certainly needed by then.

The death certificate was painful to read. The cause of death was multiple traumas, a broken leg, and internal bleeding. Then Gracie's eyes widened. A notation at the bottom of the certificate stated the decedent had been approximately eight weeks pregnant at the time of her death.

Gracie's mind was whirling with questions. Char was pregnant? Who was the father? Why hadn't Char told her? No wonder Izzy was in a tizzy. This was a major smear on the family name. Aunt Shirley had certainly been a champion at keeping this tidbit a secret. She started reading the faded police report, hoping for more answers. The bad copy was hard to make out. It looked like parts of the report had been redacted. Why? She needed to see Uncle Stan and soon.

She stood looking out into the dark backyard, holding the warm mug. Turning back toward the kitchen counter, she saw the light blinking on her message machine. Might as well find out who had called.

There were two messages. One was from Deputy Stevens. He wanted to set up a time to talk to her about the robbery. Why hadn't he called the kennel number, she wondered? The other call was from Gloria Minders. Gracie remembered Gloria's phone calls after Michael's death. They were weekly for several months. She had taken Gracie to lunch regularly and found a counselor for her. Gloria wanted to make sure Gracie was all right after the terrible robbery and was willing to help with anything she might need. Gracie smiled as she listened to the solicitous message. It never took long for the Deer Creek grapevine to swing into action. There would probably be someone with a casserole at the door tomorrow. She could just imagine the conversations at Midge's counter. She would return those calls in the morning. Tonight she needed to start piecing together the information Uncle Stan had given her.

Grabbing the paper treasures from the utensil drawer, she spread them across the dining room table. There had to be some reason he was dredging up all of this pain again after 20 years. Was it because Aunt Shirley was dead? She needed to see what Charlotte might have written in her diary. Gracie quickly undid the clasp and started reading.

July 30, 1992 Still raining today. The pool closed early, so I didn't get many hours in. Saw Lancelot and Morgan Jr. Babysitting tonight at the Grangers. Maybe I'll see L on my way.

August 2, 1992 Great day at the pool. I'll have a perfect tan to start football cheerleading. It's only a couple of weeks away. It's worse at the castle. There are always more rules. I'm tired of it all. Babysitting tomorrow night at the Grangers. The kids are good and so is the pay AND I'm out of the castle.

Nothing seemed out of the ordinary so far, just normal teenage griping, Gracie thought. Aunt Shirley's rules had been mind-numbing back then. Anybody except Isabelle would complain. She thumbed through more entries in August.

August 21, 1992 Not feeling well today. Lancelot stopped by. Morgan Sr. was there too. I wish school was over with and I was starting college. It would be simpler. I can't breathe here anymore. There's no one I can talk to except to Dear Diary.

August 23, 1992   Fainted at practice today. Heat, I guess. The coach had to call the castle of course. Big fuss over nothing. Still feeling sick, but it was pretty hot today. Lancelot left for the crusade. Can't wait for fall break. I miss him already. Saw Galahad. He makes my head spin. Not sure how I can handle all of this.

Who were Lancelot and Galahad? What was the King Arthur story all about? Morgan Sr. and Jr.? Charlotte was apparently trying to keep a few secrets herself. She remembered Char life-guarding at the Village pool that summer. Gracie had been working at the Deer Creek Veterinary Clinic, answering phones and learning how to be a vet tech. It had been a hot and hectic summer, but there had been at least a couple of family picnics with the Brownes and the Clarks. She couldn't remember anything especially eventful at either one. Charlotte had been boy crazy in high school, but she couldn't remember if there had been anyone really special.

Of course, Aunt Shirley had kept a tight rein on her daughters. Isabelle was dating Tim, but that was an approved relationship. Tim was the oldest son of the banking family of Deer Creek. They'd established the Deer Creek Bank and had run it for more than 100 years. Aunt Shirley was pleased that Isabelle was attached to wealth and the local gentry. Back then, Uncle Stan had been a successful lawyer. His law practice was booming. He was the bank's attorney, handling its corporate matters, mortgages, and foreclosures. Uncle Stan was also counsel to several of the other towns and villages in the county. His partner handled probate and real estate.

Aunt Shirley had been pretty impressed with her position in the community. She was on the library board, the Deer Creek Foundation board, and the church board. Now that Gracie thought about it, Aunt Shirley and Uncle Stan had seemed pretty happy the summer of 1992. Of course, money and prestige were plentiful at the time. Committees and boards may have been what made their marriage so successful. It sure had changed in just a few months. The Browne family never recovered from Charlotte's death. Aunt Shirley, who was overbearing and opinionated normally, became shrill and bitter after the accident. Uncle Stan, who was famous for his dry sense of humor, found solace in a bottle and watched his practice drift away. His partner left and opened an office in Geneseo, taking paralegals and secretaries with him. Uncle Stan's longtime secretary, Harriet, stayed and ran the office and probably practiced law until Uncle Stan had retired five years ago.

Gracie shook off the memories and went back to the diary. As she turned the next page, a small lock of straight dark hair fell out. It was tied with slender blue satin ribbon and had been taped to the page. The yellowed brittle tape had given way.

August 24 – I think I have a big problem. It's a huge mess. What am I going to do? The Morgan Le Fays will kill me. I am the Lady of Shalot apparently. Everything will change. There's no way out.

The entries ended. Gracie took a deep breath. Charlotte must have discovered that she was pregnant. Charlotte had been beautiful and popular. Gracie could still see her walking confidently down the sidelines at a football game, long, straight blond hair swinging almost to her waist, wearing a cheerleading outfit that didn't leave much to the imagination. Her dark blue eyes were shining and full of fun. She knew how to push her mother's buttons and constantly strained against Aunt Shirley's strict rules. There had been more than one ugly family scene about curfews and who Charlotte could date. Charlotte had a penchant for some questionable football players, and Gracie remembered talking with her mother about how different Isabelle and Charlotte were.

She'd been no saint herself, pulling some stunts that could have landed her in big trouble. She and Michael had really enjoyed high school and had probably added many gray hairs to their parents' heads during those years. They had been in love since the 8th grade, and until the accident almost two years ago, they had enjoyed life to the fullest. Gracie turned to his picture on the end table. It was the year he had taken a first prize with one of their Brown Swiss cows at Pike Fair. He had the cow's lead rope in his left hand and was holding up a large blue ribbon in his right. His beaming face made Gracie smile. He had been a very happy man that day. They'd both been very happy. The dairy farm was going well, Gracie was finally pregnant after trying for years, and life was extraordinarily good. She thought they were untouchable, but within three months, she would be a widow and would lose their baby. Gracie closed her eyes trying to erase the memories.

Walking out to the patio, she took a deep, cleansing breath. The night air was cooling, and the humidity seemed less intense. The peepers were performing a lively concert against the thrum of a lone bullfrog, all residents of the small pond beyond the backyard. Moonlight made the creamy hydrangea blossoms glow. The bushes were heavy with blossoms this year. She would have to remember to cut enough to dry, so she could enjoy them all winter. The sweet scent of stock made the air a touch heady. Gracie absently deadheaded a few snapdragons and daisies that the patio lights shone on, and then padded in bare feet back to the living room. If she could focus on the flowers, maybe the other thoughts would go away. She sipped at the tea left in the mug. It was lukewarm. She dumped it down the sink and put the mug in the dishwasher.

Trouble with Isabelle was only beginning, and the documents Uncle Stan had given her would be demanded at some point. Maybe Uncle Stan had had second thoughts and told Isabelle what he'd given away. She wasn't ready to roll over and just give them to Isabelle, but she needed to have a copy of them just in case.

Gracie took all the documents to the spare bedroom that contained her small home office. For the next hour, she carefully scanned in all the newspaper clippings and each page of the diary. There would be time to read the entire diary later, but she wanted to ensure that she had everything Uncle Stan meant her to have. She saved it all in a folder named Misc. Dog Info. Gracie was feeling like a CIA operative. The way Isabelle was behaving, she felt that she should be very careful about everything. Gracie pulled out her flash drive and copied the folder onto it. Her motto was "Always Have Plan B." You never knew when it would come in handy.

Chapter 9

Gracie stared out her kitchen window, absently buttering an English muffin. Joe Youngers was pedaling into the driveway on a black mountain bike. It was 6:45 a.m. He was early, and that was a good sign. Jim's Explorer was right behind Joe announcing its arrival with a rumble. The muffler was definitely worse. Who knew when he'd get it fixed. The day was overcast, but the clouds were breaking up, and the sun was making an attempt to shine. She'd already decided to let Jim handle the training, to give Joe a fair chance. Gracie had a million errands to do today and phone calls to make. With some luck, she'd be able to disappear for a few hours. Maybe she could even get her hair cut. She needed a trim in the worst way.

Jim jumped out of the Explorer and with a bag in his hand. "Are you decent?" he yelled as he strode up the bluestone path and up the steps.

Gracie opened the door. "Yes, as decent as it gets. What's that?"

"It's a peace offering. They're warm and the first batch out of the oven at Midge's."

Gracie inhaled deeply, enjoying the cinnamon and the brown sugar syrup smells wafting from the bag as Jim pulled out the Styrofoam container.

"Not necessary, but Midge's sweet rolls are always welcome. I've got coffee ready, if you want some."

"I'll be back in a few minutes. I'd better get Joe started on feeding the dogs and cleaning runs."

"OK. We can plan out the day when you get back."

Jim slammed the door with his usual enthusiasm and half-jogged out to the kennels. Joe was standing at the door with hands shoved in his pockets. Gracie looked at the English muffin and the white container. It was no contest. She tossed the muffin into Haley's dish, opened the container, and pulled out a warm, gooey roll. It was dripping with pecans and brown sugar syrup. Haley eagerly gulped down the muffin, and Gracie sat down at the kitchen bar to go over the appointment book and enjoy her breakfast. There seemed to be a break in the action by the looks of the schedule. There were four grooming appointments and only two pickups and two arrivals. It wasn't great for business, but all of that could change quickly. Marian would be in at 9:00 along with Beth. If it wasn't too hectic, she should be able to do some grocery shopping, banking, and talk with Deputy Stevens. She might even be able to see Uncle Stan today. Haley woofed as Jim came through the kitchen door.

"Hey, Haley." Haley greeted Jim with a wagging tail and paws on his chest.

"Get off, Haley. Jim, I swear you're the worst influence on her. Just when I think she's over jumping on people, you encourage her."

Jim pushed Haley down and rubbed her backside. "We'd better behave, girl, or we'll be in the doghouse together." He grabbed a mug off the hook under the row of oak cupboards and poured himself a cup of coffee.

"I've got him going on the runs. We'll see how quick he picks up the routine."

"It's not rocket science, but does have to be done right. We're building a pretty good reputation, and I don't want any problems. We've had enough of them for this week."

"I know, Gracie. I don't want that either. Like I said, we'll give him a week. What's the schedule look like for today?" Jim sat down next to her and pulled the appointment book over. It was a black three-ring binder with the daily appointments printed out.

"It's really pretty light, so far. As long as it's still calm by nine o'clock, I'll do my errands this morning. I think Marian and Beth can handle the phones and the grooming. They seem to have hit it off."

"Marian can get along with anybody, *and* she's a great teacher. She'll have Beth trained in no time. If it's going to be quiet, it'll give me a chance to really go over things with Joe. I want him trained ASAP. I'm still planning on that St. Lawrence fishing trip in August."

"I know. I just hope Joe works out. I don't want to be looking for somebody or training another newbie while you're on vacation."

"Not my first choice either. We'll hope for the best." He finished the coffee and tore off a piece of roll, dripping syrup on the granite counter. "These are always so messy," he complained, grabbing a paper towel and wiping up the sticky puddle.

"Yeah, but they're so good." Gracie licked her fingers and poured another cup of coffee.

"You were going to tell me about your dark family secret that Isabelle was all up in her nightshirt about yesterday."

"Oh, right. In fact, she stopped by again last night to try and get the books back that Uncle Stan gave me."

"What books? Are they valuable?" Jim wiped his mouth and helped himself to more coffee and another roll.

"Well, it's kinda strange actually. He gave me some books, but they were stuffed with a bunch of clippings and reports about Charlotte's death. He also stuck Charlotte's diary in with everything else."

"You're kidding. What's going on with that?" Jim's face and voice turned serious.

"I'm not sure. That's one thing I want to see him about today. I don't know why he gave all this stuff to me. Isabelle saw the diary last night on my coffee table, and she's on the warpath to get everything back. I told her it was my diary and hid the clippings before she came in the house. Isabelle was actually scary. I'm not sure I can hold onto this stuff without a fight."

"There's nothing to fight over. Isabelle should have her sister's stuff. Stan probably just wants to tweak Isabelle, or he's seriously confused."

"I don't know what to think, but I have a weird feeling about the whole thing. Uncle Stan wants me to have it for some reason. He was pretty intense about it. I'm going to talk with my parents when they get back this weekend. Maybe they remember something." Gracie pulled back her unruly red mane, grabbed her hair clip off the counter, and twisted the hair into a pile on her head.

Jim slid off the stool and went to the door. He pulled a Yankees baseball cap out of his back pocket and jammed it on. "I'm not sure if you want to tangle with Isabelle over Charlotte's stuff. You'd better be careful."

"I know. I'll try to sort it out with Uncle Stan today. Let me brush my teeth and then I'll meet you in the office."

Gracie headed for her bathroom and heard the door slam, announcing Jim's departure. Tail wagging, Haley followed Gracie.

Within minutes, Gracie and Haley were in the office. She began entering payments and calculating invoices for the day's pickups. She printed a copy of the day's schedule for Marian. Gracie kept trying to shake off the creepy feeling that came with the realization somebody had broken into the kennel. The experts were right; she felt violated and not at all comfortable in her own office. She was glad there were others in the building. It was way too weird to be here alone.

After sniffing every inch of the office, Haley was bored and trotted down the hallway to the runs. The barking volume in the run area rose quickly and then settled down. Haley was making her presence known. The sounds of buckets scraping against concrete and dog food hitting metal bowls echoed back down the hallway. Gracie could hear Jim yelling over the din, telling Joe how to check the feeding instructions for each dog and where to look on the run tag if a dog needed meds. It sounded like everything was going OK so far. Gracie finished up the deposit and shoved the checks and cash into the green vinyl Deer Creek Bank bag. She had to remember to call Deputy Stevens before she left. She wanted to pick up the report and then get groceries. She took a quick inventory of the grooming and cleaning supplies. She tacked up the day's schedule on the board in the grooming room and made sure the appointment book was on the desk in the reception area. Haley was back in the office, begging by the treat jar.

"Just one, my dear. You don't want to lose your girlish figure." Gracie tried to sound firm, but knew Haley would use her big, sad Lab eyes to get at least two more from her. "You can chase after them if you're going to be greedy." She threw one toward the reception area. Marian was just coming through the door and Haley momentarily left the treat to greet her with a generous kiss, whacking Marian's legs.

"Watch out for the tail of destruction," Gracie laughed.

"Ow, Haley. You're right. She's got a deadly weapon there. What a good girl! Come with Marian, and I'll give you better treats."

Haley happily bounded off ahead of the tall woman, crunching the current treat and obviously anxious for the jerky Marian kept in the grooming room.

"Morning, Marian. It's good to have you here. Don't spoil that dog."

Marian walked around the corner to Gracie's office, hands on her broad hips and looking extremely happy.

"I *will* spoil that dog, and I'm glad to be working. I thought I would go out of mind, just cleaning house and watching TV. Not healthy. I'm not retiring until the dogs are too much to handle. Besides, my husband is driving me crazy. He retired last month and is underfoot all day."

Gracie laughed. By the smile on Marian's face and the way she was playing with Haley, she would be working for quite some time.

"Today's schedule is on the board, Marian. It's not too bad, so I'm going out to do errands in a few minutes. I've got to see that deputy too." Gracie gathered the bank bag and her grocery list. She put both in her large canvas tote bag decorated with an embroidered black Labrador.

"I wonder if they're really working on finding that thief. We need a sheriff who wants to do the job." Marian unsuccessfully tucked her short platinum blond hair behind her ears. Her broad Eastern European face was stern, blue eyes dark with indignation.

"I'm sure the police are doing something, but at least the thieves didn't get the money. I should have been more careful and locked it up though. Life around here is pretty tame, so I didn't think too much about it." Gracie picked up the tote bag, searching for her keys in its depths.

"Our homes and businesses should be safe. But that Sheriff Chamberlain just doesn't care. Haven't you read about the robberies at Silver Lake? He doesn't have any suspects yet, and they've been robbing homes over there for two months."

Gracie had a feeling that once Marian started complaining about local law enforcement, she'd never get out of the office. Fortunately, they were interrupted by Beth, who looked a little glum. She had her long dark hair pulled back in a ponytail and was wearing jeans and her Milky Way Kennels T-shirt. She was slender and long-legged. Gracie imagined that Beth probably had plenty of teenage boys interested in her.

"Feeling OK, Beth?" Gracie asked.

"I guess." She was biting her lower lip as if in an effort to keep from crying

Marian put an arm around Beth. "Boyfriend trouble?" she asked knowingly.

"Well, yeah, I guess." Beth's face drooped again.

"Men are always trouble. I could tell you some stories. Come with me, and let's get going on today's schedule. I'll show you how to clip toenails." Marian's motherly firm tone left no doubt that moping wasn't allowed, and there was work to do.

Gracie smiled and made sure she had all the stuff necessary for her errands.

"I'm heading out, ladies. I should be back around one or so," she called out.

"We'll be here," Marian boomed back. "Do you want Haley in the kennel or in the yard?"

"Put her in the yard. She'll just be a pest for customers otherwise. Thanks, Marian."

"No problem. We'll handle everything here."

"That's music to my ears. Thanks." It was good to have Marian. Gracie knew that everything would be handled, and she could actually think about something other than the kennels for a while. Throwing the tote bag onto the front passenger seat, Gracie remembered she needed to call Deputy Stevens. She hurried back into the house to get the number from her answering machine. As she listened to the messages again, Gloria Minder's voice prodded her memory.

"Rats, I need to call her and let her know I'm OK," she said to herself. She wrote down both numbers and called Deputy Stevens first. The dispatcher who answered told her that Deputy Stevens was off duty, but would be in about three o'clock. She would have him call her. Gracie gave the dispatcher her cell phone number and the kennel number. Then she dialed the parsonage. She got the answering machine there, but left a message saying she was fine, and the sheriff's department was working on the case.

"Finally, I can get on the road," she said to the empty house. The phone began to ring just as she grabbed her purse and headed for the door. The caller ID said it was Isabelle.

"Forget it, Izzy. I don't have time for any threats today." Gracie stalked out and climbed into in her vehicle. She could feel the anger coming up through the roots of her hair. Gracie took a deep breath to refocus her thoughts. The grief counselor had gotten her into the habit of breathing exercises to clear her mind and refocus on positive thoughts. Sometimes it worked. Not so well today, but she really needed to see Uncle Stan and find out what he wanted her to do. Life was too busy at the moment for any more excitement. How could Isabelle and Charlotte have been so different? Isabelle was maddeningly like Aunt Shirley, following the rules and demanding that everybody else toe the line. Charlotte had been a free spirit, although a little too free for her own good sometimes. Was Uncle Stan really a free spirit too? Maybe he had been held captive by Aunt Shirley all these years, and now he was cutting loose. Hopefully he had some answers for her. Maybe he knew who the father of Charlotte's baby was.

She adjusted her rear view mirror as she backed out of the parking space by the kitchen steps. Joe was hefting a 50-pound bag of dog food from the storage shed. He threw it easily over his shoulder and walked to the kennels. Would he really work out? She wished she didn't have such a bad feeling about him. Her cell phone buzzed insistently from the depths of her bag. It had to be Isabelle. How was she going to pry Izzy off her back without having to admit she'd lied? Something would come to her. It had to. Sighing, she turned the small SUV around the driveway and sped out onto the road.

Chapter 10

Jim poured Joe a cup of coffee and motioned to a folding chair. Joe plopped down and took a sip.

"Thanks. This hits the spot. My grandmother still uses instant. Doesn't have a coffeemaker, which ticks off the other guys. I don't mind it, but this is good coffee."

"Other guys? Jim sat at the desk and popped open the top on the container of muffins.

"Yeah. A couple of guys from prison. They were released about the same time as I was. We hung out together."

"Oh." Jim said slowly. "Help yourself," he said, pointing to the large streusel-topped blueberry muffins.

Joe pulled one out and took a large bite, washing it down with another gulp of coffee.

"I think my grandma liked having the company in the beginning. But they're a little rough, and she's been complainin' about the mess they make."

"Your grandmother is getting up there, isn't she? Over 80 anyway."

"She's 84, I think."

"Right." Jim licked gooey syrup from his fingers. "That's getting up there. What are these guys doing for work?"

"Still lookin'. Brad's picked up some yard work, and Carter's trying to get a job with a construction outfit. He used to do drywall. If they don't get something steady pretty soon, they'll probably head to Buffalo."

"There's more work up that way than around here right now. Have they signed up for Second Chances?"

Joe shifted in the chair, resting his left foot over his right knee. He tugged at the hem of his jeans.

"No. They're not much interested in programs. Not into counseling or anything."

"Right. You're OK with that?"

"Doesn't bother me. I wanna get it right this time. Figured if Rev. Minders' wife was involved, that would keep Grandma happy too. She's always after me to go to church and get right with God. I know she means well, but if I stay in this program, that'll keep her happy enough."

"Makes sense. I'm not much on church myself. Gracie goes, or she used too. Michael always went, but I do my own thing."

"Me too." Joe put the mug on the desk.

There was a light tapping on the doorframe. Marian stood with a pink slip of paper in her hand.

"Sorry to interrupt, but this Isabelle has called twice for Gracie."

Jim shook his head and stood. "I'll take it. It's Gracie's cousin."

Marian handed him the message. "That's what she said, but I wondered. She wasn't exactly friendly."

"No. She's not. Her mother just died though."

"Oh. I didn't realize. That's too bad. Then the message makes some sense."

Jim glanced down at the paper. The message read: "Call me about my mother's books."

He grimaced. "Yeah. It's an estate thing. Family stuff."

"That can be difficult. I'd better get back out front. Beth is doing playtimes. Maybe Joe would like to help."

"Sure. I can do that," Joe said, smiling. "That should be fun."

"Good idea," Jim said. "We've got most of the runs done anyway. Let's go."

He shoved the paper in his pocket.

Chapter 11

Bea Youngers was methodically washing breakfast dishes in her deep cast-iron sink, etched with years of use. The dishes were piled in the old red dish drainer on the counter. She sighed as she looked out the kitchen window toward the street and wondered if she had done the right thing. She wanted to help Joe and his friends. Joe was her only grandchild still in Deer Creek, and Bea wanted to give him the best chance to get his life straight. Maybe she could get him to go to church with her this Sunday. At least he had a real job at the new kennel now. His friends seemed to be a different story though. They'd been released from prison at the same time as Joe, and even though they said they only needed a couple of weeks to find jobs, they were still here after three months. They left trash and dishes everywhere. Their dirty clothes were perpetually on the floor of the bedroom they shared. They had to watch their TV shows, and she was relegated to her bedroom to watch the tiny set in the evenings. Brad, the taller and heavier of the two, had been especially polite to start, but now they both treated her as if she were their maid. Carter, who was balding and had tattooed arms, hardly spoke, but he had a mean look in his eye. She didn't trust him at all.

She was 85 years old, she was tired, and she shouldn't have to put up with their rudeness. She would tell Joe tonight that his friends had to go. She couldn't do this anymore. They should be cooking her meals and picking up after her. She knew Joe needed friends, but she didn't think he needed these two. Joe kept trying to clean up and smooth things over between her and this Brad and Carter.

She desperately hoped Joe wasn't doing anything criminal with them. She didn't think they had real jobs, but they had money for cigarettes and beer. Joe wasn't supposed to drink while he was still on probation. Bea hoped and prayed that he was doing the right thing. Maybe she would make a special supper of chicken and biscuits, and then have Joe tell them they needed to leave by next week.

Her crooked, blue-veined fingers slid the dishrag over the last plate, and it went into the overfull dish drainer. At last the dishes were done. Maybe she could watch *The Young and Restless* before anybody got home. She wiped her hands on the worn hand towel and then went to turn on the TV. She was fast asleep with her favorite soap opera blaring when Carter and Brad slunk through the living room and disappeared into their bedroom. The backpacks they carried were quickly deposited under the beds.

Chapter 12

Midge's was hopping. Gracie took a quick look around for a seat. The steady clank of plates and the sizzle of grease in the fryers indicated lunch was in full swing. The stools at the counter were full, and Midge was flipping burgers, stirring gravy, and yelling at everyone to keep moving. Midge was vertically challenged and skinny as a rail. She had short brown hair liberally streaked with gray and a tongue as sharp as her chef's knife. In the days when you could smoke inside, she kept the kitchen blue with cigarette smoke. Now, she had to step out the back door and smoke when she had a chance, which wasn't nearly as often as she thought necessary, as she was quick to say. She was perpetually grumpy and her voice husky.

She and her husband Ernie had raised six boys, all of whom had fled Deer Creek as soon as they graduated from high school. After Ernie and Midge divorced a few years ago, Ernie took off to Alaska to make his fortune and shack up with some woman he dated on the Internet. Her chat room name was Huggy Bear. Midge had said good riddance, since he'd never helped much around the house or the restaurant.

For all practical purposes, she lived at the restaurant; a folded-up cot resided in the huge walk-in pantry. She was a terror to her wait staff and cooks, but she made the best sweet rolls in the county and had more business than she could handle most days. Her Friday fish fry was legendary, and it wasn't uncommon to see a line winding around the block, waiting for a table or an empty stool at the counter.

The men at the counter were exchanging their daily gossip with animation. Gracie caught sight of Harry, the Hillside Feeds delivery driver, who by the laughter was regaling the boys with his stories, which were probably spicy. Midge planted herself squarely in front of him.

"Harry, so help me, if you don't keep your mouth shut and mind your own business, I swear I will knock you off that stool. You're just full of you know what."

Harry frowned and muttered something unintelligible. The rest of the men at the counter shifted uneasily on the stools. A couple of them stood up to pay their bills and shuffled to the cash register. Midge happily took their money, stabbing each check on the long spike next to the register, and told them to come back tomorrow. There would be fried green tomatoes and meatloaf. Their faces brightened at that news.

Gracie shook her head, watching Midge clear the counter area. The way the woman treated customers, it was a wonder she stayed in business. Midge punched the buttons on the cash register and tucked a wad of cash in the drawer. She looked up and smiled.

"Hey, Gracie, there's a stool down here by the kitchen. I bet you want a chicken finger salad with poppy seed dressing."

"You're right as usual, Midge." Gracie walked past the row of men who eyed her surreptitiously.

"Hey, Kelly! Finger salad with poppy seed on the side," Midge called out to her kitchen help. She poured a tall glass of fresh lemonade and slid it over to Gracie.

Gracie leaned across the counter and softly asked, "What's up with the guys today?"

"They're just being stupid. They're worse than old women. That Harry gets gossip going like a grass fire. I just have to put him in his place every so often." Midge quickly changed the subject. "How's everybody holding up after your Aunt Shirley died?"

"Well, pretty good. It wasn't unexpected. In a lot of ways, it's probably a relief for Uncle Stan and Isabelle."

"Heard you and Isabelle had a few words." Midge popped a piece of gum in her mouth and chomped down hard.

"Well, yeah. You know how everybody gets on edge at a funeral." Gracie squirmed inwardly. She'd known that little scene would get around town in no time.

"You've had quite a week then, with the funeral and robbery, and all." Midge was now seriously pumping her for juicy details.

She'd have to give Midge something that would satisfy her insatiable appetite for information.

"It sure has. Fortunately, they didn't get any cash, just caused some damage in the reception area. I guess the alarm system scared them off. The sheriff's department is working on it though."

"Yeah, right. Since when have they ever caught anybody?"

"You sound like Marian. I'm talking with a deputy this afternoon. Maybe they'll have a lead or something."

Gracie poured a thin stream of dressing onto the huge salad and started munching on the pile of greens. Just as she was washing it down with the lemonade, her cell phone sang, "Who Let the Dogs Out" in her bag. Midge took a couple of steps back to create personal space, but still close enough to get the details. It was Jim.

"You're kidding. How did it...?" Gracie felt her face drain of color. "I'll be right there."

She flipped the phone shut. Gracie fumbled into her cavernous tote bag and found her wallet.

"Midge, I've gotta go. Kennel emergency. This should cover it." She handed Midge a $10 bill.

"What's the matter? Another robbery?" Midge snapped her gum, eyes shining with interest.

Although she knew better, Gracie blurted out, "Beth was bitten. They called the squad."

"Is she OK? Where did she..?" Midge was cut off in mid-sentence. Gracie was already pushing the door open to the street. The remaining group at the counter began a low hum of conversation. Midge, disappointment showing in the slump of her shoulders, headed back to the kitchen. The fire hall siren began wailing for an ambulance call, and several men followed behind Gracie to answer the call.

The SUV churned up loose gravel as she turned into the kennel's long driveway. The wail of the ambulance siren grew louder behind her. Joe was standing outside the kennel entrance, nervously scanning the road above the kennel.

"How is she? Is it bad?" Gracie's words tumbled out.

"Uh, I'm not sure. Jim and Marian are with her." Joe's face was pale, and he had to force his words out.

Gracie dashed through the door and found all three in the kennel corridor near the end of the building. Beth was sobbing, and Marian was pressing a towel on the girl's bloody thigh. Blood was slick on the floor beside them. She sat on a storage chest and bent over to examine the injury.

"It's going to be fine; the squad is here," Marian crooned to Beth. It was the soothing voice she used with skittish dogs.

"It hurts so bad. I can't stand it." Beth continued sobbing. Her face was ashen. Dogs were anxiously whining and yipping in the background.

Two EMTs strode down the corridor, with Joe tagging along behind them. Gracie didn't recognize either one; they must be new to the crew. They also looked pretty young, one with dark brown hair and the other with curly blond hair. They quickly put on gloves, and one retrieved a stethoscope and blood pressure cuff out of the kit. The blonde relieved Marian and continued to put pressure on Beth's leg.

"What happened here?" the dark haired EMT asked.

"I was just, just—oh, it hurts. I'm going to bleed to death," Beth howled.

"She was taking two dogs to the play area, and I guess they decided to mix it up for some reason. Beth got nailed trying to get them apart." Jim answered the EMT matter-of-factly over the din.

Both of the EMTs nodded. The blonde carefully began to ease the pressure on her wound, and the blood gushed again. He quickly reapplied the pressure and pulled a large pressure bandage from the kit. Even though Gracie had been a vet tech and dairy farmer's wife, she started to feel sick to her stomach and turned away. She gave Marian a lot of credit. She knelt at Beth's side, holding her hand, and patting her shoulder.

"Did anyone call her parents?" Gracie managed to get out.

"Yes, and they're on the way. They're both at work, so they'll probably get here in about 10 minutes or so." Jim's face was furrowed with worry.

"Tell them to meet us at the hospital; we're loading her up right now. We'll need the shot records on those two dogs."

"Sure, no problem. I'll get them now." Gracie headed for the reception area, glad to have an excuse to get some breathing room.

"What dogs"? She yelled to Jim.

"Barney, the Bingels' Boxer, and Smokey, the Smith's Collie-mix."

Gracie quickly printed off the vaccination records and handed them to the dark-haired EMT.

"There you go."

"Thanks." He folded the papers and stuffed them in his shirt pocket.

Beth's leg was now wrapped securely, and the men packed up their equipment. Her sobbing had stopped, and she had become quiet, wiping her face and snuffling on her T-shirt.

Emery Harwood was wheeling the gurney through the hallway. It was always a little unnerving to Gracie that the funeral home director was on the ambulance crew. It seemed like a conflict of interest.

Beth's parents were both pulling into the driveway as she was being loaded into the ambulance. They anxiously talked to the EMTs. Both were trying to be calm, but Gracie could see that Frank and Evie were far from it. The dark-haired EMT was shaking his head "no" to Evie. Gracie guessed that she wanted to ride along in the ambulance. Jim was already outside talking to them as the ambulance made a wide turn in the driveway.

"Gracie, I'll clean up this mess. Why don't you see if Jim needs help with Beth's family?" Marian spoke gently.

"Uh, right. Yes, I'd better go see if we can do anything for them." Gracie broke out of her self-induced fogginess. The blood on the floor and the ambulance had brought back memories she hoped to bury. She stopped by her office and found the bottle of Xanex in the top desk drawer. She quickly gulped down two pills with some cold coffee left in her mug and hurried outside.

Chapter 13

The four of them gathered in Gracie's office to assess the day's damage. Everybody had grabbed a can of Coke or a bottle of water and were all looking expectantly at Jim. He cleared his throat and adjusted his baseball cap.

"OK, folks, let's see where we stand." Jim said wearily. "Marian, did you see how Beth got bitten?"

"No. I found her when she started screaming. Barney and Smokey were running loose in corridor C, but they weren't fighting. Barney cowered down when I called him." Marian's expression showed the day had taken a toll on her as well.

"Joe, where were you when this all got started?"

"I was hosing out runs in the other hallway, is it B?"

"Yeah, it's B, Joe. Did you see anything?"

"No, I called 9-1-1 when Marian yelled to me. It all happened kinda fast." Joe systematically cracked the knuckles on his left hand, flexing it when he reached the ring finger.

"Sure is a heck of a way to start a new job, huh, Joe?" Jim's attempt at humor fell flat.

Gracie was scribbling notes on a yellow legal pad. "I'm going to need a boatload of detail for the insurance company. Beth has a nasty wound on her thigh." She concentrated on pad of paper. "The insurance company is sure going to love us. This will probably put our rates through the roof."

Jim lifted his baseball cap and ran his fingers over his sweat-soaked hair.

"I'll go check on those two dogs, while you finish up getting the details from Marian and Joe." He adjusted his hat and left the office without his customary whistling.

Gracie finished getting the information necessary for the insurance claim from the two subdued employees and let them return to work. With just an hour to go before closing, Marian and Joe had a lot to do. She could hear Jim and Joe feeding dogs and Marian finishing up the last grooming. Gracie painfully made the call to Milky Way's insurance agent.

"I figured I'd be hearing from you," Howard Stroud, the insurance agent, said brusquely.

"Sorry it's so soon again. How'd you know I'd be calling?"

"I heard the call on my scanner, so I've been waiting for you to let me know what happened. You got all the information?"

In her mind's eye, Gracie could see Howard leaning back in his ancient squeaky swivel chair, one pudgy hand on a well-developed paunch, the other hand smoothing his careful comb-over. He'd be looking down through his reading glasses and chewing on a disheveled cigar. Howard had given up smoking, but not cigars. Gracie heard a crackle as he adjusted his headset. He wore a headset to answer the phone, since he'd decided that his secretary had become too expensive. His wife, Polly, who was his secretary, said Howard was just too cheap and had gone to work for the competition in Warsaw.

"I've got a report from Marian Majewski and Joe Youngers, but not from Beth Simmons yet," Gracie said. "I'm going to check with her parents a little later tonight to see when I can talk to her and get that form filled out."

"Is she OK?"

"Not sure how's she's doing, but she seemed to be calming down and doing OK by the time the squad left. It's not life-threatening, but the leg was bleeding pretty good. I'm hoping there's no real damage."

"Well, get that stuff to me as soon as you can tomorrow. I'm headed out on vacation next week, so I'd like to get it moving before I go."

"I'll be over as soon as I can in the morning. Thanks, Howard."

"See you in the a.m., kid."

Gracie sat with her head in her hands, wondering why she had ever thought a kennel business was a good idea. Apparently, the string of misery that had started with Michael's death almost two years ago was continuing. She slammed her fist on the desk and mentally screamed at God to give her a break. This whole suffering thing was out of hand. Jim must think he'd gotten himself into the partnership from hell. The first three months had gone so well and now, everything was going wrong and headed down the toilet. They might as well forget trying to build the training barn and agility course next year. They'd be out of business by then. Gracie tried to stop her thoughts from careening down this angry road of depressing scenarios. She heard the bell jingle in the reception area and Marian's voice calling for her to help with a dog pickup. Gracie took a deep breath and pasted a smile on her face before she reached the reception area.

Gracie and Jim were in their usual places in the office, but there was no relaxing tonight. Jim sat on the edge of the recliner's worn seat, and Gracie was tapping her foot on the base of the desk chair. Haley chewed methodically on a large rawhide in front of the desk. They had finished talking with Beth's parents and the dogs' owners about an hour ago. Everyone was trying to appear understanding and cooperative, but Gracie and Jim knew that could disappear as fast as kibble. Dog owners and parents were going to cover their backsides and wallets on this. Milky Way Kennels would take the fall before any of them would.

"I still don't understand why Beth took two dogs at the same time. She's been told to take dogs one at a time to the play area."

"Well, from what Frank said, Beth was trying to cover the phones, and keep playtimes on schedule. Marian was in the middle of clipping the Harwood's poodle, so Beth thought she'd take as many as she could handle at once to the play area. She was actually trying to get one more out of a run at the time of the accident."

"Neither of those dogs is aggressive with people or other dogs, so I still don't get it." Gracie's voice was edgy. "Beth must have done something to get it started."

"I don't know what. She's been pretty good about handling dogs the way we've trained her to. She made a greenhorn mistake. At least she's doing all right and should go home tomorrow. She'll have some pain for a while, but there's no permanent damage."

"And the dogs are all right too. I guess we can thank the Lord for small favors on that one," Gracie grudgingly gave in.

"We're going to have to do some damage control on the PR side of this, Chief."

"No kidding. Plus we need to find a good kennel helper since Beth won't be coming back."

"I guess I don't blame her on that one. She is just a kid, and she was a little afraid of the dogs anyways." Jim eased back into the junky recliner, his jaw relaxing slightly.

"We need to get someone with animal experience of some sort. I made a mistake on getting teenage help this summer." Gracie was angry with herself. She prided herself on good hires, and both teenagers hadn't lasted a month.

"Why don't we post the job on that Deer Creek Help Wanted website?"

"That's probably a good idea. I'll get something written up and posted tonight. These incident reports will go to Howard in the morning and then I'll spend the rest of the day here."

The phone rang and startled them both.

"Milky Way Kennels," Gracie answered hesitantly.

"Gracie, I've been trying to call you all day."

It was Isabelle. Gracie grimly tightened her hold on the receiver.

"Listen, Isabelle, I really don't have time to talk."

"Yes, you do, and you can't go on avoiding me about those books. I'll be at your house in the morning to pick them up. Have them ready." Isabelle's dark tone was almost menacing.

"If it's so important, they'll be on the steps outside the kitchen door."

"All right then. It's about time you were reasonable." Isabelle voice became sugary. It was her condescending inflection that Gracie hated so much.

"Whatever." Gracie slammed the phone down with frustration.

"Ah, the pain-in-the-butt cousin finally caught up with you, huh?' Jim smirked, and his deep blue eyes flashed with humor. He eased the recliner back all the way.

"Don't get comfortable, and don't think she's getting what she wants," Gracie snapped.

"Hey, Chief, we've all had a bad day. Don't take your family troubles out on me too."

"Sorry, but she's not getting her way. I still have some leverage in this."

"Gracie, you need to take it easy on her. She's just lost her mother. Have some mercy."

"Yeah, I know I should, but I still need to talk to Uncle Stan. He wanted me to have this stuff for some reason." Gracie pulled the center desk drawer out and found a brush.

"He's a sick, sad old man. He probably doesn't even know what he's doing anymore, although he likes to tweak Isabelle." Jim grinned.

"He knows what's going on," Gracie said defensively. "I just need to find out what he wants me to do with Charlotte's stuff. I'll see him tomorrow night at the VFW. It's poker night, and he never misses. Isabelle won't go in the place, so we can talk safely."

"Good grief, you're making this all pretty dramatic. Have you been watching reruns of *Murder, She Wrote*?"

Gracie brushed her tangled hair smooth and clipped it back above the nape of her neck.

"We'll see what Uncle Stan says. If it was a mistake, I'll hand over the goods to Isabelle. But I don't think he made a mistake no matter how much beer he had. I'll bet money on it."

"All right then." Jim shifted the recliner to the upright position. "Let's make a little wager. How about twenty bucks and a fish fry from Midge's?"

"You're on, Jimmy, my friend." Gracie laughed for the first time that day.

Chapter 14

True to her word, Gracie plunked the bag of books on the steps and headed out to file the accident reports with Howard first thing Friday morning. She had filled a bag with the old romance novels. There was no way Isabelle would get the other things back that easily. Besides she wanted those dog books for her collection, and Isabelle would no doubt throw them in the garbage.

She was relieved to see that the bag was gone when she returned from her errands. Isabelle had apparently tried to pump Marian for further information, but since she knew nothing about the books, Isabelle had hit a road block. However, a tersely written note was waiting on Gracie's desk. It read, *"I know there are more things. I will call you later. Isabelle."*

Gracie crumpled the note and threw it away. The rest of the day flew by helping Marian handle grooming appointments, along with drop-offs and pick-ups. Some customers were pointedly expressing their displeasure with Milky Way hiring incompetent help. They weren't sure they could trust the safety of their dogs to a place that had gotten robbed and had a major dog bite incident all in one week. Others were sure that a nasty lawsuit would ensue, and the kennel would probably go under. Gracie and Marian patiently smoothed ruffled feathers and assured each one that it was an anomaly, and they were beefing up the staff right away. Gracie also handed out a coupon for a free day of room and board to everyone who came through the door. By closing time, Marian and Gracie were exhausted.

"I don't know how to thank you for today, Marian. You're a lifesaver." Gracie leaned back in her chair and propped her feet on the desk.

"No problem, but I'm going to need a long, hot bath tonight. My husband better be cooking supper or getting takeout, because I am one tired old woman." Marian was reclining in the Jim's ratty chair. "I don't think I can take too many days like today, Gracie."

"I hope we don't have any more days like this, ever."

Jim walked through the door, and Marian made an effort to get up.

"Don't move, Marian. I'll get the chair out of reception. Keep your feet up."

Marian relaxed back into the chair, and Jim rolled the task chair from the reception area into the office.

"Well, ladies, did we survive the onslaught of dissatisfied customers?"

"I think so. Marian is a wonder woman at customer relations. We did get a few cancellations though. Most of them said they were going to Bark-n-Lounge in Pike."

"Well, I guess it's not unexpected. Did we get any hits on the website posting?"

Marian yawned and pulled the side handle to bring the chair back upright.

"You two have a lot to talk about, and this tired old mama is going home." She stretched her back from side to side and got up with an audible groan.

"Get some rest, Marian. You're the best. You will be back on Monday, right?" Gracie asked anxiously.

"Don't worry. I will, but let's try to have a less exciting week."

"I'm with you on that one." Jim stretched his well-muscled and tanned arms over his head and pushed them back against the wall. "We'll see you Monday, and thanks, Marian."

Jim and Gracie listened to her old pickup truck chug out of the driveway.

"We're sure lucky that Marian is here right now." Gracie twirled a pencil on a yellow legal pad. "And no, we didn't get any hits on the site today."

"We *are* lucky. Let's hope we can keep her on board for a while. People know and trust her, so we've got that advantage. When she retired from Pawsitively Puppies, they had a heck of a time replacing her. I'm hoping we can find another gem like Marian." Jim leaned forward and placed his hands on his knees. "I'm beat, plus I'm supposed to meet Laney at Midge's and then head out for a movie. Can you lock up?"

Laney was Jim's latest girlfriend. They'd been dating for about six months, and so far, he hadn't made excuses to break dates, like he usually did when things started to get serious. From what Gracie had seen of Laney, she was an approved girlfriend. She gave Jim the breathing room he needed, but they were spending more and more time together. He stood and rolled the chair back to reception.

"No problem. I'm picking up fish fries from Midge's and taking them to my parents. They got back this afternoon. I'm going to try to see Uncle Stan too. We're only at half capacity tonight, so it won't take me long to do bed checks and set the alarm."

Gracie locked up the day's receipts in the small safe under her desk. Jim was already headed out the driveway, his disintegrating muffler marking his progress down the road when she made her rounds to see that everybody was secure, had water, and looked comfy. Haley, who had been sleeping in reception most of the afternoon, sniffed and licked muzzles on her way down the corridors. Satisfied that everyone was settled, Gracie punched in the security code and locked the front door. Haley ran ahead to the kitchen door, anxious to get to her supper bowl.

Her parents looked surprisingly relaxed and well-tanned when she opened the kitchen's screen door, carrying the pile of take-out containers. Her mother's gray and fading auburn hair looked freshly done. It was a new cut, but no new color. Theresa had recently announced she was done being a slave to the monthly coloring drill. Her father was in stone-colored Dockers and a blue golf shirt that complimented his wavy silver hair.

The fish was excellent, as always, and Gracie updated her parents between bites on the events of the past week— funeral, Isabelle, robbery, and bite incident. Bob Clark looked at his daughter with concerned eyes.

"Are you doing all right then, Gracie?"

"Well, I've had some moments, but I think it's under control." Gracie plunged a fork into the coleslaw dripping with mayo.

Gracie's mother wasn't convinced, by the look she exchanged with her husband.

"You probably need to get some reliable, experienced help, so you can concentrate on running the business," her mother said, taking a bite of her broiled fish.

"We're working on it. I put a posting on that new Deer Creek Help Wanted site, an ad in the Pennysaver, and I called the employment agency in Warsaw. With Marian, things are off to a good start. We'll see how Joe works out." Gracie closed the lid on the take-out container. "I need one more full-time person, and I think we can handle things. Of course, it depends on whether we have any business after this week of major disasters."

"It'll work out. You and Jim have good business heads. And, Gracie, you need to take care of yourself. You don't want to end up with...umm, problems again." Her father wiped his mouth with the paper napkin and threw his container in the kitchen's stainless steel trashcan.

"I'm fine and don't worry." Gracie's voice was sharp. "I need to be busy, which reminds me, I've got to see Uncle

89

Stan. He should be down at the VFW tonight. I'll let you both get caught up on some sleep." She picked up her mother's container and hers, tossing them in the trash. Haley scrambled from under the kitchen table, her toenails clicking on the hardwood floor.

"Here's my roll, Haley," Theresa laughed. "You're always so good until we clear the table. What do you need to see Uncle Stan about?" she queried as she wiped down the blue laminate counters and table.

"Well, I didn't tell you the part about the books."

"What books?" Her father put the newspaper he was reading on his lap and raised the recliner.

"Uh, well, Uncle Stan gave me a bunch of old books the day of the funeral. Isabelle is hot to have them back. She's practically threatened me."

"Are they valuable or sentimental to Isabelle?"

"Not really, but he had newspaper clippings about Charlotte's accident, her death certificate, and some other papers stuck in the books. I gave some of them back already to keep the peace."

"Really!" her mother exclaimed. "Bob, can you take the garbage out?"

"And the strangest part is that Charlotte's diary was in there too." She pulled Haley's leash from her large bag.

Theresa clutched the dishrag and leaned against the counter. "No wonder Isabelle is upset. That should all be hers. Stan is really having a hard time and isn't thinking clearly. Plus you have a gift for getting her going, but I think this may be over the line." Theresa rinsed the cloth under faucet, draping it over the sink divider. She wiped her hands on an apple-patterned kitchen towel.

"Well, I don't think so. I think he wants to keep Charlotte's things away from Isabelle, but I need to know why he gave them to me. Was there anything fishy about Charlotte's death?"

Her father stepped back into the kitchen with the newspaper in his hands.

"Fishy?" He folded the paper and threw it in the recycling box by the trashcan.

"Well, wasn't the investigation cut short? Didn't Aunt Shirley just want to move on?" Gracie clipped the leash on a squirming Haley.

"It was so long ago now, Gracie." Her mother rubbed her forehead and put a stray lock of hair behind her ear.

"As I remember, the police ran into a dead end with no real witnesses." Her father pulled the white garbage bag from the trashcan.

"But didn't somebody give them a partial plate number?" Gracie let the leash drop to floor as she searched for her keys in the over-sized tote bag.

"Hmm, yes." Her father tapped his forehead with his index finger. "I think somebody did spot a car speeding along Mill Street that night and remembered two or three numbers on the plate. Nothing ever came of it though."

"I think it was Matthew Minders who reported that," her mother interjected. "Maybe it wasn't enough for them to go on. Those weeks after Charlotte's accident were pretty awful. Shirley and Stan had a lot to deal with. With your Uncle Stan's reputation then, the police wouldn't have cut corners. Everyone wanted to find the driver, but it was a horribly rainy night, and no one saw it. It was such a terrible loss for all of us." Her voice suddenly quavered, and she quickly grabbed a tissue from the box on the counter. Her husband put his arm around her.

"Sorry, Mom. I shouldn't be dredging this stuff up. You've got enough on your plate, losing Aunt Shirley." She decided that it wasn't the time to drop the bombshell that Char had been pregnant, but maybe they knew. She'd save that for another time. Her mother had truly loved her sister, and the reality of her loss was sinking in.

"It's OK, Gracie. I'm tired, and Shirley's death is kind of hitting me now that we're home. I went to call her to tell her we were back and..." Theresa's voice broke.

Gracie hugged her mother.

"Get some rest, Mom." She glanced at her watch. "I guess I'll catch Uncle Stan tomorrow. It's getting late, and this will keep another day." Gracie swung the bag over her shoulder and whistled for Haley. With tail thumping against the screen door, Haley stood panting with a silly Lab grin and leash dragging on the floor.

"Come on girl, let's hit the road. Love you both, and I'm glad you're back."

"Love you too," her father said as he rubbed his wife's back. "Be careful, Gracie."

"Sure thing. See you later."

Chapter 15

Stan put the receiver down slowly. He wished Gracie was home. He needed to talk to her about Charlotte. Rubbing his jaw, he stood by the phone, pondering his next decision. He picked up the portable phone again and then put it down.

With Shirley gone, a weight should have lifted from his shoulders. It was a weight that had been there for way too many years. But the pain of losing Charlotte had never dissipated. The guilt and questions remained. He'd been afraid of the truth since the accident, but now he needed to know. Didn't Charlotte deserve some justice after all these years?

Stan could still clearly see the large dent in the grillwork of Shirley's car the morning after Charlotte's death. She said Isabelle had hit a deer and they needed to get it repaired quickly. In the numbness of grief and haze of funeral arrangements, the car had been repaired before the funeral service. Shirley hadn't wanted to discuss the car or report it to the insurance company. He'd put in the claim with Howard though. Shirley had been stoic and in control during the funeral and the investigation. How could he have been so weak? He'd let Shirley make too many decisions, and now he was left with a pile of regret.

He was too tired to deal with Isabelle anymore, and by giving Gracie the information, he knew he had disturbed a hornet's nest. He needed to explain to her the suspicions he'd carried around for 20 years. Why wasn't she home?

Stan took the phone into the living room and sat heavily into the deep-cushioned, buttery leather club chair. He thought about getting a beer, but he needed to think clearly. The pain he so often anesthetized with alcohol would keep him sharp tonight. He punched in the numbers again. He looked at his watch. It was almost nine. After four rings, the call went to Gracie's answering machine. He decided to leave a message, although he hated talking to a machine.

Stan leaned his head back against the comfortable chair and closed his eyes. He jerked awake to find that it was after 9:30. He'd call her in the morning.

The yard and kennel area looked normal when Gracie drove into her driveway. Haley bounded out of the back seat and loped to the office door with Gracie. It still felt creepy, even though all seemed secure. Goose bumps raised on her arms when she unlocked the door and turned off the alarm. She was grateful for the lingering twilight that still glowed in the western sky. Her fingers were actually shaking as she punched in the code. She took a deep breath and tried to get her heart to slow down.

"Let's take one more look around before we go in, girl."

Haley waved her straight, broad black tail in agreement. A chorus of whining and barking began the moment they walked through the doorway to the runs. Everybody and everything did look fine as she checked each run.

"Well, boys and girls, sleep tight. Come on, Haley." She tried to keep her voice lighthearted, but the words caught in her throat. Gracie switched the main corridor light off. She suddenly felt the need to get inside her house and lock herself in. She carefully set the code before locking the door.

"Come on, Haley, race you to the kitchen." She took off with Haley who sprang ahead of her with ease. The shiny Lab leapt up the steps and then down again, butt-tucking in circles before she flopped on the ground at Gracie's feet.

"Girl, you are a clown." Gracie was laughing hard at the typical Lab comedic antics, one of the endearing qualities of the breed. "Let's go in before the mosquitoes eat us up."

Haley trotted through the kitchen door and headed for the cool tiles.

The message light was blinking on the answering machine. Gracie groaned. Isabelle had probably left another message. Maybe her mother was right, and she should give everything back to Isabelle. She had copies now, but she still wanted to talk to Uncle Stan before that happened. There was a reason he gave it to her and no one else. She'd listen to it later.

After a long hot shower and cup of tea, she relaxed watching the local news. The light on the answering machine was in her direct line of vision. The blinking was making her crazy. She punched the button to listen to the playback.

"Hey, Gracie, it's Uncle Stan. Say, uh... I'd like to talk, uh... to you about those books. Maybe you can, uh... give me a call." His speech was halting, and he sounded stressed.

"That call I *will* return," she said out loud grabbing the handset. Then she looked at her watch. It was 10:15. Uncle Stan would either be still playing cards or in bed. She'd make a point of seeing him tomorrow and get some answers. She also needed to check on Beth and talk with the deputy investigating the robbery. Her head began a familiar throb. *I need to just take things one at a time. Why didn't things happen one at a time instead of in batches? That old saying about things happening in threes should have said things happen in fours or fives.*

The ibuprofen bottle was on the kitchen counter, and she quickly downed four tablets to ward off a full-blown headache. She checked to make sure the kitchen door was locked and then settled in with the diary and clippings. There must be something funny about the investigation, or

Uncle Stan wouldn't have given her all of this information. Gracie reread the newspaper clippings and the police report. Everything looked so ordinary. There wasn't anything that jumped out and shouted cover up or that the sheriff's department had botched the investigation. She flipped the diary open to the October entries.

Oct. 4 – I'm going to have to talk to Mother. I don't know how I can tell her. Maybe I'll talk to Dad first.

Oct. 8 – Talked to Dad, but I couldn't tell him everything. There's no way I can talk to Mother. I don't know what I'll do. I wish I was dead. I wish I'd never believed him.

Gracie's throat constricted at Charlotte's pain and her prophetic statement. She drew her legs up and hugged herself. A list of questions flooded her mind. How much did Isabelle know? Who was the father? What had Uncle Stan and Aunt Shirley known? But the big question was still, why had Uncle Stan handed this to her?

Her racing mind would never settle down to let her sleep, so she made a trip to the medicine cabinet again. Looking at the pills in her hand, she almost put them back in the bottle. But she didn't. The pills slid down easily with the glass of cold water. When had medication become such a routine? Migraines and panic attacks had all come after Michael's death. It would be two years in August. Why couldn't she hold it together? Maybe running another business was a mistake. Jim had been hesitant about the kennel. He loved dairy farming, but he'd agreed to sell the farm and be a partner in the new venture. It hadn't been fair to him. He was only doing this to keep her happy. She should get a job where there was no responsibility. No pressure. Something mindless would be good. Life insurance and the sale of the farm had left her without the pressure of even having to work—at least for a while. Jim could get back to farming where he was truly happy. She could just get on with her life without so much drama and relying on Jim for everything. It was time for a real conversation with him. No emotional outbursts or demands. She was sick of her behavior, and so was everyone else. Her parents tiptoed around her, and probably everyone else did too. She huffed at her reflection in the mirror over the sink. Opening the medicine cabinet, she took the brown plastic container, unscrewed the lid, and dumped the remaining pills into the toilet. Staring at them floating around in the water, Gracie bit her bottom lip and flushed. It was time to get back to real life.

Chapter 16

Haley jumped in the back seat and sat on her red plaid blanket, while Gracie finished loading the front seat with the bank bag and her Lab tote. She tucked a grocery list under the visor strap.

"Sorry, girl. You need to stay home today. Too many errands, and it's too hot in the car."

Haley whined in disappointment, but her tail still wagged furiously.

"I know, but I'll be back soon. You can play in the backyard."

Haley jumped out and ran to the gate.

"Be good, and I'll bring you a new bone." Haley's tail thumped heavily on the white vinyl fencing. Gracie gave Haley's rump a scratch and opened the gate.

After dropping the bank bag in the night deposit slot, she turned onto Route 19A toward Warsaw to do her grocery shopping. The next priority was to spend a little time with Uncle Stan to get things sorted out. Then she'd talk to Jim.

Tops supermarket was bustling with harried moms and whiny kids, who wanted to be anywhere else but grocery shopping. Summer didn't last long in Western New York, and good weather weekends were precious. No one wasted a minute of summer. Gracie hoped she could get through the aisles without running into anyone from Deer Creek. Of course, that was wishful thinking.

"Hi, Gracie." It was Gloria Minders.

"Hi." Gracie pretended to study the label on a jar of spaghetti sauce.

"The kennel has had quite a week."

"Sure has." Gracie grabbed another jar of sauce and stared at the list of ingredients. Why was she giving the silent treatment to her pastor's wife? Where was the new Gracie Andersen she'd committed herself to last night? She turned and smiled at Gloria. "We'll get through it."

"We're praying that things work out and that Beth is all right."

"I talked with her mother this morning, and Beth is doing well. She's home and on the mend. But more prayer is always appreciated."

"I'm glad to hear she's doing all right." Gloria put six boxes of spaghetti in her cart. She grabbed several large jars of sauce and added them to the load.

"Looks like you're planning on a big dinner."

"Yes, it's our turn to host the County Clergy's Association dinner this week. I'm cooking. Midge is supplying the dessert."

"I guess you'll be busy with that." Gracie made an attempt to wheel her cart around Gloria's.

Gloria moved her cart aside and then patted Gracie's arm as she went past her.

"I will. Preachers always seem to have good appetites," she laughed. "Have you found anyone to replace Beth yet? I'm sure you need help during this time of year." Her face showed concern.

"We're looking, but so far no applicants."

"I might have some help for you."

Gracie groaned inwardly. She didn't want another ex-con on staff.

"I'm sorry, but probably not from your program. No offense," she added quickly "We hired Joe on a trial basis. I don't know if he'll work out yet. I really need a person who has experience with dogs."

"We've got people from all walks of life. I'm sure we've got some clients that have experience with animals. Second

Chances will work with the employer to get more job training, if it's needed." Gloria's mouth was pressed into a firm line, and her eyes shone with excitement.

"Let me send a couple of people over on Monday. Just talk to them and see if they're a good fit."

Gracie sighed. She didn't need to hire any of them, so why fight?

"Sure, OK. Look at the posting we have on the Deer Creek Help Wanted website and see if you have any qualified people." With any luck, she'd have a line of non-criminal applicants Monday morning, so the Second Chances people could be dismissed before an interview.

"Wonderful! I'll have the counselors send their best people on Monday. You won't regret this, Gracie." Gloria pushed the shopping cart toward the checkout lines with unexpected speed.

"Thanks, Gloria." Gracie shook her head and continued to tick items off her list as she hurried through the rest of the store. Fortunately, no one else appeared from Deer Creek, and the dreaded grocery shopping was finished.

She pressed her foot down on the accelerator as the SUV climbed Rock Glen Hill on Route 19 in record time. There was still a lot to do on her list. Flashing lights suddenly appeared in her rear view mirror, and she glanced at the speedometer.

"Just great," she said aloud.

She pulled over on the gravelly shoulder. The deputy put on his hat as he stepped out the patrol car with lights still flashing.

"Could I see your license and registration, ma'am?" He took off his dark sunglasses.

Gracie gasped in surprise to see that Deputy Stevens stood by her window. He was even better looking in the daylight. His uniform fit perfectly.

"Sure thing, deputy. Uh, remember me?"

He smiled in recognition.

"Sure do. Mrs. Andersen, right?"

"Right. Was I speeding, Deputy?" His eyes were a dark blue, and his arms were well-muscled. He must work out regularly.

"Well, I clocked you about 10 miles over the speed limit back there."

She gulped. "Sorry about that. Not paying attention, I guess. You know, I haven't seen a copy of the break-in report yet. Is there any progress?" She reached in the glove box to grab the registration and insurance card, hoping that they were there and not expired.

"It's all finished, but no real leads. There was another break-in at Silver Lake, and some computer equipment was stolen, so we're checking that one out too. Weren't you going to pick up a copy?" The deputy quickly scanned the two cards Gracie handed to him.

"Yes, but things got crazy at the kennel, and I haven't had a chance to get it. Could it be mailed to me?" She flashed her best repentant smile.

"Sure, I'll see if Administration can get that out to you on Monday. Well, Mrs. Andersen, why don't we forgo the ticket today, and you just make a promise to slow down?" His smile was amazingly attractive, and he sure did look good in that uniform.

Gracie swallowed hard. "Sure thing, Deputy Stevens. I appreciate that."

"No problem. Just so you know we're making sure a nightly patrol goes past your kennel. We're keeping an eye on things. Just call us if you see or hear anything suspicious."

Nodding, she rolled up the window while watching the deputy get into the patrol car in her rear view mirror. Her heart was beating like a drum, and she gripped the steering wheel to keep her hands steady. Was it the deputy or almost getting a ticket? Maybe a little of both. She wouldn't mind if Deputy Stevens made the nightly patrol. Gracie mentally shook herself. It was the first time another man had entered her head since Michael's death. Was she moving on or just lonely? The deputy touched the brim of his hat as he pulled around Gracie. She waved and then slid the gearshift into drive. She wasn't sure if she liked the feeling she had just experienced, but, then again, she hadn't gotten a ticket either. Things were looking up.

She dropped the groceries off at the house and turned back for town to see Uncle Stan. There was no answer when she tried calling him on her cell, but he might be on the back porch, enjoying a cold one or snoozing. His car was in the driveway when she pulled up. There was no answer to the doorbell and the newspaper lay in front of the door. She walked around to the backyard to check the porch, but there was no sign of him. Two empty brown bottles stood on the glass-topped, circular metal table, and the ABA Journal was on the chair. The screen door was unlocked, so Gracie stepped into the big country kitchen and called out. No answer. A greasy frying pan sat on a cold burner, and there was a little coffee left in the glass carafe under the coffee maker. She could hear the TV in the living room. Uncle Stan must be passed out in front of the TV again. She pushed the swinging door from the kitchen and stepped into the large sunlit dining room. The half-walls and white columns at the end of the dining room led to the foyer, which opened to the curved staircase opposite the living room. The announcers for the Yankees game were discussing a double play.

"Hey, Uncle Stan, are you awake? It's Gracie."

Gracie stopped short as she passed through the opening to the foyer. Her legs froze, and she couldn't quite take in the scene in front of her. The familiar surroundings were suddenly foreign and surreal. The floor lurched and rose up to meet her. She grabbed at the large oak newel post at the end of the curved banister.

"Uncle Stan," she groaned.

Stan lay at the bottom of the stairs; his eyes wide open as if he were surprised. His left leg was twisted back at an unnatural angle.

Gracie couldn't get her breath, and her throat felt like it was closing up. She dropped to her knees, stretching her fingers toward the still form. She drew back her hand and ran outside.

Chapter 17

Gracie stood numbly with her parents, as the EMTs wheeled the sheet-draped form of Uncle Stan out to the ambulance. The only sound now was the pendulum clock in the hallway; the ticking was like a dripping faucet. The coroner made notes on his clipboard and cleared his throat to speak.

"What happened?" Tim barreled through the front door, slightly out of breath as his head swiveled back toward the ambulance.

"Well, it seems that your father-in-law took a bad tumble down the stairs here." The coroner, Ralph Remington, pushed his reading glasses up onto his broad forehead and gazed impassively at Tim's ashen face.

"Is he..?"

"I'm sorry, but he's gone, Tim. Looks like he broke his neck and leg in the fall." Ralph was not known for his bedside manner, but he had been the coroner for 30 years and had seen just about everything. From farm accidents, car accidents, suicides, and a few murders, Ralph had long ago developed a crusty shell that distanced him from viewing a victim as a real person.

Tim rubbed his forehead, "I knew his drinking would get him, but I thought his liver would go, not this."

Bob Clark put his hand on his nephew-in-law's shoulder. "Have you gotten a hold of Isabelle yet?"

"She's on her way, but I didn't know it was this bad." Tim sat down heavily on a dining room chair and put his head in his hands. "Who found him?"

"I did," Gracie's voice quavered. "He was just lying there." Gracie began to cry, and her mother quickly put an arm around her waist.

The ambulance was slowly pulling away from the curb. Ralph walked back into the house.

"Gracie, I need you to sign the report. Sorry."

She quickly wiped tears from her eyes, trying to focus on the paper. She scribbled her name.

"Thanks." Ralph shifted his weight and turned toward Tim. "You know, Tim, there'll have to be an autopsy, so you and Isabelle call the hospital morgue tomorrow to see if it's been done. We'll try to push it through."

"All right, I understand. Isabelle won't like it though. I'm sure you'll find plenty of alcohol in his system."

"We'll see. I know Stan sure did like to knock 'em back."

With that, he gathered the rest of his equipment and headed to his shabby black county-issued station wagon parked behind Gracie's SUV.

Gracie found a clean tissue in her bag and blew her nose. She wasn't sure that facing Isabelle and possibly creating another ugly scene was something she could handle. She really needed to get home; there was a lot to do in the kennel and around the house. Her resolve to control her emotions last night was quickly dissolving.

"I'd better get going. Tim, I'm so sorry. I can't believe..." Her voice broke, and flashes of finding Michael in the hayfield under the tractor flashed through her mind.

"I think I'll go with you," Theresa said firmly. "Your dad can pick me up later. Let me drive."

"I'll stay here with Tim then." Bob was equally as firm and hugged Gracie. Gracie nodded and handed the keys to her mother. Theresa gave Tim a quick hug and followed Gracie through the front door.

Exercising the dogs in the play yard helped Gracie regain some emotional control. Haley joined in the fun, and the motley crew of canines ran after balls, stuffed animals, and each other in the large grassy area, shaded by two silver maple trees. It was over all too soon, and the vision of Uncle Stan at the bottom of the stairs made her stomach lurch. Why hadn't she stopped by sooner? He'd probably been drowning his sorrows again. He shouldn't have been by himself. Maybe it was time to show Mom all the stuff Uncle Stan had left her. The smell of homemade macaroni and cheese filled the kitchen.

"Mmmm good, Mom. How'd you know that would hit the spot?" she said a little too brightly. She had to try and keep it all light, or she'd really lose it.

"Comfort food is needed today. Your pantry is pretty well stocked right now, so I didn't have to improvise."

Gracie laughed. "I did do some shopping today." The last time she'd made mac and cheese, she had to use cheese topping from a spray can. It had been an interesting dish with a peculiar texture. Her father pulled up just as they sat down to eat.

"Is there enough for me?" The screen door slammed behind him.

"A ton. You're just in time, Dad."

Her father said a quick blessing and her mother began dishing up the casserole. Gracie thought she'd have no appetite, but the food tasted good. Haley slept under the table, snoring contentedly.

"I think I'd better show you both all the stuff that Uncle Stan gave me. I won't ever know now why he handed it to me, but maybe we can sort it out." Gracie scraped back her chair and pulled out a gallon-sized zip-lock bag from the refrigerator.

"Expecting Maxwell Smart?" Her father was shaking his head.

"No, but I *am* expecting Isabelle. She came right into the house the other night and tried to take these back."

"You watch way too much crime TV, my dear," Theresa admonished her daughter.

"Maybe, but I'm not taking any chances."

Theresa quickly cleared the table as Gracie spread out the clippings, death certificate, police report, and the diary.

"Oh, my! Stan gave you Charlotte's diary?" Her mother's voice suddenly cracked.

"I told you that he did. That's why I wanted to hang on to all of this. She had some weird code going on in the diary, and I'm not sure who she's talking about. And did you know she was pregnant?" This was the bombshell she'd been holding back.

"Pregnant! No. Shirley never said a word."

"Here, look through this and tell me what you think."

Gracie settled into her chair and watched her parents read through the papers.

"Well, I'm sure your Aunt Shirley didn't want anyone to know about the pregnancy. In fact, I can almost guarantee she'd have driven Charlotte to a clinic for an abortion if she had known." Bob took his reading glasses off and leaned back on the Mission-style chair.

"Unfortunately, I'd have to agree with your dad. My sister was hardnosed about appearances and family honor."

"Really, Mom?"

"No need for sarcasm, Grace Marie."

"Well, from what I can decipher from Charlotte's diary, Aunt Shirley was making her life miserable."

"You need to be careful too. Teenaged daughters are not the easiest to reason with or keep on the right path sometimes. If you remember, your parents were pretty mean too." Her father was trying to lighten the tone.

"I know, but if it was just general teenage angst and a hormonal mistake that turned into a surprise pregnancy, why did Uncle Stan give all of this to me?"

"Who knows? Stan had been slipping for awhile now, and maybe Shirley's death triggered something about Charlotte. I really don't think it means anything, other than maybe he wanted someone to remember Charlotte or maybe know about the pregnancy. I don't know, Gracie," her father answered.

Theresa stood and began rinsing dishes and loading the dishwasher.

"I agree with your dad. I think Stan had some kind of remorse or just sadness about Charlotte and Shirley, and for some reason, gave all of this to you. You and he always had a pretty close relationship when you were growing up."

"I guess, but I think there's more to it." Gracie was feeling stubborn, and a nagging in her gut told her there was more here than met the eye.

"I doubt it, and at this point, it's the wrong time to aggravate Isabelle. She now has to plan another funeral. Losing both parents in one week is pretty horrible." Theresa's brow furrowed and met Gracie's gaze.

"I know. I know. Take it all back to Isabelle." She'd been the bad guy long enough, and it was time to do the right thing.

"I think that's wise, Gracie. I'll give them to Tim and keep this low-key for Isabelle's sake. She's taking her father's death pretty hard." Her father began piling the papers and slid them back into the bag. "Now that they're room temperature, we can return them. You just beat all sometimes." He arched an eyebrow at his daughter, and Gracie shrugged.

"Are you going to be OK?" Her mother's voice was full of concern. Worry lines were etched in her forehead.

"I'll be fine. I really am feeling better, and Jim is going to stop by later, so we can go over the week's excitement and figure out what we're going do staff-wise." Gracie was suddenly eager to have her parents go and leave her to her own thoughts. Maybe Jim could shed some light on things.

"Well, that's good. Come on, Theresa, let's head home. We still have to stop in and check on Isabelle and Tim and the kids. Don't worry, Gracie. I'll give the papers to Tim tomorrow, so as not to cause a scene. You get some rest and don't worry about everything. And *don't* make too much of these papers. Your imagination is way too active."

"Yeah, right, Dad. Thanks for everything. I'll call you tomorrow."

She hugged them both, and the car was out of the driveway before Gracie had finished dumping food into Haley's bowl. She was printing out the scanned documents when Jim yelled through the screen.

"Hey, are you decent?"

"Mostly. Come on in." She flopped down on the couch, sipping on icy lemonade.

"Want something to drink?"

"Whatever you're having is fine." He rubbed Haley's ears, and she immediately went back to the bowl of kibble.

"Help yourself. It's in the pitcher on the counter."

Jim poured himself a large glass and joined her in the living room.

"Are you doing all right, Chief?"

"I'm OK. I can't believe all the stuff that's happening at once. I haven't had time to check on Beth today."

"She's doing fine. I called this afternoon and talked to her. Beth is young and bouncing right back."

"Good. I'm glad you called her. The family stuff going on is way too much." She saw the immediate concern in his eyes. "And I'm handling it. I'm sick of not dealing with my life, so don't worry."

"All right. But you know how's it's been."

"I do. I'm sorry for all of it too. Let's not talk about me anymore. I want to show you this stuff and get your take on it." She spread out the scanned documents on the coffee table for him to read.

"Wow, I don't know, Gracie." Jim put the copy of the death certificate back on the table. "It sounds like there was a lot going on with Charlotte right before she was killed. I don't understand why your Uncle Stan gave this to you, but maybe Isabelle will calm down now that she's getting the diary back."

"I hope so, but I don't think I can count on it. I still think Uncle Stan wanted me to have these for another reason than just fond memories. Maybe there was a cover-up, or something was done wrong in the investigation, and he wanted me to find out what really happened."

"You do have a great imagination. Who are you, Agatha Christie?"

"Thanks for the vote of confidence. I'm still going to do some digging and see what I can find out. I owe my uncle." She tightened the loose ponytail that threatened to slip from the band.

"You'd better be careful. Give Isabelle some consideration. I hate to bring this up, but what if Charlotte...well, stepped in front of the car..." He paused. "Her diary is kind of disturbing." Jim tapped the diary entry on the coffee table.

"I can't believe she'd do that. Charlotte wouldn't have..." Her voice trailed off. This was something she hadn't even considered. But Jim was right. Her cousin was over the edge about her situation. But just as quickly, Gracie decided against that theory. She didn't want to even think about that possibility.

"I've got to find out more about Charlotte's death, now more than ever. Uncle Stan wouldn't have given me her diary if he thought she'd jumped in front of the car. There's something that doesn't feel right. Plus I need to find out who she was seeing."

"I don't think that'll be easy after all these years. Anyway, we're not going to figure it out tonight. Can we go over the financials and the schedule for next week?"

Gracie brought her laptop out, and the evening sped on as they poured over the spreadsheets of income and expense. Income was down for the week, but it was understandable. When she brought up the subject of letting

Jim out of the partnership, he refused. It was way too early to make that decision in his opinion.

When Jim finally left, it was almost 10 o'clock, and Gracie was exhausted. The emotional rollercoaster day had taken its toll. But, before she could go to bed, she needed to check on the dogs and double-check the alarm.

The night air was permeated with eau de cow manure wafting from the dairy farm a couple of miles down the road. She could also smell the heavy scent of the cornfield behind the kennel. Nothing was as invigorating as good country air. Haley trotted across the driveway to the office door. A car drove slowly down the road as Gracie's sneakers crunched on the gravel. She swung her flashlight toward the road as it passed. The car braked and then backed up. Gracie stood still, her heart racing. She grabbed Haley's rolled leather collar as the car swung into the driveway, its headlights bathing her in brightness. Haley growled, and her hackles rose.

"Hey, Mrs. Andersen, everything OK?" It was Deputy Stevens.

"No problems, Deputy. Just making the final bed check." There was relief in her voice, and her pulse still pounded in her ears.

"Would you mind some help?" He was already getting out of the car and putting on his hat.

"No, in fact that would be great. It's been a little spooky out here at night, since the robbery."

Haley sniffed the deputy's pants, and he stroked her head. Haley leaned into his leg, begging for more.

"I can imagine. You are pretty isolated in this spot." He pulled a long flashlight from the front seat. "Great dog you've got here. What's her name?"

"Haley, as in the comet. She's a good dog most of the time and then..." Haley whined and pushed her cold wet nose against Gracie's palm. "All right, I won't turn you in to the law," she laughed.

"You're working a long shift today," she observed.

"Yeah, a couple of guys called in sick tonight. I went home, grabbed a few hours of sleep, and got back on the road about an hour ago."

"Your wife must love those double shifts."

"Well, no worries there. Never been married. Law enforcement isn't always conducive to long relationships, but maybe someday. It would make my mother happy." He laughed and held the door for Gracie as she punched in the code on the keypad.

Dogs were barking and whining when they entered the kennel corridors. The bed check didn't take long, and everything was in order. Haley ran up and down the corridors, sniffing and joining in the canine chorus. With the kennel secure and the dogs tucked in for the night, Gracie felt that the late night encounter with Deputy Stevens had been way too short. There was no reason for him to stay, but then she remembered the redacted police report on Charlotte's accident and the mention of the incomplete license plate.

"Deputy, I do have a question for you." He was back in the cruiser, fastening his seatbelt.

"Sure. Shoot."

"Do you have any idea if the DMV keeps records back 20 years or so, and if I could get a copy of an old police report from about the same time?"

"Any particular reason?"

His facial expression was hard for her to see in the darkness away from the mercury vapor light by the kennel. She imagined he must've thought she was slightly weird.

"Well, I'm trying to get some answers about my cousin's death. It was a hit-and-run that was never solved. And it was 20 years ago."

"Oh." He was thoughtful. "Well, we can probably dig up the incident report, if the sheriff's department investigated, but I'm not sure about the DMV records. I can do some checking and let you know."

"I'd really appreciate that. Let me run in the house and write down the information about the accident."

"Sure. I've gotta check in anyway."

Gracie hurried to the kitchen and quickly wrote out on a sticky note Charlotte's name, the date of the accident, and where it happened. She added her name and phone number at the bottom. He was talking on the radio when she returned with the note. He took it from her hand and stuck it to the dashboard.

"Sorry, but I've got to run. Another break-in."

"Is it close?"

"Not too far. The Jorgensen place by the lake."

"Jorgensen? That's only three or four miles from here. You know, I've got their dogs here. They're on vacation this week."

"Thanks for the info. I'll call you." He backed the car out of the driveway and sped with lights flashing in the direction of Silver Lake. Gracie shivered, even though the night air was warm. Another robbery and so close. She hurried into the house with Haley and locked the door.

Chapter 18

Sunday morning was a blur of activity. The phone calls had started by seven—first from her mother, then the church ladies, followed by an abrupt call from Tim informing her how upset Isabelle was because of Gracie's thoughtless actions. Then Isabelle called her to say she was no longer speaking to Gracie. At that point, Gracie was ready to disconnect every phone she owned.

According to the church ladies, the rumor mill was working overtime about how Gracie had found her Uncle Stan. The prayer chain at church included a request that Isabelle and Gracie mend their fences and put their feud to rest. Her mother called again to say Isabelle was fighting with the medical examiner to get Stan's body released before the autopsy was completed. It was all a little much. She felt like she was living some bizarre reality TV show. Who were these people?

At 11 a.m. sharp, the Clarks were sitting in their usual pew at Deer Creek Community Church. She really didn't want to be there, but Gracie sat stiffly with her parents, looking straight ahead, deliberately not singing the hymns. She hadn't been able to sing a hymn without crying since Michael's funeral. With the vision of Uncle Stan at the bottom of the stairs fresh in her thoughts, today was not the day to try again. Isabelle and Tim were absent, which made the service bearable. When it was time to greet each other, Gracie noticed that Joe Youngers was with his grandmother in the back row. She gave him a quick smile, and he raised his hand in greeting.

"Who's that?" Theresa whispered as they sat down.

"Joe Youngers. We hired him on a trial basis as a kennel helper," Gracie whispered back.

"Oh. Well, I hope he works out."

Rev. Minders' sermon was, unfortunately, on loving your enemies. Gracie guessed that he'd dusted that one off for just her. She was sure that was what the rest of the congregation was thinking too. When the coffee hour started, Gracie slipped out the side door to the parking lot. She didn't want to face the condolences and questions. It was probably cowardly, but she didn't feel like being a hero. There were certain ladies who loved the gory details. They'd want to know if Stan had a peaceful look on his face, if he was dressed, and if he smelled of liquor. These were conversations she didn't want to have today.

The Deer Creek streets were relatively quiet on Sunday mornings. Driving home, Gracie enjoyed the well-kept lawns on Main Street, until she reached the railroad tracks. There was the proverbial wrong side of the tracks in Deer Creek. The houses in the section closest to the deteriorating depot looked tired and run down at the heels. The depot was finally scheduled to be razed, much to the relief of the Village Board. It was a haunt for kids who needed a place to smoke dope and who knew what else. Graffiti flourished on the weathered clapboards. The depot was at the head of a short dead-end street called Rail Avenue, which curved to accommodate the bend in the tracks. Gracie remembered a train derailment or two growing up, when a tired engineer hadn't negotiated the curve in time. Then she remembered it was where Bea Youngers lived. She craned her neck to see around the curve, but was unsuccessful in catching a glimpse of the Youngers home.

A large, muscular man walked down the sidewalk, keeping his eyes fixed on the uneven pavement. Gracie didn't recognize him, but then she couldn't see his face very well under the baseball cap. There were no trains to wait for today, and she slowly drove over the bumpy tracks. The phone message Uncle Stan had left her ran continuously through her mind. No matter what anyone said, there was more to Charlotte's death. What if there was more to Uncle Stan's death too?

Gracie made a quick decision to turn around and go to Uncle Stan's house, while everyone was still at church. Hopefully, Isabelle and Tim weren't already there, cleaning everything out. Maybe he had left a note or some other bit of information for her. If Isabelle found anything, it would be lost forever. She'd have to make a quick job of it and hope no one saw her. The spare key was under a large rock by the garage, so there wouldn't be any problem of getting in.

The house looked quiet when she parked across the street. Deciding it was too chancy to leave her vehicle where everyone could see it, she drove back around the corner and parked in the driveway of a vacant house with a for-sale sign stuck in the front yard. Slipping through two backyards, Gracie pushed through the hedge into her uncle's yard. Plucking the key from under the sparkly pink rock nestled in the snow-on-the-mountain groundcover that edged the front of the garage, she got into the kitchen, dropping the key in her tote. The frying pan was still on the stove, the smell of stale bacon still clung to the area. It looked like Isabelle hadn't been over to clean yet. Gracie felt like throwing up when she reached the bottom of the stairs. There was no sign of yesterday's horror, and the clock still ticked the seconds off with a steady beat.

She forced herself to climb the stairs. There were many happy memories of running up and down these stairs, playing hide-and-seek in the rambling Victorian. Aunt Shirley had always decorated the banister with extravagant garlands at Christmas time, filling the house with scent of pine. Now the house seemed draped in sadness. When she reached the top of stairs, Uncle Stan's bedroom door was open. The bed was made, and the room was in perfect order. A large blue braided rug covered a good portion of the polished wood floor.

His rolltop desk stood in a corner by the south window, overlooking the side lawn. She quickly went through the few papers on the desktop. There were only medical bills for Aunt Shirley. Gracie rifled through the drawers and cubbies, still not finding anything of interest. She glanced at her watch. The 10 minutes she'd allowed herself were ticking by. She rummaged to locate the key in the bag. Finally grasping the silver key, it slipped from her fingers and clanged onto the hardwood floor, skittering underneath the desk as her tote spilled out on the floor. The sound of a car coming down the street sent panic through her as she snatched up the key and stuffed the spilled contents back in the tote.

Jim looked like a kid, throwing tennis balls and running with a dog pack that eagerly watched his every move inside the large fenced play area. Haley was in the middle of it all, soaking up the excitement and chasing tennis balls. He looked up with a big grin on his handsome face when he saw Gracie walking to the fence.

"Hey, Chief, how was church?"

"OK. I slipped out when the coffee hour started. When are you going to stop being a heathen and go?"

"The steeple would fall down if I ever darkened the door. Besides, who'd give these guys a really great playtime if I was in church?"

For all the years Gracie had known Jim, the only time she'd seen him in church was for a funeral or wedding. Since Michael's death, Jim had seemed even more adamant about staying away from church. Gracie couldn't say much; she was just as guilty. It had been too painful to attend after losing Michael and the baby. But that was going to change. Life needed to be normal again.

"You're working up a real sweat."

"Yeah, I know. It's been a danged humid summer, but the dogs don't seem to mind."

"I think they're slowing down though," Gracie laughed. Two Golden Retrievers were stretched out on their bellies, panting furiously; three mixed breeds and a small beagle were lapping water from a large bowl by the fence.

"Hey, before I forget, that Deputy Stevens stopped by." Jim mopped his sweaty face with his T-shirt, his well-defined six-pack in full view.

"What did he want?" Gracie was careful to keep her voice measured.

"He said he had information about an old DMV record or something like that. Does that have anything to do with the robbery?"

"Not really. I had a couple of questions about Charlotte's stuff, so I thought I'd ask him."

"Come on, Gracie, you need to let that whole thing go. It's not healthy for you."

"I'm a big girl, and I can handle it. Something is not right with what happened to Charlotte. Uncle Stan trusted me with all that information, and I'm going to find out what happened. Is he stopping back?"

"He said he might. Listen, Gracie, it was a stupid, awful accident, and the driver didn't get what he deserved. You're not going find out anything new now. Let it go."

"Not your call, Jimmy. Thanks for the advice though."

Sometimes Jim was a little too protective, but he meant well.

"Whatever. I'll put the dogs back. I've gotta run. I'm meeting Laney. We're headed for the lake this afternoon. Joe's coming to feed and bed everybody down around five. You'll just have to set the alarm."

"Sounds like fun. I'm hanging out here today with Haley. A dog is always the best company. Have a good time." Gracie flashed a warm smile. "You'd better shower before you pick up Laney."

"Nah, good old lake water will take care of it." He smelled his armpits and made a face. "Pee yew... maybe not."

"Maybe not indeed, Pepe LePew. You don't want to scare her off first thing."

"She's a farm girl. She can take it."

"I hope so. Come on, Haley, let's go." She opened the outside gate, and the big dog ambled through the gate to the kennel.

Gracie spent the afternoon with the sheaf of printed diary entries and scanned documents. They were scattered over the floor, as she searched for anything that might help identify real names from the King Arthur code.

There didn't seem to be any more statements in Charlotte's diary that helped her figure out who Lancelot and Galahad were. She racked her brain to remember Charlotte's closest friends. Heather Martin came to mind, but she wasn't sure if she was still in the area. She grabbed her senior yearbook from the bookcase and looked back at the sophomore class to see if any faces clicked. She easily picked out Charlotte on the JV cheerleading squad, along with Heather. She looked through the pictures of the Varsity and Junior Varsity football teams. No players jogged her memory, but then she recognized one. A tall, lanky, blond Matthew Minders stood in the back row.

He had hung around Charlotte, although she had pretty much ignored him. He had been a bench warmer most of the time, only playing when victory was truly out of reach or victory was totally assured. He was the youngest of the four Minders' children. He might be a possibility, plus her mother had mentioned he'd given the police a partial plate number. She wrote his name in a small spiral notebook, along with Kelly and Heather. Miss Russell stood beside the cheerleading squad. She'd been the coach in the 70s and 80s, and was the 10th grade English teacher. Maybe she was still around, even though she had retired from teaching and coaching several years ago now. The school might know for sure. Another note went in the book.

The phone started ringing again late in the afternoon. Gracie had dozed off on the living room floor, leaning against the sofa. She jerked awake and grabbed the phone that was on the floor. Her mother informed her that the medical examiner was not going to release Uncle Stan's body today or tomorrow. There were some questions that needed answers before that happened.

"What do you mean he has questions?"

"He's not really saying. Isabelle is beside herself. She just wants to get the funeral planned."

"I can imagine."

So Uncle Stan's death wasn't falling neatly into place. Maybe she wasn't imagining things after all.

"We're not sure what this means, but hopefully they'll clear it all up quickly." Her mother's voice was weary.

"I hope so too. You sound like you could use some rest."

"I know. I'm pretty tired."

"Get some sleep, Mom. You can't solve all the family crises on your own. I'm sure the medical examiner will figure it out."

"You're right. They have to make sure nothing is missed. We'll just have to wait an extra day or so. It's just so much to deal with right now."

"I know, Mom. Please get some rest."

Gracie heard a car turn into the driveway.

"Somebody's here. I'd better go. Rest. Go to bed." Haley was already barking.

"OK. I'll call you tomorrow."

The car was one Gracie didn't recognize, but she did recognize the driver. It was Deputy Stevens. What was his first name anyway?

It turned out that Deputy Stevens' name was Marc with a "c," and he did have some information on old license plates. He wore a fresh white golf shirt and jeans that looked as good on him as his uniform did. Gracie invited him to sit on the back patio, while she grabbed a pitcher of lemonade and a couple of glasses. Haley was busy smelling his jeans and looking for more of the treats that filled his pockets. His sunglasses were pushed up onto his head, and he stretched out his legs as he settled back in one of the Adirondack chairs.

"Hey, thanks," Marc said appreciatively when Gracie handed him an icy glass of lemonade. "Just the thing to cut the humidity today. What a summer it's been." He took a long, deep drink.

"It sure has been sticky and hot. We'll probably pay for it this winter. We'll have six feet of snow from Halloween to April."

Were they really talking about the weather? Gracie wished the conversation would move to a more relevant topic.

"I hope you don't mind me stopping by like this."

"Not at all. I'm really glad you did." Gracie hoped that her T-shirt was clean and her hair presentable. At least she had some makeup today. With any luck, she hadn't rubbed mascara all over her face.

"Well, there's good news and bad news on the DMV front. Which do you want first?"

"Might as well get the bad news over with. I've had plenty of that this week."

"Sorry to hear that. More than just the robbery?"

"Plenty more." Gracie suddenly launched into a litany of the business and personal disasters that had overflowed her life during the last week.

"Uh, wow. I'm really sorry about your uncle and..." Deputy Stevens face looked bewildered and a little overwhelmed. "I didn't realize..."

Gracie was shocked at herself, that she had just shared a torrent of complaints and grief with a total stranger.

"I'm really sorry. I don't know where all that came from. I guess it's the lemonade talking." She feebly tried to make a joke.

"Sounds like you've had a pretty bad week, so a little venting is understandable." He sat forward in his chair and took another drink from the glass dripping with condensation.

"What's the bad news then about the DMV?" She was anxious to focus on Charlotte, not her current life.

"Well, the DMV doesn't keep records that far back, so looking for a partial plate that old is pretty impossible." He set the empty glass on the small wicker side table.

"I thought that would be the case, so that's not a big surprise. Is there any good news in any of this?"

"The good news is that, with a little digging, I think I can find the original incident report without the redactions. Maybe that will help you sort things out."

"Is that something I can request, or do you have to do that?"

"Since I go in Tuesday morning to catch up on my paperwork, I can do a little research in the office at the same time. If I find it, I'll make a copy."

"Thanks, that sounds great." Then Gracie's mind flashed to the little snag in getting Uncle Stan's body released. "On another subject, can you also find out why the medical examiner won't release my uncle's body?"

Marc looked surprised as she explained about the holdup in getting the body to the funeral home.

"I'm not sure about that," he said hesitantly, his eyes narrowing. "Could be a lot of things to delay the release. It happens all the time."

The moment suddenly seemed awkward, and he stood saying he needed to get going. Gracie felt her face flush. She had the distinct impression she'd scared him with her multiple personal and business issues. Not very smooth.

She watched him get into his car and then walked back to the patio door with Haley close at her heels.

"That went well! I'm almost 40, but socially, I'm about 15. I've got to get out more. What do you think, girl?"

Haley merely wagged her tail and flopped down in front of the fan on the living room floor.

Chapter 19

Joe Youngers chewed the inside of his cheek. His grandmother had given him the ultimatum. His Uncle Ron was coming to make sure it happened too. He had to get Brad and Carter out within the next week. He knew they'd been on thin ice for a while. He had warned them, but their slovenly habits, odd hours, and rough language were well-ingrained. Joe also knew there would be threats that Brad would not hesitate to carry out. He needed to choose his words carefully.

Carter and Brad were usually together, but Carter came in alone.

"Where's Brad?" Joe said offhandedly.

"He's finishing up at the depot. Should be back in a few minutes. There were some kids hanging around he had to deal with."

Joe's stomach lurched. So far, there hadn't been trouble with the local kids. They had been able to store the "inventory" without too much curiosity. They had found a section of the crumbling depot that wasn't used by transients and dope-smoking kids. It was dry and fairly secure. Joe hoped that Brad wasn't being too rough, arousing suspicion. He figured he might as well get started on the conversation he dreaded. He cleared his throat and shoved his thin, sinewy hands deep into his jeans pockets.

"You know, I've got some stuff to talk to you and Brad about."

"Whaddaya mean, Joe? You don't look so good." Carter stared blandly at Joe.

"It's my grandmother. She's not doin' so well lately. I might have to put her in a home or somethin'."

"That's too bad, but we'd have the house to ourselves then, so that would be good, right?" Carter ran his thin hand through the shaggy brown hair that fell haphazardly into his eyes.

"Yeah, but we've got a problem. My uncle is coming to stay for a while, and he's not going to like you and Brad living here. You're going to have to..."

Brad came through the front door. His shaved head was streaked with dirt and his AC/DC black T-shirt clung to his bulky torso.

"Have to do what?" he demanded.

Joe swallowed hard. He casually stepped nearer to the back door, hoping to give himself room to run if necessary.

"It's not what I want, but you guys have to move out, for a while anyway. My uncle could cause a lot of problems. He's a retired state trooper."

"Where'd we go? Your uncle is just going to have to deal with it." Brad's brown eyes were sharp and belligerent.

"You're goin' to have to find somethin'. You don't know my uncle. He doesn't mess around, and he wouldn't think twice about puttin' us all back in prison."

"Maybe we can just take care of that problem." He flexed his right arm, well-developed muscles popping.

"Hey, Brad, I don't want to go back to prison. We can find something." Carter was getting nervous. The mention of a cop in the house didn't appeal to him at all.

"Call that program that got me hooked up, you know...Second Chances." Joe tried to sound hopeful.

"That old bag, the preacher's wife, is a nut case. What good will she do?" Brad was sneering.

"She's a little loony, but she's got connections. She can probably find you a place to stay for a while." Joe was getting desperate.

"Come on, Brad, we can check it out. I really don't want any trouble." Carter was looking more anxious. He wiped sweaty hands on his faded jeans.

"Well, I guess we can check it out and see. She might set us up with a good situation like you. You're still in this, Joe. I'm expectin' you to keep us in the loop."

"Yeah, I know. Don't worry about that. If you're outta here, it'll be easier to keep things quiet." Joe was starting to feel a little more relieved. He grabbed a can of beer for each of them from the dingy white refrigerator and headed to the back porch.

"To better days," Joe said lightly, raising the can to the air.

"Yeah, whatever," growled Brad.

Carter drank his beer slowly, watching a stray cat saunter across the yard. He grabbed the pellet gun propped against the house.

"Watch this." He quickly took aim and shot the gray cat in the head. It fell to the ground, spasmed, and then lay still.

"Not bad, Carter." Brad was smirking and then crumpled the empty can in his paw-like hand.

Joe winced and stretched out arms on the weathered railing. White paint chips, flaking off the porch railing, speckled the dirt below.

"Hey, take care of that before my grandmother sees it. She feeds those strays, you know."

"Maybe she'll just have to boo-hoo over this one," Brad sneered.

"Yeah, that'll teach her," Carter snorted.

"Just take care of it. I gotta go to work." Joe said. He suddenly felt weak and shaky. "The shovel is in the shed."

"Sure thing, boss. Make sure you come back with some fresh info tonight." Brad took his crumpled can and twisted it in half.

Chapter 20

Gracie sat straight up in bed, gasping for air, as if she had been underwater. She was running through the hayfield, trying to get to Michael. The rear tractor tires were spinning in the air as it lay upside down. Everything was slow motion, and she couldn't reach the tractor. Michael's voice kept calling for her, but her legs were like lead. She kept running, never making enough progress to get to the tractor. When she looked down, she wasn't running through grass, but mud that was knee high.

She looked at the clock. It was 5:30, and she needed to get up anyway. She hadn't had that nightmare for many months, and now it was back. The hot, sharp spray of water from the showerhead felt good on her face, as she tried to wash away the horror of the dream and the memories of real life. Maybe it had been stupid to flush the medication. There had to be an emergency stash of pills somewhere in her desk or purse. She closed her eyes and shook her head. "No. I am fine," she told herself, rinsing the shampoo from her hair.

Jim and Gracie shuffled four applications between them as they sat in the office, discussing the best choice.

"Here's the one I like," she said pushing the paper to Jim.

"Cheryl Stone?" He scanned her resume and application.

"Yeah, she's got the most experience with dogs. She takes overflow dogs from the county shelter, teaches 4-H dog obedience, and isn't a criminal."

"You can't blame Mrs. Minders for trying." Jim adjusted the Yankees cap on his head and leaned back in the black task chair.

"I guess not, but those two she sent over yesterday were pretty bad. The one with the messy hair wasn't especially bright, and Haley didn't like him. Always trust a dog's instincts about people."

"I'll go along with you on that one; Carter was his name, I think. The other one wasn't too bad though. At least he had some animal experience." Jim smiled, anticipating Gracie's response.

"Turtles and canaries don't count. Neither one is a mammal." She looked up from the last application and saw Jim's grin. "OK, who do you think?" Gracie said teasingly with hands on her hips.

"I say call Cheryl Stone. See if she can start this week."

"Good, at least we agree on this one. Isn't Joe's review coming up today or tomorrow?"

"Tomorrow, I guess. He's doing fine. He's caught on to everything I've asked him to do. He's on time every day, and he's willing to work weekends. Any complaints on your side?"

"None that I can put my finger on. It's just a feeling I have. But he was in church with his grandmother Sunday, so maybe I've been too hard on him. Watch him though; I just don't trust him completely."

"Right, Chief." With a quick salute, Jim was out the door, whistling *American Pie*.

Marian stuck her head in the doorway, pointing to the portable phone in her hand.

"It's your Mom, Gracie. I think they've got the funeral set."

"Thanks, Marian. I'll take it in here." Gracie picked up the receiver and punched the blinking button.

But the funeral wasn't set, according to her mother. It was Wednesday and still no Uncle Stan to bury. Isabelle was fuming about the incompetence of the medical examiner and the impropriety of not being able to lay her father to rest. The latest development was that the sheriff's department was doing a little more investigation. The M.E. found some unexplained bruising, and there was a minimal amount of alcohol in his system. He was ruling it a suspicious death.

"You're kidding, right?" Gracie's voice rose in disbelief.

"I'm afraid not. You can expect an investigator to ask you some more questions. They've already talked to Isabelle and Tim. They'll probably talk to us too. It's a real mess. I don't see how they can think it was anything other than an accident." Theresa's voice matched the timbre of her daughter's.

"I guess I'll make sure I'm around today. It's gotta make you wonder." The wheels were turning, as she chewed on the eraser of the pencil in her hand.

"What do you mean?" Theresa sounded puzzled.

"Nothing, Mom. Just thinking out loud, I guess. I'll let you know if anyone from the sheriff's department shows up."

"OK, I'll talk to you later. Bye."

Gracie heard the click at the other end and slowly put the receiver back in the cradle. She suddenly had the urge to get Charlotte's diary from the living room and read it again. Things were hectic in the kennel though, so there was no way she could leave. She hurried back to the reception area to relieve Marian of phone duties so she could get the grooming customers back on schedule.

When the phone calls slowed down, she gave Cheryl Stone a call to see if she'd accept the job offer. When she did, Gracie yelled out, "Hot dog!" and danced around the desk. Haley jumped up with enthusiasm, her front paws hitting Gracie's stomach. She laughed and grabbed the dog's paws and continued dancing. Jim came in with work gloves stuck in his back pocket, as Marian was driving out to pick up lunches at Midge's.

"Good news?" he asked. He stood with hands on his hips and a hopeful expression in his eyes.

"Yes. Good news," said Gracie, her eyes bright. Haley sat panting by her knee.

"Cheryl can start tomorrow since she's not working. I should be able to get her trained in a week or two." Gracie felt more lighthearted than she had in days.

"All right! We're going to see light after all." Jim went to Gracie's office and pulled a Coke from the small refrigerator. "Want a diet?" he called back.

"Yes, thanks. Wait till I tell you what else is going on, though."

"What now? Something about your Uncle Stan?" He handed Gracie a bottle of Diet Coke and sat in one of plastic brown chairs in the waiting area.

"His death has been ruled suspicious. The sheriff's department is still investigating. They'll probably talk with me. They've already seen Isabelle and Tim." She took a long swallow of the icy cola.

"You're kidding. How could they think that? He must have had a few beers in him."

"Not from what the medical examiner says. Plus there's some kind of strange bruising."

"I don't know, Gracie. Sounds like they're making a mountain out of molehill. He fell down a flight of stairs; he would have bruises."

"There must be something different about them."

"Sorry to interrupt, but there's an Investigator Hotchkiss out here," said Joe, who was hauling a 50-pound bag of kibble. His face was white, and he shifted the weight of bag on his shoulder uneasily.

"Thanks, Joe. I'll go see him." Gracie tucked in her T-shirt and ran her fingers through her unruly red hair. It was curling out of control in the humidity.

"Uh, it's a her." Joe quickly turned toward the runs.

"I'll catch the phones while you go and chat." Jim slid into the task chair behind the desk.

"Thanks. Hopefully, this won't take long." Gracie was suddenly nervous, a million jumbled thoughts sparking in her brain.

Two hours later, Gracie was back in the grooming area with Marian. The Sheltie standing on the grooming table licked Gracie's hand. She absently rubbed the dog's ears.

"I've never been so insulted in my life. The questions she asked. It was unbelievable. She acted like I killed Uncle Stan." Gracie's face was redder than her hair.

"Cops are always like that. Everybody's a suspect. You watch *Law and Order,* don't you?"

"I can't believe that's actually real life. Investigator Hotchkiss has got some real attitude," Gracie huffed.

"And you don't?" Jim had just come in at the tail end of Gracie's tirade.

"No comments from the peanut gallery, thank you."

"Lighten up, Chief. She's just doing her job."

"I suppose, but if Uncle Stan was truly..." She couldn't bring herself to say "murdered." "I think it must have something to do with Charlotte. I need to figure out why he gave me those papers."

"Gracie, let the cops do their work, and all of this will get sorted out. I'll bet they change their minds soon. Who would hurt Stan?" Jim sounded so logical and calm.

Right now, logical and calm seemed annoying, but she decided to stay cool herself and surprise everybody.

"We'll see. But, hey, boys and girls, it's time to close up, so let's go home."

"You don't have to tell me twice," Marian said, sighing. "I'll get Sam kenneled, and then I'm outta here." She easily lifted the Sheltie from the table and led him down the hallway on a blue leash.

"Good night, Marian. Thanks for another great day." Gracie was sincerely worried that Marian would quit the kennel, given all of the turmoil. She was looking pretty weary.

"I'll go check on Joe and lock up the barns." Jim left through the front door.

"Great. I'll do bed checks after I count the receipts."

There weren't as many checks and credit card slips today. She hoped this wasn't a trend. There were footsteps in the reception area as she finished putting the deposit in the safe.

"Hey, Jim, is that you?" she called out. There was no answer.

"Who's there?" She felt the hair on the back of her neck rising.

"Uh, just me. Joe."

"Oh. Is there something you need?"

"I was just getting my hat. I left it in reception. Good night."

Relieved, Gracie exhaled slowly. The kennel still gave her the creeps when she was alone.

"Good night, Joe."

Old yearbooks and the diary entries were scattered over the living room floor. An open phonebook was on Gracie's lap. She finally found the name she was looking for—K. Russell. It had to be Kay Russell, long-time cheerleading coach and English teacher. She lived in Perry on Marquis Avenue. There was no answer, but the voicemail confirmed her hopes. Gracie left a message, explaining she was doing some research on cheerleaders and football players back in the early 90s.

She hoped that the retired teacher wasn't on vacation. Some quick answers about Galahad and Lancelot were needed, and maybe Kay could supply them. Gracie had no idea where Matthew Minders was these days. He hadn't been in Deer Creek for many years. She really didn't want to call Gloria Minders to ask about her son and have to explain why the kennel hadn't hired either of her two candidates. She typed in his name on the search engine page that was already loaded on her laptop. She uncrossed her legs as 20 possibilities appeared on the next screen.

There were two good prospects: one in Jamestown, New York, and the other in Denver, Colorado. The one in Jamestown was mentioned in a newspaper article from a year ago. He was a counselor and had spearheaded a new program for victims of domestic violence. The other Matthew was an electrical engineer for a large firm in Denver. Gracie would bet the farm that her Matthew Minders was in Jamestown. He was a lot like his mother; always involved in social justice programs. She quickly dialed the number in Jamestown. Her heart was pounding as the phone rang. What was she going to say? Suddenly, it all seemed pretty awkward and far-fetched. What was she doing?

"Hello," a female voice answered.

"Hi. Is Matthew there?" Gracie bit her lip.

"Sure, just a minute. Who's calling?"

"An old friend, Gracie Andersen."

"Oh." the friendliness in the voice changed slightly.

"Uh oh," Gracie whispered to Haley, who watched her with interest, while chewing on a rawhide. Haley's warm, liquidy brown eyes followed her mistress as she paced with the phone.

"Gracie, what a surprise! How are you?" The warm male voice was familiar. She softly let out her breath.

But the conversation didn't stay as relaxed as she'd hoped. The memories of Charlotte were painful for both of them, but in the end, Matthew agreed to make the two-hour trip on the weekend to go over the police report and

Charlotte's diary. Within minutes of hanging up with Matthew, the phone rang as Gracie pored over the police report once again. It was her mother.

"The funeral's on. They're releasing the body tonight. Isabelle wants the funeral tomorrow night at the church."

"Why so quick? That hardly gives any time for visiting hours."

"There won't be calling hours. Isabelle feels everybody is just waiting for the word, so the sooner the better. She's really been through enough. The police questioned her for quite a while today."

"I had the same treatment. Was it an Investigator Hotchkiss?"

"That sounds right. We had Deputy Stevens here. He seemed very nice. He asked if we knew where Stan was Friday night and Saturday morning. He also wanted to know where Isabelle and Tim were too."

"Deputy Stevens! He's the one investigating the robbery here. Do you know where they were?" Her curiosity was piqued, and a flush of embarrassment came back at the memory of Sunday afternoon.

"Not really. We assumed Stan was at the VFW, like he usually is on Friday nights. I don't know about Saturday. Your dad checked on him Friday morning, and he seemed to be doing pretty well. Isabelle says she was over earlier that afternoon, but I don't know where she went after that. She and Tim usually go out to dinner on Fridays.

"I'd be interested to know what Isabelle was doing Friday and Saturday."

"You can't be implying what I think you're implying." Gracie was familiar with the tone and softened her answer on the fly. She'd dropped her gaze and noticed that more freckles had appeared on her arms. She must be spending too much time in the sun.

"It's probably sour grapes after my experience with Investigator Hotchkiss this afternoon. She made me feel like the prime suspect."

"Well, it's a suspicious death, so I think they're just covering all their bases. Since they've released the body, they must be satisfied with everything."

"Not necessarily, Mom, but let's hope so."

After getting the details on the funeral, Gracie said good night, and then it flashed back—Uncle Stan's message was on her machine. She'd forgotten to tell the investigator, probably because she was so irritated at the time. She pushed the button to replay messages. It was eerie to hear his voice. The timestamp was 8:57 p.m. She'd left the house at 6:30 to pick up the fish dinners and go to her parents' house. Uncle Stan's habit was to eat at the VFW by six, and then play cards until 10 or 11 p.m. Lord knew Gracie had heard Aunt Shirley complain about his boys' night out often enough. So why was he home before nine? Or had he skipped the poker all together? Why hadn't she called him back? When did he die? Was it Friday or Saturday? Why hadn't she asked her mother if they'd talked to or seen Uncle Stan on Saturday? A shiver ran over her spine, contemplating Uncle Stan lying at the bottom of the stairs all night. She'd have to tell the investigator about this, but maybe she'd just call Deputy Stevens and give him the information. Hopefully, she wouldn't make a fool of herself if she got a second chance.

On her way to the sink with the empty glass, headlights swept into the driveway and Haley woofed her alarm. Peeking through the curtains on the kitchen door, she saw it was a sheriff's cruiser. Deputy Stevens was apparently brave enough to visit again. She opened the door just as he raised his hand to knock.

It didn't seem nearly as awkward as Sunday afternoon had been. Gracie decided that Deputy Marc Stevens looked something like Harrison Ford in his younger Indiana Jones days. He even had a dimple in his chin. No wonder he made her nervous.

He said he didn't have much time, but the visit was to drop off a copy of the un-redacted police report. Gracie hurried to find the scanned copy she had on the living room floor. They quickly compared the two on the dining room table.

"It looks like it's the vehicle information and license plate they've blacked out," Marc commented.

"It's a WY plate. They're hard vanity plates to get. You have to be somebody or know the right person at the DMV to get them." Gracie's mind whirled through possible reasons the plate number was obliterated in Uncle Stan's copy.

"A lot of them go to county employees. The County Clerk is WY 1. The judges have special plate numbers too. This plate number isn't complete, so I don't understand why they'd bother to redact it."

Marc shoved the chair back and ran his fingers through his short blond hair. There was just a sprinkling of silver showing at his temples. He stood and picked up his hat from the table.

"I need to get back on the road. Maybe we can talk about this some more, if you want, this weekend. It would be great to solve a cold case like this one, especially after all that's happened. It won't be easy though."

"I know. My family and business partner are telling me to let it go, but since my uncle gave me all this information, I need to find out what really happened. The weekend is great, but I do need to tell you about the message my Uncle Stan left me on Friday night. I completely forgot to tell Investigator Hotchkiss."

"A message?"

"He left a message on my machine. I can replay it for you."

"I'd better take it down. The investigator will want that." He was all business in his demeanor, as he took out a small spiral notebook that was in his shirt pocket. Marc listened carefully to the message three times and jotted down his notes.

"OK, I've got it. Don't erase it. Investigator Hotchkiss will probably want to hear it herself." He shoved the notebook back in his pocket.

"No problem. Just take the machine. It's as old as the hills. I should set up the voicemail on the phone anyway, and let's just say the Investigator and I didn't exactly hit it off. It'll be a peace offering of sorts." She could only hope that the policewoman would take it in the spirit it was given.

"Thanks. That'll save her a trip."

"No problem. Always glad to cooperate."

Marc looked at her skeptically.

"Cooperate, huh?"

"Yes, cooperate. If someone hurt my Uncle Stan, I want you to find out who did it. Investigator Hotchkiss is a little rough in her approach though, and I don't appreciate being treated like a suspect." Gracie could feel the color start to creep up her neck.

"She's a tough cookie, but she's a top-notch cop." His voice was even and cool.

Gracie could tell the conversation was over in that area, so she moved on. Other questions about the investigation would have to wait.

"Is there a good time we could get together about Charlotte's stuff?"

"I'm not sure of the weekend schedule yet, so I'll give you a call." He carried the answering machine under his arm and started for the door.

"Great. I'll wait to hear from you." Haley thrust a cold nose into her hand and whined.

"OK, I guess I'd better let you out." Gracie turned to the patio door and opened the screen slider.

"Goodnight then, and thanks for this." He waved the answering machine in her direction.

"Goodnight, Deputy."

"It's Marc," he said, shutting the kitchen door.

Chapter 21

The whole village turned out for Uncle Stan's funeral on Thursday evening. Even though the ceiling fans were running at top speed, people fanned themselves with the funeral bulletin. The air-conditioning had conked out a few hours before. Even Isabelle looked wilted in the humidity. She had another new suit. It was black linen with a short sleeved jacket and large obsidian buttons. Tim kept his arm around her shoulders throughout the service. His brown hair, with gray at the temples, looked freshly cut since Gracie had seen him at Aunt Shirley's funeral. He had recently grown a mustache, which Gracie thought made him look older, and his black suit coat was open to accommodate his middle-aged spread.

Greg and Anna were once again in appropriate mourning clothes, looking uncomfortable. Greg pulled at his tie throughout the service and looked down at his feet during the eulogy. His brown hair was the same shade as his father's, and he was now the same height too. Anna twisted her long honey-blonde hair around her fingers. Her petite features reminded Gracie of Charlotte at the same age. Anna, however, was quiet and studious, very unlike her late aunt. The poor kids had been through hell in the last week. She really needed to take the time to talk with them. How Isabelle had ended up with such good kids was a mystery, but then again, Tim was all right when he wasn't bragging about how much money he made.

Rev. Minders did a fine job of laying Uncle Stan to rest, reminding them of the life to come and the grand reunion of Shirley and Stan in the heavenly realm. He offered the standard scriptures, Psalm 23 and John 14, to give them all comfort. Gracie wasn't sure she believed those anymore. She had never questioned them until she had lost a husband and an unborn baby within days of each other. If she hadn't fallen scrambling up the bank to get to her cellphone in the SUV, she would have a son. The cramping hadn't been severe until two days after Michael's funeral. And then there was nothing the doctor could do. At the time, she'd felt that God had played some cruel joke on her. Her counselor had said she was stuck in the grief process and was hanging on to a lot of anger. She'd stopped seeing the woman after that session.

But in the last couple of weeks, it was evident that anger and fear were running her life. Even if that life seemed to be unraveling again, she wasn't going to revisit those dark thoughts. They made her feel helpless and so alone. She wasn't alone, and she wasn't helpless. She needed to focus on that. Michael would have told her to snap out of it. His faith had been so strong and it had been easy to rely on his confidence in God. It was time she figured out where she stood with the Almighty for herself.

Her mother's touch on her arm brought her back to the present moment, and she stood as the casket was carried out by the pallbearers, which included Tim and Greg. There was no graveside service, but there was a private service for the immediate family Friday morning. Gracie hoped that didn't include her. Another scene with Isabelle was undesirable, and walking by Michael and Andrew's graves was not something she was ready to do again. There was no funeral dinner tonight, but Gracie knew the church ladies were in overdrive, since her own refrigerator was filled to capacity with casseroles and Jell-O salads. What was Jell-O anyway, and why was it a designated funeral food?

The organ finished a somber postlude of *Guide Me, O Thou Great Jehovah,* and the congregation began filing past the family. Gracie was at the end of the family receiving line, staying as far away from Isabelle as possible. Theresa

Clark had declared a truce between her daughter and niece for the night. As the new matriarch of the family, her word on sticky family relationships would reign on this public occasion. There were to be no scenes or displays of anger. Theresa had always been skillful at managing Isabelle and smoothing her ruffled feathers. In fact, she'd managed her sister Shirley with the same aplomb.

The line of people seemed endless, and Gracie's emotional energy was flagging. Out of the corner of her eye, she observed Investigator Hotchkiss melting into the crowd, moving toward the exit. What or who was she watching? Gracie wished she too was exiting, but there was really no way to escape. Her mother had seen to that. Theresa and Robert graciously greeted everyone and talked in low tones to Greg and Anna, who were struggling with issues of their own. Uncomfortable clothes, no cell phones, and an adult crowd were testing their endurance. Greg did look handsome in his dark suit, and Anna was charming in her black sheath dress and sandals. Gracie gave them a quick, understanding smile.

The crowd was thinning into the darkness and sounds of car engines starting up and down the street, when Gracie saw an opportunity to slip away. Her mother turned to talk to Isabelle, and Gracie stood on tiptoes to kiss her father's cheek.

"Gotta go, Dad. I've got an early day, and I need to check the dogs and the alarm system."

"OK, my girl. You've stood the test long enough for Mother, I think. We'll stop by tomorrow after the graveside. You're not going, are you?"

"You know me well, Dad. No, I won't be there, so give my apologies to everyone."

"I think they understand; don't worry." He gave her a quick hug and pushed her toward the side entrance.

ঌঌঌঌঌঌঌঌঌঌ

Cheryl Stone was a quick study in the kennel business. Already, Gracie and Jim were sure this hire was a good one. Cheryl loved dogs, and they loved her. She already knew all the dogs' names and was teaching them tricks while they were in the play yard. She was tall and willowy, with dark brown hair cut in short layers, framing a constantly smiling face that was almost pretty. Gracie and Cheryl hit it off immediately and were trading stories about high school. Cheryl had graduated from Warsaw, while Gracie had from Letchworth. They had both been in 4-H and decided they'd competed against each other in dog obedience at Pike Fair.

Cheryl was recently divorced, with a teenage daughter, and had moved back with her parents in Warsaw. Her ex lived in Buffalo and taught at Erie Community College. Cheryl had Marian's seal of approval, and the work was settling into the efficient rhythm that Gracie thrived on. The only worry now was rebuilding the business that had suffered because of the bite incident and robbery.

Jim brought in the mail and dumped it on Gracie's desk.

"A lot of bills today, Chief."

"I know. It's been that way all week."

"What's the checkbook looking like?" Jim was uncharacteristically concerned. He left most financial matters to Gracie.

"We're all right for now. If we have another month or two like the last couple of weeks though, we could be in trouble. We might have to dip into the reserve account if that happens." She pushed back a lock of hair that had escaped the large hairclip holding the rest of her hair in check.

"Do you think we need to get some more advertising out there or offer some added-value service?"

"Wow, Jim you're getting all business-like here," Gracie laughed.

Administration was not Jim's forte. He enjoyed the physical work, the dogs, and the people, not the paperwork.

"Hey, you two. How's business?" Bob Clark walked through the doorway. Gracie could hear her mother talking to Marian and Cheryl. Jim shook Bob's hand.

"A little slow, I'm afraid." Gracie was separating the bills and the junk mail into two piles.

"We're trying to figure out what we need to do to get a positive spin on Milky Way back out there." Jim took off his Yankees cap and scratched his head.

"Have a seat, Dad." Gracie pointed to the ugly recliner.

"Thanks, I think," Bob laughed.

"It's broken in just right for my taste. Gracie keeps telling me it doesn't go with the décor, but hey, this is a kennel." Jim gazed fondly at the chair.

"I'm tolerating the chair because he's such good help. Most of the time." Gracie teased.

"It wasn't here the last time I was in the office."

"I've been negotiating with the Chief for a while, and I finally wore her down." Jim looked pleased with himself.

"He brought it over right after you left for your cruise."

"Good job, Jim. Anybody who can talk my daughter into allowing that chair in her office has great persuasive powers."

"Is everybody hungry?" Theresa walked bearing a large pan covered in aluminum foil.

Gracie groaned. "Not another casserole."

"No, it's really lasagna, and I brought paper plates. Clear off your desk so I can set this up."

Gracie quickly swept the pile of mail into the top desk drawer to make room for the food.

"All right," Jim said with anticipation. "Real home cooking from Mrs. C. Thanks."

"You're welcome. Except it's not mine—it's from Gloria. My refrigerator is so full; I had to part with something. This pan just wouldn't fit."

"That's good for us," chimed in Marian who came in carrying plates, napkins, and silverware. Cheryl was behind her with a cooler of iced sodas. The conversation lulled as they loaded plates with the rich layers of sausage lasagna. Gracie was mid-mouthful when she realized Joe wasn't there.

"Where's Joe?"

"I'll go get him. He's probably in the barn." Jim left his plate on the task chair.

"Anybody home?"

Gracie recognized Deputy Stevens' voice.

"Back here in the office," she called.

"Have some lasagna." Theresa was already on her feet, grabbing a plate and spatula.

"I'd love to, but I don't have the time, Ma'am. Mrs. Andersen, could I speak to you?"

He sounded official, and Gracie rose, expecting to see a smile, but his face was deadpan. "Sure, Deputy. Let's go in the reception area."

Deputy Stevens stood straight and tall, looking extremely law enforcement-like by the reception desk. He pulled a set of papers from his clipboard.

"I'm sorry, Mrs. Andersen, but I have serve you with these papers."

"Serve me with what?" She tried to keep her voice controlled.

"It's a summons. You'll probably want to contact your attorney."

"My attorney! What are you talking about?"

"You'll have to read it."

Gracie scanned the front page of the document stapled in a blue litigation cover.

"You've got to be kidding! They're suing us. It was an accident, and they're suing."

"I'm very sorry. Like I said, you'll want to contact your attorney."

"I can't believe this is happening." Gracie's voice was no longer as controlled as she wanted.

Bob Clark came around the corner.

"Is everything OK?"

"Not really, Dad. Frank and Evie are suing me for Beth's accident." She sat down in the molded, brown plastic reception chair, staring at the paper in her hand.

"Don't panic, Gracie. Just give Nathan Cook a call and put him to work. It's not unusual for this to happen after any accident."

"You're right about that, Mr. Clark. Happens all the time. I'm sure it'll work out. I'd better be going." Deputy Stevens opened the front door and strode toward his car.

Everyone was silent in the office when Gracie returned. Theresa was picking up the plates and collecting silverware.

"Well, I guess Milky Way has some more doo-doo to deal with." She threw the paper on the desk.

"It'll be OK, Gracie," Marian said confidently.

Cheryl nodded in agreement. "People do it all the time to get more insurance money."

"I know, but the last people I expected to play that game are Frank and Evie." Gracie shrugged and picked at the cold tomato sauce, puddled on the saturated plate.

"What's going on?" Jim searched the unsmiling faces watching him and Joe.

"I just got served with a lawsuit. Frank and Evie are suing us for Beth's damages, whatever that means. Our insurance will cover all her medical bills. What else do they want?"

"Great. Although I expected it before now."

"Well, I didn't. I still can't believe they'd try to milk this thing. Beth is most likely to blame for the accident, plus she's OK." Gracie was beginning to boil.

Theresa grabbed another plate and landed a huge square of lasagna in the center.

"Here, Joe. No sense in letting all of this go to waste."
Theresa gave him a motherly smile.

"Thanks. I can just take it with me back to the barn."

"Stay here, Joe. Don't leave on our account." Bob stood
and offered the recliner.

"That's OK. I'm not sure..."

"Have a seat, Joe. Enjoy your lunch." Theresa was firm.

"OK, thanks." He sat ramrod straight in the recliner,
discomfort oozing from every pore.

All eyes were focused on Joe as he lifted a forkful to his
mouth. The silence was awkward. Amazingly, Joe spoke
and broke the spell.

"Wow, this is good. I haven't had homemade lasagna in
a long time."

"It's compliments of the pastor's wife. Eat up and get
some meat on your bones." Theresa had her mother hen
hat on now.

"Well, let's give the man some peace while he eats." Bob
admonished his wife.

"Of course, dear." Theresa gave her husband a good-
natured glare.

"How did the graveside service go?" Jim broke in and let
Joe off the hook.

"It was fine. Isabelle held up pretty well. It's a good
thing Tim is so steady. She's going to need him to help her
sort everything out." Bob helped himself to another hunk of
lasagna.

"Poor Uncle Stan. This whole thing is surreal. Have you
heard if they've finished up the investigation?" Gracie
settled back into her desk chair.

She thought she saw a flicker of fear on Joe's face. A
sheen of sweat crossed his upper lip.

"I don't know. I'm assuming no news is good news."
Theresa dabbed at a spot of sauce on her black skirt.

"I guess we'd better get back to work." Jim adjusted his
baseball cap and dumped his plate in the wastebasket.

"I'm right behind you." Joe quickly shoved the last bite in his mouth and stood to leave.

"Jim, wait a second before you go. We need to put in a call to Nathan."

"Right. Go ahead, Joe. Finish cleaning the runs."

"All right."

"There aren't any more grooming appointments this afternoon, so I'm going home if you don't need me," Marian said.

"Fine with me. If one comes in, I can handle it. See you tomorrow." Gracie let out a sigh.

"Cheryl's up front, so the phone is covered."

"Thanks, Marian."

With good-byes out of the way, and her parents on their way home, Gracie and Jim spent some time talking to Nathan Cook, Esquire. She faxed the summons and complaint to him, and gave him Howard Stroud's number.

"I'll get with Howard, and I'm sure we'll work this mess out. Don't talk to the Simmons family or their attorney and make an appointment to see me next week." Nathan's voice was firm and confident. He had handled all of their legal affairs for years and had always come through. This was the first lawsuit though. It seemed immensely scary to Gracie, not like a partnership agreement or probate.

"Thanks, Nathan. We'll see you next week." Jim hit the speakerphone's "Off" button, disconnecting the call.

"It's Nathan's problem now. I hope he can get this settled quickly."

"It's *our* problem, and I still can't believe they'd do this. We've been friends for years... or so I thought." Her brown eyes flashed with anger and hurt.

"Gracie, take a deep breath. Let Nathan do his job and we'll get on with business. We do have a PR problem, which this lawsuit isn't going to help. Any ideas?" His eyebrows were furrowed, and his blue eyes were dark with worry.

"I was thinking about hosting an obedience match here, but I need to get in touch with the Valley Kennel Club." Gracie was trying to cool down and focus.

"That's a great idea. How about adding agility?"

"We'd have to get a spot ready for that. We need more fencing installed, too."

"Not a problem. There are a few rolls of livestock fence out in the barn."

"OK, that's good. I'll give them a call and see what we can work out."

"All right then. Get crackin', Chief." Jim adjusted his cap to a jaunty angle, winked, and whistled his way out of the office.

"Sure thing. You too." Gracie felt a surge of excitement. It would be a feather in Milky Way's cap to host a match. If they made a good impression, who knew what else could happen?

Gracie's mind was still whirling with organizing the obedience and agility match set for six weeks away when she sat at the kitchen counter to sort her personal mail. The Kennel Club had readily agreed and would do the advertising. Milky Way just had to supply the venue.

The copies of Charlotte's diary were still scattered on the coffee table like pieces of an unsolved puzzle. Maybe digging up the past wasn't a good idea.

"Let sleeping dogs lie, right, girl?"

Haley looked up from her rawhide chip and thumped her tail on the floor.

Gracie spotted the flashing red light on the phone as she went back to opening the mail. It was her buddy, Investigator Hotchkiss, leaving an official voicemail. She wanted to see Gracie tomorrow. How could she prove that she hadn't had anything to do with Uncle Stan's death? Of course, she might be reading into why the investigator wanted to talk to her.

Chapter 22

Investigator Hotchkiss snapped her notebook shut. Her almost military-cut, dark brown hair was threaded with silver. Gracie guessed she was probably in her late-forties. She wore a plain gold wedding band and was trim in a navy blazer and skirt. A short, upturned nose and fine-boned face with piercing brown eyes, met Gracie's gaze. Did this woman ever smile?

"Thanks, Mrs. Andersen. I think that's about it."

"Sure. Glad to help," Gracie said through clenched teeth.

The questions were no less threatening than the first interview. The investigator wanted to know why Gracie had kept Charlotte's papers from Isabelle. Why was her uncle so eager to talk to her about Charlotte's death? Since she had such a hot temper, as witnessed by many at the funeral dinner, did she get into an argument with her Uncle Stan? It appeared as if Isabelle had tried to implicate Gracie, in some twisted way, in Uncle Stan's death. It was unthinkable. Investigator Hotchkiss had thanked Gracie for turning in Uncle Stan's message though, so maybe being helpful was making some points.

"One more question before I go." The investigator stood with her left hand draped over the doorknob.

"Sure, why not?" Gracie scratched Haley's head nonchalantly.

"Did you notice anything missing when you were in the house? Was there anything out of place?"

"I don't think so, but I wasn't really looking at the time."

"If you think of anything, please give me a call. You've got my card, right?"

"Yes, I'll be sure to let you know."

Gracie hesitated and then decided to ask the question she was dying to ask.

"Investigator?"

"Yes?"

"Where does all of this stand? Is my Uncle Stan's death still suspicious?"

Investigator Hotchkiss was clearly all business, and Gracie doubted she'd get a straight answer, but she still needed to ask.

"We're following up on all our leads right now. I think we'll have things wrapped up pretty soon." The investigator sounded confident, but unhelpful.

"Well, that's good. I hope you find some answers soon."

"Thanks again, Mrs. Andersen. I'll be in touch."

Investigator Hotchkiss shut the kitchen door quickly.

"OK. We made it through another interview. Maybe this time I lost the job as suspect."

Gracie flopped onto the sofa and pulled absently on Haley's soft ears.

"Isabelle has some explaining to do though. She's got to be smoking dope to tell the police I could hurt Uncle Stan." She felt her chest tighten, as Uncle Stan's sad face flashed through her mind.

Gracie decided to focus on her deceased cousin. Thinking about Isabelle only made her angry. Charlotte's diary entries and the police report were now stacked neatly on the coffee table. The license plate number was making her crazy. The WY vanity plate was probably her best clue, but without DMV records to check it out, the task seemed impossible. It might not even be the car. Maybe Matthew could shed some light on things. Who knew what he'd seen that night? Sometimes you blocked bad things out of your mind because they were just too awful. He might remember something significant after all these years.

Matthew Minders hadn't changed much. He was tall and lanky, but a little heavier than in high school. His curly blond hair was still out of control, although it was much shorter now. He was dressed in faded jeans and a green T-shirt that sported a white dragon logo with "Coach" embroidered underneath.

The Village Park was full of T-ball players and parents. Cheering rose from both fields, and it looked like the short, helmeted players, in bright red and blue uniforms were actually advancing around the bases. Gracie and Matthew had been catching up on life, and why he didn't show up very often in Deer Creek as they watched the two games from a distance. Haley sniffed an invisible trail through the dense grass and then flopped in the shade of a half-dead elm near the picnic area. Matthew stood with his right leg propped on the seat of the redwood-stained picnic table. Gracie watched Haley sleep.

"So, what do you want to know about Charlotte? You sounded a little mysterious on the phone."

"I know. As a matter of fact, it is a little mysterious. My Uncle Stan, now my late uncle, handed me a bunch of information about Charlotte's death with no explanation. Unfortunately, we didn't get to talk about it before his untimely death last week. Your name has come up a couple of times, and I was hoping you could shed some light on that night."

"It was terrible. The wind and rain were really something. I saw a car and got part of a license number."

"Did you see it happen?" Gracie asked softly, swallowing hard.

"No, but..." His voice shook, and pain showed in his eyes.

"Did you—?"

"I found her in the street. It was the most awful thing I've ever gone through. She was so still. It didn't look like Charlotte when I first got there."

"What about the car? Did you see the car after you found her?"

"No, it was before. I was walking up Mill toward Main Street, when a car flew past me, fishtailing on the wet leaves. I turned around to look at it because it was so out of control and caught a glimpse of the plate, as it passed under a street light. I really didn't get a good look at the car because my head was down. When I got up to the intersection, I saw something in the street; I wasn't sure what it was. At first, I thought it was a dog. The streetlight was out at the corner, so it wasn't well-lit. A car was coming down Main toward her, and then I could see it wasn't a dog. I flagged the car to stop, and then we checked on her. It was pretty bad, Gracie. I haven't ever talked about that night much, just to the police, and then I just wanted to forget it." He sat down on the bench with his back to the table and leaned back. Gracie did the same.

"I can understand that." Gracie's mind flew to the day she found Michael. If only she could forget that hellish scene.

"What did the police say about the plate number?"

"Not much. I gave them the information, but nothing ever came of it. I could've made a mistake, but I don't think so. If only I'd gotten the whole thing. WY 7. I'm not sure if the number was the first or the last. It was pretty fast."

"Seems like the cops could have figured something out with that much."

"I thought so too, but nothing happened. I really wanted to help, but I guess the information wasn't enough. Charlotte was such a good friend. I was having a hard time that last year of high school, but she was always there with a good word and that beautiful smile. She wouldn't go out with me though." He rubbed his hand over the light stubble on his chin and smiled.

"Who was in the car that stopped?" Gracie hadn't ever heard this information before.

"I'm not sure. It wasn't anyone local—a couple from out of town. I think they were staying at the Glen Iris Inn to see the leaves or something like that. I ran to the Randall's, which was the closest house, and called the ambulance."

"Did they see or hear anything? Their house was pretty close to the corner."

"They said they'd heard some tires squealing, but they heard that all the time, so they didn't think anything of it."

"I guess that makes sense. Plus the wind was blowing pretty hard."

"It sure was. It was an icy rain, and the wind was whipping like it was November or December already."

"Why didn't the sheriff's department keep pursuing the case? It was a hit-and-run after all. I can't believe my Aunt Shirley and Uncle Stan would have just let it drop." Gracie picked at a rough cuticle on her index finger.

"I don't know. I remember my parents talking about their wanting resolution and the sheriff had done his best, but it was just going to drag on and on."

"There was never any resolution, though, if the driver was never caught. It just doesn't make sense to me."

"It didn't to me either. But what did I know? I was just a 17-year-old geeky preacher's kid, hoping to graduate and get outta here." He gave her a crooked grin.

Gracie laughed, remembering excruciating Sunday school classes as a teenager. Matthew took all the pressure for the right answers. The teacher, Mr. Bannister, loved asking tough questions of the pastor's son. One favorite was if the Nephilim in Genesis were some aberrant race of human giants.

"I guess you had the short end of the stick on that. Remember those challenging Sunday school classes?"

"Yeah, they were great. I guess good old Mr. Bannister thought I'd been to seminary already. That class pretty much cured me of any thoughts of the pastorate. My mother was bucking for the only son to go to seminary, but by high school, I was tired of life in the fishbowl. You spend a lot of time being a good example and keeping a low profile." He dropped his foot from the bench and hoisted himself on the table top.

"I can imagine. At least you've got a real life now."

"Yes, and it's one of the reasons that Deer Creek isn't high on my visiting list. My parents come down to Jamestown every other month. They see our kids, and we have a good visit. It's good for them too. They get a day out of the public eye."

"Your mom is still coming up with new programs. We've even got one of her projects working for us."

"Second Chances, right? She needs to keep busy so that the church doesn't suck all her time. It gives her an excuse to not attend every Missionary Circle meeting or organize every fundraiser. Of course, Dad depends on her for a lot of things. He's not the most organized person, and she keeps him focused and on time for things."

"Sounds like my parents. Mom runs a tight ship, and Dad benefits. If she didn't, Dad would just putter around the house and never finish anything. They've been traveling a lot since they both retired last year."

The conversation rambled to more pleasant memories. They both had a good laugh remembering long summer afternoons when they were kids, biking down to the creek to swim with the gang that included Charlotte, Matthew, Jim, Michael, her brother Tom, and Gaile, one of Matthew's three sisters. Sometimes they'd get a watermelon from Hatfield's long gone little grocery store that had the best produce. One of the guys always had a jackknife, and they'd cut it up into big slices and eat the whole thing. The juice was cool and ran from their hands to their elbows, creating a sticky mess. Inevitably, there was a seed-spitting contest. The boys were proud of their prowess and ability to disgust the girls. They'd swim again to dissolve the sweet glueyness and make themselves presentable to their respective mothers. Matthew broke her reverie.

"Well, sounds like families are pretty much the same everywhere."

"Not exactly. I do have some other questions about Charlotte...and Isabelle too."

Matthew shot her a quizzical look. "OK. I'm not sure what else you want to know. I really don't know any more about the accident."

"Not the accident, but what was going on with Charlotte right before she died. Do you know if she was dating anybody?"

"No...." he said slowly. "She was a real flirt with the football team, but I don't know if she was dating anyone in particular. She used to wait for a couple of different guys from time to time. I don't even know if I can remember their names."

"Did she ever talk to you about a Lancelot or Galahad?"

"As in King Arthur?"

Gracie nodded.

"Sometimes Charlotte talked like she was the princess in a tower. She could be a little dramatic."

"She came by that honestly. Isabelle is certainly a drama queen, and my Aunt Shirley...well, I shouldn't speak ill of the dead."

Matthew laughed. "My mother has a few stories about your Aunt, I'm afraid."

"I always thought they were pretty tight."

"Well, you could say that. I shouldn't say it, but it was more like Lincoln who said something to the effect of keeping your enemies close, so you know what they're up to."

"Oh, uh, well, that puts a different light on things."

Gracie's admiration meter went up the scale exponentially for his mother. She also wondered why she hadn't seen this side of Gloria Minders before. Gracie mentally chided herself for being so dense. She decided to go for the shocker question and see how Matthew reacted.

"Did you know that Charlotte was pregnant when she was killed?"

"Really." Matthew's tone was flat and un-shocked. Slightly disappointed with his reaction, Gracie forged ahead.

"From Charlotte's diary entries, I think it was this Lancelot or Galahad she wrote about, but I can't be sure. I'd sure like to piece more of what was going on with her that last summer and fall. My Aunt Shirley kept both of her daughters on a short leash when it came to boys. Of course, Isabelle was smart enough to hook Tim in college and marry a week after she graduated. The Bakers were upper crust enough for Aunt Shirley. Money and prestige were what it was about for her."

"Not bitter or anything, are we?" Matthew gave Gracie a sideways glance reminiscent of his gloating at the seed-spitting contests.

Gracie laughed, "I guess I get on my high horse when I'm talking about my family. They mostly drive me crazy."

"Your parents are pretty laid back people and so is your brother."

"Yeah, well, they are, but the rest of my mother's family, the zillion cousins in Wyoming and Allegany Counties, are all a little different, and Isabelle has always had my number."

"Isabelle has always had everybody's number."

"She *is* a piece of work. She's even trying to implicate me in my Uncle Stan's death."

"You're kidding. What's she doing?"

"She's been feeding bits of half-truths to the investigator, who keeps coming back to ask me a few more questions."

"I thought it was ruled an accident, from what my parents just said."

"Since Isabelle has been so upset by the Charlotte papers and now with the stunt she's pulling with the police, I'm beginning to think there's more to everything than meets the eye."

"You can't think that Isabelle—"

Gracie interrupted, "I don't know what to think, but I do know I need to get to the bottom of what happened to Charlotte. Uncle Stan felt it was important enough to entrust this information to me and not Isabelle, so I have an obligation to him and Charlotte to figure it out. Maybe it wasn't an accident for Charlotte, and maybe it wasn't an accident for Uncle Stan. It's pretty strange that he's at the bottom of the stairs the day I stop in to see him about Char's papers. The sheriff's department is still investigating his death."

"Wow, Gracie, I don't know about all of this. Those are serious accusations." Matthew stretched his long legs out and flexed his left knee a couple of times.

"Everybody else thinks I'm overreacting, but maybe there's more to Charlotte's death than a hit-and-run driver. That's why I'm hoping you can help unravel what happened that night with Charlotte."

"I've told you what I know, Gracie. I couldn't say who Char was dating, and I didn't know she was pregnant. She didn't confide in me like a girlfriend. Maybe her friends knew, but I don't know what difference that would make after all these years."

Gracie could feel Matthew's exasperation.

"I'm sorry, Matt. I know it's something you don't want to think about. Believe me, I understand."

"I know, Gracie, and I'm sorry about that. You must still be dealing with stuff yourself. You've experienced a lot of personal loss. It's understandable."

"It's better than it used to be, but Charlotte and Uncle Stan don't have anything to do with Michael or the baby."

People forgot that she lost the two people she loved most in the world. The tiny baby wrapped tightly in a hospital receiving blanket looked like he was just sleeping. But he never opened his eyes or drew a breath.

"Right." He paused. "And the baby. Gracie, you have been through more than I realized."

She scuffed the dirt under the bench with her sneaker. She needed to regain her composure to continue.

"Life goes on, or so they tell me, but I seem to be dealing with a lot of death lately. Some old history and some fresh. I'm hoping you can help figure some of it out. Do you remember anything else about the car?"

She had to get back on track and not allow her emotions to rule. Matthew adjusted his position on the table and made a visible effort to relax.

"Like I said, I didn't get a good look at it—just that partial license plate. I think the car was a dark green or blue. It was a big car, maybe a Buick or Chrysler. It looked like a lot of cars around town, I guess, but it might not have been the car that hit Char."

"Did the car look familiar? It had a WY plate, so it must have been somebody from Wyoming County."

"It looked like a lot of the big cars around, I guess. My father, your father, even your uncle and a lot of other people in town had big dark cars back then."

"Did Charlotte ever talk about Isabelle or her mother?"

"It was the usual teenager complaints—not enough freedom, parents are unreasonable—you know the stuff we said. Char did get pretty quiet when school started. She kept to herself, which, now that I think about it, was really out of character for her. I guess finding out you're pregnant would change your perspective."

"Pretty much. I wasn't around, so I don't know how she was acting or if family tensions were high. That's why I was hoping you'd shed some light on what she was talking about or to whom before she was killed."

"Sorry, I haven't been more help, but that's about all I remember. Although now that you mention who she was talking to, I think she was really close with Miss Russell, the cheerleading coach. I do remember Charlotte hanging out to talk with her when practice was over."

"I left a message for Miss Russell the other day, but haven't heard back. I guess I need to call her again."

"She might be a good one to talk to about what was on Char's mind during those last few weeks."

Matthew slid from the picnic table and brushed off the backside of his jeans. "Well, Gracie, it was good seeing you, but I'd better get going."

"Thanks for taking the time to talk, Matt. I really appreciate it. I know it wasn't easy."

Gracie whistled for Haley, who jerked her head up, stood, shook, and then trotted to the picnic table. They walked slowly across the grass, noticing that the T-ball games were over, and everyone was headed to their vehicles too.

"It's OK. I'd like to find out who the driver was myself. Those were bad times for everyone. I wish I had been a few minutes earlier. I might have been able to stop it from happening. I wish I had seen the driver, or at least, known whose car was speeding down Mill that night. I wish a lot of things were different. But you'd better be careful, Gracie. Sometimes it's better to let things be, you know."

His eyes were sad, and he shoved his hands into his pockets. Gracie was unable to formulate a comeback. Everyone was telling her the same thing. Matthew broke the awkward silence.

"Well, I'd better pick up Cindy and the kids at my parents. We're headed to Letchworth Park for a picnic at the Lower Falls. I do have to show the kids my old stomping grounds every so often."

He stopped on the edge of the asphalt in front of his mini-van and turned to Gracie.

"Keep in touch, Gracie."

"I will, and if you remember anything else..."

"I will call you. Take care of yourself." He slid into the van and shut the door.

Gracie opened the back door of the RAV4 to let Haley in.

"Hi, Gracie."

She turned to see Greg, Isabelle's son, walking toward her.

"Hey, Greg. How are you holding up?"

"OK, I guess."

"Do you help with T-ball?"

"Yeah, I started this year. Mom says I'd better make sure I've got lots of community activities and good grades to get into the best colleges."

"She's right on that. It's pretty competitive anymore. Not like the olden days when I went."

Greg laughed and brushed his thick brown hair from his eyes. He wore jeans shorts with a red T-shirt that said Hawks on it.

"I thought it would be a pain, but I kinda like coaching the little kids. They're pretty funny, most of the time."

"I'm a little surprised that your Mom allows you to talk to me."

"Well, she didn't say not to, and you are one of my coolest cousins, so..."

"Thanks. I'm not feeling so cool these days, though. Has the sheriff's department finally finished with your Grandpa's investigation?"

"Mostly, I think. Mom said that they think it was a robbery. Maybe Grandpa tried fighting the robber, and he fell going after the guy or something like that."

"Was something stolen then? I hadn't heard that there was anything missing from the house."

Gracie was wondering what could be missing. The house looked in order to her, but then the shock of finding Uncle Stan wiped attention to detail from her mind that day. Everything looked normal on her secret trip to the house too.

"I think she said that some of Grandma's jewelry was gone. A cameo and pearl necklace and a couple of other things—a watch and a bracelet, I guess.

"Really? Maybe it's connected to all the robberies that are happening around the area, although it's been electronics and cash in the others, from what the newspaper reported."

"Grandpa and Grandma didn't have a lot of that stuff. They were pretty old-fashioned. I can't see Grandpa fighting with a robber though. He was pretty wasted most of the time. I would've guessed that he just fell down the stairs, but those bruises around his neck were shaped like hands, I guess. So must be he got into it with somebody."

"Handprints on his neck? I guess there was somebody else in the house. Do you think it was a robbery then?"

There was something about Greg's tone that prickled the hair on the back of Gracie's neck. She wanted to know what was running through this bright teenager's mind.

A shadow crossed through Greg's eyes.

"I...really don't know." His reluctance was palpable.

"That's OK. I never did hear when the medical examiner said he died."

"Oh, it was about 10 o'clock Friday night, I guess. It's pretty weird to think about that. Mom had me check on him in the afternoon, and he was fine. He was just watching TV and sleeping. It's just creepy to think that he was dead a few hours later. If I had hung out with him, maybe it wouldn't have happened." Greg's head went down, and he kicked some loose gravel with his sneaker.

"Don't beat yourself up over that, Greg. I'm a champion at guilt trips and know. I felt the same way, because I was going to see him Friday night, but then didn't make it."

"He did say something about wanting to talk to you while I was there. Grandpa wondered if I'd seen you."

"Did he say anything specific?"

"He was talking kind of funny. It didn't make a lot of sense to me, but he'd probably had a few."

"Was he drinking then?"

"Now that I think about it, I didn't see any beer bottles around. He usually had two or three at least by his chair, but there weren't any. There was just a can of Coke. That was pretty unusual."

"Really? So what was he saying then?" Gracie tried to contain the eagerness in her voice.

"Well, he was rambling about Grandma and Charlotte. Grandma had gone too far or something like that. He wanted to make things right and had to do the right thing. He said something about my Mom being on the wrong side, and that justice needed to be done. It was really crazy talk. It didn't make any sense to me. It kinda freaked me out, so I told him I had to get going. When I told my Mom what he said, she freaked on me."

"You got stuck in the middle. Nice. Not an easy place to be."

"Not an easy place to live. There's always drama with my mother. I try to stay out of her way mostly and disappear as often as I can." Greg took a quick look around the parking lot. "Well, I'd better get home to report in." He smiled, but his eyes looked wistful.

"Take care of yourself, Greg. If you ever need to talk or whatever, give me a call, day or night."

"Thanks, Gracie. It's good to know that not all of my relatives are strange."

"Uh, thanks, but we all have our quirks. And you probably don't want to mention that you talked to me today." She winked and gave him a quick slap on the back. She watched him in her rearview mirror as he left in a black pickup.

Matthew Minders hadn't been much help at all, but Greg had opened the door to some new information. She needed to plan her next move. There were a lot of jumbled ideas running around in her head at the moment, and each included Isabelle. And now Aunt Shirley.

Chapter 23

Brad and Carter were moving to Buffalo. The constant churning in Joe's stomach had slowed down after they'd told him when he'd gotten home from work. He had no idea how they'd talked their probation officer into letting them leave the county. He was probably grateful to hand them over to Erie County. The inventory at the depot was also leaving. Carter had bought an old junker 15-passenger van, pockmarked with rust and a questionable engine. Miraculously, it passed the state inspection, and now it was parked at the depot, hidden by the jungle of weeds that were tangled around the rear of the building. They'd stripped the seats out the night before and tossed them in the weeds along the tracks.

Joe had to help them load everything, and then he was off the hook. His grandmother calling his uncle had been a stroke of genius. Brad wanted no more of Uncle Ron's pointed questions and suspicious looks. Maybe his uncle had helped the probation officer get them moved to Buffalo. However it happened, he just wanted them to hurry and get this over with.

The night was cloudy, and there was no moon. Carter had shot out the streetlight next to the depot and the one on the corner with the BB gun weeks ago. The Village DPW hadn't replaced the bulbs yet, so the whole area was soaked in darkness. Someone was cooking burgers nearby and the smell made his stomach growl. He wiped the back of his hand across his forehead, catching drops of sweat before they stung his eyes.

Where were they? Sweat trickled down his torso, making his T-shirt stick to him. Joe needed to get back to the house to avoid any questions about why he was out. Sneaking out the bedroom window may have worked when he was a kid, but he was sure his uncle would do a bed check before he turned in. He also needed a cigarette. He didn't light one for fear the glow would be visible to the street.

Joe hoped they weren't trying to pull one more job before leaving. And he hoped no kids would show up to party at the depot tonight. The depot's secret storage area was piled with iPods, laptops, flat screen TVs, DVD players, speakers, DVDs, and who knew what else they'd ripped off on the two-month burglary spree. The cash they'd stolen along the way was long gone, helping Brad and Carter buy cigarettes, a little weed, and plenty of beer. He drew in a lungful of air and hugged himself.

Why were they so late?

Headlights suddenly swung up the street from Main. Joe felt the stereo's vibrating rap beat as the car turned into a driveway two houses up from the depot. He crouched in the shelter of the tall weeds by the steps of the rear entrance. Kids laughed and slammed doors, and the music blared. A porch light came on and a man yelled, "Turn that down, Chris. I've got enough complaints already." The music went silent, and the laughing faded after the screen door slammed. Joe stood up gingerly and flexed his stiff right knee. The porch light was still on, and Joe cursed under his breath at the thin pool of light in the blackness.

The street grew quiet again, and the drone of peepers gradually provided steady background noise. Another vehicle made the turn onto Rail Avenue. The headlights were immediately cut, and a pickup with a cap on the back crept into the parking area. Joe eased out of his hiding place in the weeds.

"It's about time. Where've you been?"

"Keep your shirt on, bucko. We had some business to take care of."

"Let's get this stuff loaded. I gotta get outta here." Joe couldn't wait for them to be on their way to Buffalo.

Brad swore and grabbed Joe's damp shirt, jerking him almost off his feet.

"We'll get it done, so simmer down, Joseph. Is your Granny waiting for you or something?"

"My uncle is, and I don't need any more trouble." Joe was tired of being afraid of Brad and his bullying.

"Come on, let's just get the stuff in the van and get outta here, Brad." Carter threw the stub of his cigarette on the gravel and rubbed it out with the toe of his work boot.

Brad grunted and pushed Joe back toward the broken railing of the steps into the depot. The rough wood scraped the back of his arm. The three men worked in silence, hauling boxes of electronics to the van. They dropped to the ground when another carload of kids sped by, stereo cranked high. More car doors slammed, and young voices echoed in the still air. They waited until the sounds dimmed, and everyone was in the house. Joe exhaled slowly and knocked off the gravel stuck to his hands. Carter pulled a pile of old blankets out of the back of the pickup to pad the TVs and speakers. It took the three of them to put the last TV in the overcrowded vehicle.

"That's it." Carter stuck his thumbs in the belt loops of his jeans, surveying the tightly packed cargo.

"You're sure?" Brad growled. He was breathing heavily and sat down on the steps.

"I'm sure."

"OK, Joe, scamper home to Grandmaw and give our regards to your uncle the parole officer."

"Sure, whatever." Joe's shoes crunched on the stones and then were silent when he reached the uneven sidewalk.

"And don't worry. We'll keep in touch," Brad hissed.

Joe melted into the night, staying well out of the reaches of the porch light across the street. With any luck, the backyard dogs wouldn't hear him. His gut twisted with the knowledge that Brad wouldn't let him off the hook so easily. The local business had just gotten a little too hot, and a change of scenery would cool things down. They would be back. He needed a plan to avoid them at all costs. It didn't look good, though. Brad had his thumb on Carter and Joe the entire time they were in prison together. It was easier to go along with Brad than stand up to him. Maybe he should ask his grandmother to pray that Brad went back to prison. If that happened, he'd have a chance at a normal life. But then again, why would God answer a prayer to benefit Joe Youngers?

With headlights off, the truck and van slowly eased onto the street. Joe turned and saw the taillights come on once they got to the intersection and turned onto Main.

"Getting some fresh air, Joe?"

Joe jumped and turned around.

"Hey, Uncle Ron."

His uncle's large hand clamped onto his shoulder. "Your grandmother was little worried about you, so I said I'd go look for you. You're not waiting for anybody are you?"

"No. No. I just thought I'd take a walk around the neighborhood. I was just coming back."

"Good. I'll walk back with you. That'll give us a chance to talk."

Chapter 24

Gracie was finishing the last forkful of a chicken finger salad at Midge's. It was fairly quiet, with just a handful of tables occupied. Midge was wiping down the worn, yellow speckled Formica counter. Gracie was the only customer sitting there. She had the lucky squeaky stool. Midge was uncharacteristically quiet, chomping on her gum and cleaning with a vengeance.

"I guess I need the check when you get a chance, Midge."

"Comin' right up." Midge sprayed the counter again with cleaning solution and kept wiping it down.

"Kind of quiet today."

"Yeah, everybody's on vacation or fishin', including my waitresses," she grumbled.

"Wish I could say the same." Gracie pulled out her wallet, hoping Midge would take the hint.

"You probably could use one after all the excitement your family has had the last two weeks."

"And how. It's still hard to believe that Uncle Stan is gone."

"I bet. I hear the sheriff is still investigatin' how he died. How'd that turn out?"

Midge was now on her own fishing expedition. She pulled the check pad from her apron pocket and started writing nonchalantly.

"I think they've just about finished their investigation. I can't imagine anyone hurting Uncle Stan, but I guess anything's possible."

"You think it was somebody who knew him?"

"I really don't know. An accident makes more sense, but the sheriff doesn't seem to think so."

Gracie didn't want to mention Greg's revelations about the investigation until she could find out more. That information didn't need to be on the evening news at Midge's tonight.

"Heard that Frank and Evie were suing you." Midge changed the subject suddenly, apparently giving up on Uncle Stan's death. She stopped mid-chomp, her brown eyes bright with interest.

"Just one of those things. It's a lawyer matter, so we're letting them fight it out." Gracie had successfully pushed that problem to the back burner, but a rush of emotion over old friends actually suing her gave her instant indigestion. Now she was really anxious to go home.

"I'd better go. Lots to do yet." She pulled out a $20 bill as Midge tore the check off the pad.

"Sure thing. Surprising what folks will do for some money." Midge rang up the ticket on the cash register.

"Yeah. We'll have to wait and see what happens." It was harder to be non-committal and cool than Gracie thought. She felt her face start to flush from the roots of her hair as she took the change from Midge. She placed a tip by her plate and slung the tote over her shoulder.

"See ya, Midge."

"Okie doke, Gracie." Midge was already headed to the kitchen.

"Gracie? Gracie Clark?" A voice from a back table caught her attention.

"Yes," she said hesitantly. The voice did sound vaguely familiar.

"Come and join me. It's Kay Russell."

Kay Russell sat at the table by the front windows hung with red gingham curtains, in the larger "dining" section. She hadn't changed all that much. She was a little heavier, and her short hair was now totally gray, but Miss Russell still had a perky smile, striking blue eyes, and flamboyant clothes. She wore a pink tropical-print capri ensemble. Her makeup was perfect, albeit on the generous side, maybe even on the body armor side. Her nails had a French manicure, and Gracie caught a whiff of Chanel No. 5 as she sat down at the small table.

"I couldn't help but hear your conversation with Midge. I thought it must be you. I've been meaning to call you, Gracie, but I got so busy this last week, I just forgot. It was such a surprise to hear from you."

"No problem. I've been doing a little research on high school, and I thought you might be able to help me with some names from back in the early 90s." Gracie was frantically trying to formulate the questions she was so anxious to ask Charlotte's old cheerleading coach.

"I'd be glad to if I can. My memory isn't the best anymore, but I had some great girls on the squad then. In fact, your cousin Charlotte was one of the best. Such a shame and such a waste. She was so full of life." A deep sadness clouded the retired teacher's face.

Gracie decided honesty was the best policy and forged ahead. "I know. It's really Charlotte I want to talk about. I have some questions about her I hope you can answer."

"What do you want to know?"

Gracie put her tote on the crumb-strewn floor and settled into the chair. Midge's waitresses must really be on vacation. Midge would have a fit if she saw the mess. She had her fingers crossed that Miss R. had some answers.

"I've been reading through some old family papers, and I found out that Charlotte was pregnant when she was killed. It was a surprise to me. Did she tell you anything about that?"

"Why, yes, she did. It was obvious by the end of September that she wasn't herself and needed someone to confide in. I was worried about her and tried to talk to her, but she kept to herself. It was very unlike Charlotte. She finally told me after I found her throwing up in the locker room one day after practice. Charlotte was petrified to tell her parents. She said they would make her get an abortion, or they'd throw her out, and she'd be disowned by everyone, including her sister."

"That's probably true, knowing my Aunt Shirley and Isabelle. Did she say who the father was?"

"No. Charlotte wouldn't tell me. She said the father didn't want the baby or her. He'd offered to pay for the abortion, but that girl truly wanted the baby. There was no way she would give it up. I offered to go with her to talk to her parents or the father of the baby, and Charlotte absolutely refused every time. I should have been more persistent."

"I wish I'd known. My parents didn't know either. Apparently, my aunt and uncle never said a word about the pregnancy. Did Charlotte say what she was going to do?"

"She was in the process of making some sort of plan the week before she died. I do know that she had decided to talk to her father and go from there. Charlotte's relationship with her mother wasn't the greatest, from what she told me. She thought her father might be more supportive. You know, Charlotte still planned on going to college and raising the baby somehow." Miss Russell's brow furrowed, creasing her makeup.

"Charlotte was in a world of hurt if my Aunt Shirley knew about the pregnancy. Good families don't have illegitimate babies pop up, and people would have talked up a storm about one of the Browne girls getting pregnant. It wouldn't have been pretty. Aunt Shirley had so many rules, and appearances were so important.

Gracie's mind was racing with visions of Aunt Shirley screaming and throwing Charlotte out onto the street. Hadn't Charlotte known she could have come to Gracie or her parents? They would have helped her.

"Then it sounds like Charlotte didn't exaggerate her family situation. That's very sad. Her parents were quite active in the community, weren't they?"

"Yes, and that was the problem. Being so prominent in all the right circles didn't allow for their children to make mistakes. Isabelle was much better at being the perfect daughter."

"Isabelle. Yes, I remember her. She was Charlotte's older sister, right?"

"Three years older."

"I seem to remember that Charlotte was having a hard time with her sister too. Isabelle must have been in college, wasn't she?"

"Isabelle went to Niagara University. She got her teaching degree there."

"OK. I do remember Charlotte mentioning that now. You know, Isabelle stopped by to watch Charlotte practice with the squad right before the accident. Charlotte wasn't too happy to see her, and I think they had some words when we were going into the locker room. It may have been the same day Charlotte told me she was pregnant."

"Really? Did Isabelle say anything to you?"

"No, I don't remember that she did. Maybe she went to watch the football team practice. I'm not sure. It was a long time ago, but I'm sure now that Isabelle was there the day Charlotte told me her news. It was such a shock. I benched her, but we did it discreetly. I didn't want her to suffer any more than she was already. I taped up her ankle, and we said she'd sprained it and would be out indefinitely. She could go to games and help with other things, but no flips and splits. I couldn't allow it."

"I wonder what she told my aunt." Gracie was musing about the little deceptions that were piling up.

"Her parents didn't come to football games, so I don't think she had to explain anything to them unless she wanted to."

"Did the other girls on the squad ask questions about her ankle, or did Charlotte seem especially close to any of them?"

"Charlotte was always good friends with Heather...somebody and another girl. Can't remember her name, but they did a lot of things together. The squad was sympathetic about the ankle injury. It was a bad break in your senior year and all that. There are always a couple of girls who are catty, but I handled that kind for many years and survived. I have the scars to prove it." She laughed and sipped the last of her ice tea.

"Did she ever talk about a Galahad or Lancelot?"

"Hmmm." Kay leaned back against the chair and fussed with her seashell earrings. "She was totally enamored with King Arthur and Camelot. She read Tennyson's *Idylls of the King* in her junior year. Oh, you know, I think she called Bryan Murdock, 'Galahad'."

"Who's he?"

"He was a substitute English teacher while Katie Reding was out on maternity leave."

"I guess I don't remember either one of them."

"Katie must have started right after you graduated, but never did come back after she had the baby. Bryan was young and very popular with the girls. They all had a crush on him. He was very good looking. Sort of a Heathcliff look and temperament. Very romantic, but not a terribly good teacher." She stopped. "Oh, dear."

"What? Was Charlotte involved with..."

"How could I have been so blind?" The woman paled under the makeup. "Bryan always seemed to be running the indoor track above the gym while we were practicing. It would have been easy for them to well...see each other after practice."

"So you think he was Galahad?"

"There's a good possibility. I can't imagine him doing anything inappropriate, but Charlotte was a beautiful girl."

"What happened to him? Is he still teaching?"

"Not at Letchworth. He left after that year for another job. Let me see. I think he went to work for a newspaper, or was it a TV station? I can't remember now. But he really wasn't cut out for teaching."

Gracie glanced at her watch. It was past time to be home. She had two play sessions to supervise and an obedience training session with Haley to get ready for the match that was only six weeks away. Plus there was a pile of paperwork waiting for her, including payroll. Gracie drummed her fingers on the red-checked vinyl tablecloth. At least she had another name to check out. He might still be in the area. She'd have to see what the computer could bring up on Mr. Murdock.

"I've taken up enough of your time. Thanks so much for talking with me, Miss Russell. It was great to see you."

"It was very nice to see you, Gracie. You would've made a great cheerleader, or I always thought so."

"I played softball, I'm afraid. Cheerleading was a little too girly for me. I was always a tomboy." Gracie smoothed her hair back and redid the clip holding it in place.

Miss Russell laughed. "You're right. It probably wouldn't have been a good fit for you."

Gracie grabbed the tote and stood, shoving her chair under the table. "If I have a few more questions, could I give you a call?"

The clatter of pots came from the kitchen, and she heard snatches of conversation from the same area. One voice sounded distinctly like Isabelle's. She glanced at the doorway of the kitchen, but couldn't see anyone. She swallowed hard. If Isabelle had overheard this conversation, it wouldn't be good. Gracie turned back to Miss Russell, who was leaving a tip on the table.

"Sure, that's fine. I'd love to know what's going on with you these days. Maybe we could have lunch here sometime."

"Things are pretty busy for me right now, but that would be fun. Thank you for filling me in on Charlotte. You've been a great help."

Gracie looked back toward the kitchen. She caught a glimpse of a woman leaving by the back door.

"Glad to help."

Miss Russell grabbed her straw handbag, with bright, pink hand-painted flowers, and made her way to the door.

Gracie's cell phone started ringing as she turned onto Kennedy Road. She had to dig around in her bag to find it. By that time, the caller had gone to voicemail. It was Jim.

"I'm almost home, Jimmy," she said to the message.

She turned into the driveway. Jim was standing by his Explorer.

"Sorry. I know I'm late, but I hit the mother lode of information today."

"Good for you, but you'll have to explain that to the kith and kin of Laney."

"Ohhh, a family event, eh?"

"Yes, eh. What are we Canadian?"

"Well, I'm home now, so you're free as a bird."

"Watch me fly then."

"Don't get a ticket."

"Yes, Mom." Jim tipped his baseball cap and started the engine.

"And get that muffler fixed," Gracie called over the rumbling.

Jim merely smiled annoyingly, shrugged, and started to back up. Haley was barking and had her front paws over the backyard gate. More barking came from the kennel. A line of wagging tails greeted her.

"I'm coming, everybody."

The stack of paper lying in wait on her desk was without a doubt going to take several hours to take care of.

She put on a pot of coffee while Haley roamed through the kennel. Jim had left a note taped to the phone that all playtimes had been taken care of, which meant she could get started on clearing away the mess. Haley's obedience session would have to wait until tomorrow.

The sun was sliding behind the woods to the west when she finally finished the last of the paperwork. She leaned back in the chair and stretched her arms overhead. Haley got up from her green L.L. Bean bed in the corner and licked Gracie's hand.

"OK, girl, I guess we can head to the house now. We'll say good night to everybody and set the alarm."

Haley wagged her tail and started down the first corridor. At least the kennel didn't seem quite as creepy now. The current guests were anxious to sniff and lick Gracie and Haley. On the final corridor, Haley ran ahead and stopped at the run housing Stinky, a brown and white terrier of uncertain heritage. His face had a Bull Terrier look, but his coat was wiry. He was usually pressing his nose against the wire, anxious for attention. Haley whined and pawed at the gate.

"Where's Stinky?" She called out, expecting his excited bark.

Haley woofed again, and Gracie ran to Stinky's run.

"Oh, Stinky, what's the matter with you?"

Stinky was lying on his side, his breathing labored. The run smelled terrible. His eyes were closed, and he didn't move when Gracie gently put her hand on his head. He had lost control of his bowels and was lying in his own mess. She ran for the phone with Haley at her heels. She got through to the Countryside Vet Clinic's answering service. Taking the phone with her, Gracie grabbed a towel from the grooming room and ran back to Stinky. He lifted his head, but seemed disinterested in her presence.

The vet on call was coming. From Gracie's experience, Stinky had probably had a seizure. She put the towel over him, stroking his head and talking to him in low tones. His breathing was less labored and seemed to improve as she sat next to him on the concrete floor. Haley lay down in the hallway, watching with a worried expression.

The vet arrived within twenty minutes and examined Stinky, who was now on his feet and looking a little confused. Gracie hosed down the run and disinfected it while the vet, who was new to the Countryside practice, examined the dog.

"Looks like it was a seizure. Could be epilepsy or just a one-time event. I'm Kelly Standish, by the way." She held out her hand.

"Nice to meet you, and thanks for coming so quickly." Gracie wiped her wet hand on her jeans before she shook hands.

"I live over on Middle Reservation, so it's not far. Do you know who his regular vet is?"

"I'll get his file for you."

Stinky's file revealed he was a patient at Countryside.

"He usually sees Dr. Smallwood. Do you have Internet access here?"

"Yes, we have wireless. My computer is still on, if you need it."

"Let me get my laptop and check his records."

Dr. Standish set her laptop up in the reception area and quickly checked Stinky's medical history.

"Nothing here. Hopefully, it's just a one-time event, but he needs to see Dr. Smallwood as soon as possible."

"Let me give his owner a call, while you're still here, so you can explain what's going on."

Although Stinky's owner seemed satisfied by the vet's diagnosis, she expressed some doubt that Milky Way could handle the situation. Gracie assured her again that Stinky was well cared for, and she would personally take him to the vet on Monday morning.

Dr. Standish smiled understandingly as Gracie finished the call. "If you could just take care of the dogs, it would be easy. It's the owners who are difficult." She smiled as she shut down her laptop.

"How true. How long have you been at Countryside, doctor?"

"Call me Kelly. Just about two months. I came back home after 10 years of practicing in Pennsylvania. My parents are getting older and need a little help these days, so I decided to move back. I couldn't get them to move near me. Nothing has changed since I graduated from high school in '93."

"It's pretty much the same. Did you go to Letchworth?"

"Yes. Did you?"

"Yes. You graduated the year my cousin would have. Did you know Charlotte Browne?"

"Charlotte? She was one of my best friends. Remembering her accident was one of the hardest things about moving back here. She had a lot of stuff going on in her life, and then it was over, really over. It all hit me again when I drove down Main Street on my first day back." She lowered her eyes and fell silent.

Gracie was momentarily speechless. Thoughts sprinted through her mind before she replied.

"You know, I've been looking at what happened to Charlotte, due to some unusual family circumstances over the last couple of weeks. Would you be willing to get together sometime soon? Come over, and I'll cook."

"I'll give you a call. A home-cooked meal sounds good. With my hours, I live on frozen dinners and salads. Let me check on Stinky before I go."

The little terrier jumped on the gate and barked. Stinky wagged his stubby tail furiously and pressed his nose through the wire.

"That's the Stinky I know." Gracie opened the gate and bent down to scratch his ears.

He wiggled his way to greet Kelly.

"All his vitals are normal. Just keep an eye on him and call us if you see anything out of the ordinary."

"Thanks, Kelly. Hopefully, he'll be fine."

"I hope so too. Once we get some blood work done, we can make a better diagnosis. You're a funny little dog, with a lot of personality. Behave yourself, now." She rubbed his belly, and he squirmed with pleasure.

"Please give me a call, Kelly. I saw Miss Russell today, and I can catch you up on Deer Creek, if you'd like." Gracie hoped the mention of Miss Russell was the hook she needed to find out what Kelly Standish knew about Charlotte.

"Miss Russell. Wow! I haven't thought about her in a long time. I would like to know what's she's doing. I'll give you call when I check my schedule for the week."

"Great. Call either the kennel or my cell. I'll give you my numbers."

Her watch said 10 p.m. by the time she was setting the alarm. As the door clicked shut, Gracie realized she'd forgotten to turn on the outside lights. The mercury vapor light outside the reception area lit the driveway well, but the side lawn to the house was inky. There was no moon, and the stars didn't illuminate the bluestone pathway to the kitchen door. Haley trotted confidently ahead of her. Gracie wished for dog night vision, as her toe hit the broken edge of the path.

"Ouch! Haley, wait up. Where are you, girl?" Haley might as well be invisible tonight.

Haley suddenly gave a deep-throated bark and ended it with a growl. Gracie stopped.

"Haley, come." She knew her voice was uncertain.

What or who was in the dark? Why hadn't she turned the lights on? Haley barked again. Gracie heard stones scattering, and she caught a glimpse of Haley running across the driveway toward the cornfield. She wasn't going to stop. Gracie ran the width of the driveway, straining to see.

"Haley, come here. Haley." There was no way she wanted to venture into the cornfield at night, but that's exactly where the dog was headed. A flashlight was a necessity. After tripping over the edge of the path again and bruising her shin on the way up the steps, she dug a flashlight out of the junk drawer in the kitchen. She flipped all the outside lights on, setting off the dogs, and they began howling, barking, and baying. What a choir! The neighbors would probably complain for sure tonight.

The corn was well over her head, and the leaves arching over her reminded her of the trees at Manderly in the movie, *Rebecca*. The batteries in her flashlight weren't top-notch, and the beam was weak. She could only hope it would last while she was in the maze of rows that whispered and waved like long tentacles in the light breeze. Hide and seek in the cornfields when she was a kid was spooky, but fun. This was not fun in any form. Where was Haley? What had she gone after? Was there someone out back just waiting for them? A knot formed in the muscle from her neck to her left shoulder. Her heart was racing. Haley didn't respond to any of her calls. She was so far in the field now, she wasn't sure which way was out. Why hadn't she kept her bearings? Maybe staying in one row would keep her from getting more confused. The flashlight flickered, and she hit it against her palm.

"Come on, don't quit now."

The flashlight gleamed a little brighter. She called again to Haley. The sound of a cornstalk cracking came from behind. She swung the flashlight around, but didn't see anything. Then she heard another crack and what sounded like footsteps. She clutched the flashlight tighter. She could at least give whoever was out here a whack on the head.

"Haley, come here. Enough fooling around. Come on." Her heart still pounded, and her head was whirling. This was stupid. She needed to find her dog and go home. Another crack of a cornstalk was now ahead of her. Something or someone was in here. It was probably an animal. A four-footed one was preferable. She squatted down and turned the flashlight off. If someone was in here, the darkness was her friend. The swish of leaves moving continued, and then she heard whining. It had to be Haley. She heard something running through the corn to her right. Two shiny eyes gleamed right in front of her. She flicked the flashlight on. It wasn't Haley. The skunk looked directly at her, and the tail rose. Before Gracie could move, the white-striped critter turned and sprayed with vigor.

The biting, acidy smell hit the air, and droplets of skunk stink hung on the corn leaves above her, burning Gracie's nose and eyes. She fell backwards onto the rocky soil. The odor was overpowering, and she was coughing and wiping her face with her tank top. Scrambling to get up, she scooped the waning flashlight from the ground, pushing through the rattling green dagger-like leaves to get out of the cornfield. Gracie's throat burned so badly that she couldn't get more than raspy cough out. Tears streamed like a fountain, making her vision blurry. The rough corn leaves with their sharp edges cut into her arms and legs. She had to find the end of a row so she could escape the field from hell. Breaking through the last of scratchy corn leaves, her flashlight gave out. Shaking and tapping it didn't work this time. With some effort and a few stubbed toes, she finally made it back to the steady light by the kennel. On the concrete pad in front of the entrance, Haley lay panting heavily. She thumped her tail and smiled, holding her nose high and sniffing with interest.

"You've got to be kidding."

Haley got up, tail still wagging, but making a good attempt to look properly chagrined.

"Stay there. Don't get near me. You'll smell just like me if you do. Of course, I couldn't tell if you did or not. " Her nose was in massive overload.

Gracie started peeling off her jeans and tank top. There was no way she could go in the house like this. The smell would be everywhere. She turned the alarm off, ran to the grooming room for the "Skunk Off" shampoo they kept for unlucky dogs, and grabbed a large towel from the storage rack. Using the outside hose and generous amounts of shampoo, she lathered and rinsed twice, wearing just her underwear in the darkness behind the office. At least the water was lukewarm in the hose. Haley stood in wonder, wagging and sniffing throughout the process.

"This is all your fault, Haley. What were you thinking?"

Haley ran to backyard fence and came back with her mouth full. Gracie tried to make out the shape. She squinted through the sting of the shampoo running into her eyes.

"A raccoon! I got sprayed because you had to go hunting? You've got to be kidding!

Haley dropped her trophy at Gracie's bare feet.

"Haley, take it away. It's great. Good job, but get it out of here."

Obediently, the big Lab picked up the limp raccoon and took it back to the fence. She lay in the grass, nosing her catch as if deciding to eat it or save it for later.

"And don't you dare eat it. I don't need guts all over the lawn."

The offending clothes were dispatched with a stick she found on the lawn and tossed in the dumpster. Gracie couldn't be sure how badly she still smelled, since her olfactory system was officially out of commission. After a short discussion with Haley, she decided that camping on the back patio was probably the best idea, and a quick trip to pick up some clothes and her sleeping bag wouldn't damage the air quality of the house too much.

When the kitchen door swung open, she caught her breath and almost dropped her towel.

The house was a mess. Chairs were tipped over, and papers were scattered. Mugs she had left in the sink lay shattered on the kitchen tile.

Chapter 25

Police car lights flashed, and dogs barked furiously, while Gracie talked to Investigator Hotchkiss in the driveway. The investigator was standing a judicious distance away, asking questions in between coughing and frowning at her notepad. It was all fairly embarrassing. There was no doubt that Gracie stunk to high heaven. Her parents arrived right behind Jim, and they were greeted with the same force field of skunk power.

"What happened here?" Theresa demanded. "Did someone hit a skunk in the driveway or something?"

"No, Mom. It's me. I managed to get sprayed and robbed all in one night."

At least Gracie had been able to put on a pair of shorts and a T-shirt before the sheriff's department arrived. Her laptop sitting on the coffee table and the MP3 player were gone. The TV in the living room hadn't been touched, but then it was attached to the stereo system, with a web of wires only an engineer could untangle. It was one of Jim's technology masterpieces. The laptop was a major problem. It held all her personal financial information, the scanned copies of Charlotte's documents, and an archive of family pictures. She had backups of her financial information, but she hadn't backed up the pictures. She'd been scanning them for her parents, but needed to purchase an external hard drive for complete storage.

Another encounter with Investigator Hotchkiss wasn't high on her list, and unfortunately, Marc wasn't on duty tonight. Gracie would have felt better if he were here to run interference for her. However, she didn't smell very nice, so maybe it was just as well.

The house had been unlocked. She hadn't even given it a thought. The robbery must have happened while she was in the cornfield. How would they have known unless they were watching her? It was unnerving to think that criminals had actually been in and out of her house in such a short time. She was also hopping mad. How dare they come back and do this? Maybe they had been in the backyard when Haley started barking. Had they, him, or whoever set her barking?

"You really do stink." Jim leaned backward in awe of her aura.

"I know. I used the Skunk Off, but it doesn't seem to work very well."

"How about not at all? You were sold a bill of goods there, Gracie."

She could see her father holding a hand over his nose, pretending to rub his face. He was wisely not saying a word.

"Gracie, you must have some peroxide, baking soda, and dish soap," her mother demanded.

"Yes, of course I do. It's in the kitchen and bathroom."

"I'll be back in a minute with a bucket and a brush." Theresa pushed up her sleeves and headed to the house.

She marched back with a bucket of sudsy solution, a towel, and a bath brush.

"Get yourself out back, and we'll do this again the right way."

"Mom, not now, I've got..."

"Please, Gracie your mother is right on this." Jim covered his nose.

"Yes, go ahead, Mrs. Andersen. I can wait." Investigator Hotchkiss put her notepad to her face. Was she laughing or what?

Gracie stomped off with Theresa leading the way. They reappeared 10 minutes later.

"It's better." Her father let his breath out audibly.

"It *is* better." Jim sniffed tentatively.

"That solution works every time," Theresa beamed.

"You should market it, Mrs. Clark." Investigator Hotchkiss lowered her notepad and actually smiled.

"It's an easy recipe. A quart of peroxide, some baking soda, and two or three good squirts of dishwashing liquid. Cheap and effective. Remember Daisy? That dog loved skunks. I found this concoction early on, and it's a good thing."

"I thought tomato juice was the cure for skunk," Investigator Hotchkiss said.

"No, that doesn't work; it just makes you smell like tomato juice and skunk. Well, Gracie, you smell almost human again."

"I *should* smell better. You probably scraped off most of my skin. I must be bleeding."

"You're fine, but there could be a slight alteration in your hair color."

"What do you mean slight alteration?" She asked warily.

"Well, you could be a strawberry blonde or something like that by tomorrow."

"You're kidding! Mom, why did you do that to my hair?" Gracie knew she sounded like a whiny five-year-old and didn't care.

"Do you want to stink for days, lose all your friends, and annoy your family?"

"Uh, excuse me, Mrs. Andersen, could we get back to a few more questions?"

Investigator Hotchkiss had her pencil warmed up again.

They decided that Jim would camp out at Gracie's for the night. Eau de skunk lingered in the house, so Jim opened the windows. Gracie took a raging hot shower and sprayed herself liberally with vanilla and lavender body spray. Now that she felt more human and wrapped in her soft blue terry bathrobe, she was wired and ready to talk about her fruitful detective work. Jim was already sound asleep in the recliner, his head tipped back, mouth open, and his long legs comfortably stretched out. Haley snored deeply, lying full length on the couch. What a pair! No stamina.

The copies of Charlotte's diary pages that the robbers had scattered through the house had been put on the kitchen counter. She grabbed them and found her notebook under the coffee table. With papers stacked in front of her, Gracie sat cross-legged on the floor and began piecing together the conversations of the day.

Gracie groaned and tried to straighten up. She'd fallen asleep amid the papers sometime during her all-nighter, and slats of sunlight shot through the half-open blinds. Her back was knotted and her legs stiff from camping out on the floor. Jim was gone, but Haley was on her back, still sleeping on the couch. She flipped over and jumped down to lick Gracie's face as Gracie tried to stand.

"Okay, girl, let's go out."

She left the patio door open and started making some sturdy coffee, while Haley finished her morning constitutional. Gracie needed to hurry. It was 7:30, and the one pick-up time on Sunday was 8:00 to 8:30. No church today. She needed to call Marc and let him look over her notes. The pieces of the puzzle Uncle Stan had given her were just the frame. Yesterday's wagonload of information was filling in the middle of the picture. Maybe with Marc's help, she could get the last few pieces in place.

Stinky was happy and eating his breakfast. His stubby tail was wagging like a flag, and his appetite was good. There was no trace of the seizure from the night before. Three dogs were picked up before 8:30, and the pack scheduled for a morning play session was sufficiently tired out. Joe had cleaned all the runs and double-checked water dishes by 9:30. Jim had asked Joe to start putting up the fence posts for the agility course, so he'd be around until noon or so. Jim was taking the day off, transferring the evening feeding and afternoon play sessions to Gracie's calendar, but, with any luck, she could meet Marc before Joe left.

She suddenly realized that she didn't have Marc's home number. She'd have to see if he was on duty. Gracie doubted the dispatcher would give her his personal number, but it couldn't hurt to ask. She left a message with the dispatcher, who promised to pass it on to Marc. Now she'd have to sit around, waiting for his call. Since she needed to find the flash drive that held her backup information from the stolen laptop, she might as well look for it while she waited for the phone to ring. All the usual storage places yielded nothing, and her frustration was rising. She was checking the bathroom drawers in desperation when she caught a glimpse of her hair in the mirror over the sink.

"AGGGH! It's pink! I've got a pink stripe! Are you kidding me?" A few other words came to mind as she glared at the thick ribbon of pink hair on the right side of her head.

"I look like a punk rocker or a Halloween reject."

Haley whined and wagged her tail, banging it against the door.

"The customers must have thought I'd lost my mind this morning. Just great!"

No amount of braiding or twisting hid the pink, so finally Gracie pulled it back in the clip as usual.

"Well, Haley, your adventure last night sure landed me in a fine mess. No more running after raccoons or other creatures of the night. Deal?"

Haley looked properly interested in Gracie's admonition and then found her raggedy monkey toy, ready for a game of fetch.

"Sorry, girl, you'll have to amuse yourself right now. I have to find that flash drive. My tote, that's it. I took it with me to meet Matthew, and then we decided on the park instead of the parsonage."

She dumped the contents on the bedroom floor, the green and black flash drive skittering across the hardwood floor and under the bed. Haley sniffed through the rest of the inventory, snatching a small piece of paper. She wagged her tail and trotted toward the living room.

"Hey, come back with that. I need all my stuff."

It was probably a receipt she hadn't dropped off in the office. Haley sat by the patio door, eager to play.

"Drop it, Haley. You're not at the top of my favorites list today."

Haley opened her mouth with the paper stuck to her long pink tongue.

"Yuck, why did you have to slime it?" Gracie pulled the strip off. It was certainly no receipt. It was a ticket. A ticket from Delicious Delights Theatre.

"How did *this* get in my tote? And who went to see *Wanda Does Albuquerque?*"

Further inspection gave her the date—the day Uncle Stan died. It was a four o'clock matinee. Gracie carefully laid it on the kitchen counter to dry. How did this end up in her stuff? The phone rang. It was Marc, and he was on his way to talk with her. It was about the robbery.

They sat at the dining room table—Marc, Gracie, and Investigator Hotchkiss. Marc was in uniform, looking fine, while the investigator was surprisingly casual with jeans and white golf shirt.

"We've got a pretty good idea of what's been going on, but we need your help, Mrs. Andersen." The investigator looked over her reading glasses at Gracie and glanced back at her notebook.

"OK, but I'm not sure how I can help."

"Gracie, it looks like the kennel has been used to target individuals to rob." Marc spoke quietly, watching Gracie's face for a reaction.

"What do you mean? How could the kennel be used for that?"

"Well, the robberies escalated in the last couple of weeks, and all the victims were out of town at the time. We had a couple of them mention their dogs were at your kennel. Could we take a look at your records and see if there is some connection?"

Gracie could see that the investigator was letting Marc take the lead. Not only was she a suspect in her uncle's death, but now she was somehow also involved in robbing houses.

"Am I being accused of something here?"

"No, Mrs. Andersen. We just want to see your records, if you don't mind." Investigator Hotchkiss attempted to sound almost friendly.

"All right. Let's get this over with."

Gracie watched Joe pound a metal post in the soft ground on north side of the kennel. He looked up briefly and picked up another post.

"Who's that?" the investigator questioned.

"That's Joe Youngers, our kennel helper. We're getting ready for a dog match in a few weeks."

"He hasn't worked here very long, has he?" Marc watched Joe with curiosity.

"No. He's been here two or three weeks."

"Any trouble with him?"

"No, although he's on probation. I wasn't sure about him when we hired him, but he seems to be doing OK. Jim likes him. He's willing to work anytime, which is a big help."

Gracie pulled up the occupancy records on her office computer. Investigator Hotchkiss thumbed through her notebook, while Gracie printed off the last two weeks of kennel activity.

"Here you go." She handed the stack of paper to the investigator.

"Thanks for your help, Mrs. Andersen. We'll get back with you in a day or two." Her eyes were steady and unsmiling. Why couldn't this woman lighten up?

"No problem. I hope you catch these guys. I'd like my computer back, but I hope the kennel isn't involved in this. We don't need any more bad publicity. A connection could ruin us." The implications of what they were suggesting hit Gracie like blizzard-force winds, chilling her even in the summer heat.

"I understand, Mrs. Andersen. But we're trying to solve this case and stop any more robberies. We're just following every lead." Investigator Hotchkiss left Gracie and Marc standing in the driveway and climbed into her unmarked black sedan.

"This is a disaster, Marc. If people think the kennel is connected with these robberies, they'll never leave their dogs here. We'll be out of business in no time."

"Sorry, Gracie, but we have to look into it. I'm not a big believer in coincidences. I think I'll have a chat with Joe before I leave."

"All right." Gracie stopped short. "He's...gone."

Joe was nowhere in sight. His bike had been leaning against the building, but now it was gone too. She glanced at her watch; it was only eleven.

"Where does he live?" Marc was already getting into his cruiser.

"On Rail, in town."

"Thanks. See you later."

"But, wait... I need..."

The car was already backing out of the driveway. Why couldn't they have a conversation without interruption or something stupid happening? She stood, looking at him turn onto the road with her hands on her hips. And, if Joe had something to do with these robberies, she was going to deck her partner. Michael had always told her, "Trust your gut." Right now, hers didn't feel so great.

She needed to talk to someone, so Gracie left a message on her parents' answering machine to come over for steaks after church. Knowing her Dad wouldn't turn down steak, she started chopping veggies to grill with the meat. Their car pulled into the driveway just as she finished sealing the foil packet of summer squash, onions, and green beans.

They sat enjoying the shady patio and the afterglow of a good meal. There was a light breeze, and the smell of grilled beef lingered in the air. The pink stripe had been talked to death, and Theresa promised to call her stylist to see if she could fix the color. Bob was dozing with the Sunday paper draped over his lap in the lounge chair. The conversation was at a lull, but Gracie was dying to share her information bonanza. Her mother wouldn't be happy about her suspicions. But she'd let them draw their own conclusions.

"You know, I had some interesting conversations yesterday," Gracie began tentatively.

"Really?" Her mother was relaxed and only half-interested. She was watching a pair of finches play in the hydrangeas.

"I saw Matt Minders and Miss Russell, the old cheerleading coach."

"Oh? I rarely see Matthew around. Was he visiting his parents?"

"Yeah, but we'd made arrangements to get together and talk about Charlotte."

"You're still messing with that?" She turned to face her daughter.

"Yes, I'm still messing with that, and I found out a couple of things I didn't know. For one, Matt is the person who found Charlotte in the street. And he's the one who saw the car going down Mill Street that night."

"That's right. Matthew was the one who got the license plate number. It wasn't advertised though."

"It was storming so badly that he really didn't get a good look at the car and wasn't able to see the whole plate. It was a WY plate though, so it had to be someone local."

"It must have been horrible for Matthew to find Charlotte." Her mother shuddered. "So did Matthew have anything else to say?"

"According to him, Aunt Shirley was anxious for resolution, so the investigation was shut down pretty quickly. And maybe Matt's parents tried to protect him by just keeping that part quiet. He was a kid. He still has a pretty hard time talking about it."

"Rightly so. I'm not sure how you ever get over something like that." Gracie's father opened his eyes and folded up the Sunday paper that had started sliding off his lap.

"Miss Russell had some interesting things to say too."

"I always liked her. Kay was a good teacher, and she treated the office staff like gold, unlike some other teachers." Theresa had worked in the school office for more than 25 years, retiring three years ago.

"She knew Charlotte was pregnant. Charlotte was really afraid of Aunt Shirley and didn't know what to do."

"Not surprising. Shirley was pretty tough on her daughters." Her dad adjusted his reading glasses and pulled out the comic section.

"I'm not sure what 'really afraid' means, Gracie." Theresa sounded a little defensive, and Gracie could tell her hackles were slowly rising.

"If Aunt Shirley knew about the pregnancy, she would have made things pretty awful for Charlotte." Gracie didn't want to go any further with her suspicions. They were pretty shocking, and Aunt Shirley was her mother's sister, after all.

"If she did, I'm sure she was just upset, which is how any parent would react. Parents want the best for their children."

Gracie chewed the inside of her cheek. Aunt Shirley would have always taken care of Number One. But how far would Shirley have gone to protect her own reputation? She had no proof anyway.

"You're right. Sorry, Mom."

She rose to pick up newspaper section that had fluttered to the ground from table next to her father. The coupon for free popcorn at the drive-in caught her eye. She folded the paper, placing it back on the table.

"You know I found, or rather Haley found, a ticket stub in my bag today. It was for the Delicious Delights Theatre in Geneseo."

"That's a porno theatre. Where did you get that?"

"I don't know. It was for the day Uncle Stan died, though. I'm wondering if it was in the house and somehow found its way into my bag. I dropped everything when I found him...there." Gracie swallowed hard with emotion.

"Your uncle never went any place like that. I can't imagine..."

"Your mother is right. Stan was never interested in that kind of entertainment." Her father pulled his glasses off and set them on the side table. "Maybe you picked it up somewhere else."

"Possibly," Gracie said slowly. "I can't imagine where. It's quite a coincidence that it's the day Uncle Stan died, don't you think?"

The phone rang, and Gracie jumped up to answer. She was hoping it was Marc, and she wasn't disappointed.

"Gracie, I need to come back and fill you in on your employee Joe. Is now OK?"

From Marc's tone, her gut must have been right all along.

"Sure, now is fine. It's not good, is it?"

"Afraid not. I'll be there in a few minutes."

"Bad news?" Her mother was now picking up dishes to carry into the house.

"Yes. I knew my instincts were right about Joe, unfortunately. I think he's been involved with the robberies and was using the kennel somehow."

"Oh, no, Gracie. I thought he was doing so well."

"He was, or at least, we thought so. Marc is on his way over to fill me in."

"Marc?" Bob asked looking over his readers.

"Deputy Stevens, Dad."

"Oh." His short answer spoke volumes, and he gave his wife a knowing look.

"I'll get these dishes in the dishwasher, and then we'd better get going, Gracie. Unless you need us here for some reason." Her mother's curiosity was growing.

"No, Mom. I think I'd better hear this on my own anyway."

"We understand. See you later, kiddo. Thanks for lunch." Her father hugged her and headed for the car. Gracie saw him yawn and rub his eyes. He would continue his Sunday afternoon nap on his own couch.

Marc was true to his word and showed up just minutes after her parents left. His face was grim, and his jaw tense.

"So here's what we know so far." Marc smoothed back his short hair and sat down on the sofa.

"OK. What's the story?"

"Joe has been keeping tabs on the reservation book and feeding the information back to these two other felons, who've been living with him and his grandmother. Then this pair takes a midnight drive, and they help themselves while no dogs or people are home."

"Not a bad setup, but this is going to ruin Milky Way. There's no way I'm going to be able to fix this PR nightmare. Leave your dogs here, and our employees will rob your house while you're away." Gracie kneaded the familiar knot in her neck. "I'd better try to get a hold of Jim. This is one time I wish I'd been wrong."

"From what Joe tells us, I'm pretty sure that he's been coerced into doing this. These two guys threatened to hurt his grandmother and a few other things. The one 'friend' is a pretty violent person. No excuse not to report them, but prison pals have their own code of honor and obligation."

"So what does this mean for us? Do you have to advertise what was going on?"

"Not necessarily. Joe is cooperating fully. His uncle is seeing to that. We've got a good idea where these two are headed, so we may be able to wrap this up quickly and quietly."

"That would be the best thing for the kennel. I appreciate anything you can do."

"No problem."

When she grabbed the pitcher of ice tea off the kitchen counter, the ticket stub caught her eye. She picked it up carefully. It was almost dry.

"You said one of these men was a violent type?"

"Yes." Marc looked at her quizzically as she placed the stub on the dining room table.

"I think I found this in my uncle's house the day he died. Could he have been a victim? My uncle wasn't into porno, just beer."

"You *think* you found this in your uncle's house? What does that mean exactly?"

Gracie cleared her throat. "I, uh, I dumped my purse while I was in the house and kind of shoved everything back into it. It must have been on the floor."

Marc examined the ticket as she talked. She could only hope he wouldn't ask for more details. How would she explain breaking and entering while everyone was in church?

"It's entirely possible that they tried robbing your uncle, so I'll take this with me, if you don't mind. From what your cousin tells us, a few things are missing at the house. Do you have a plastic bag?"

"Sure." Gracie pulled a sandwich bag from a drawer and handed it to him. His hand brushed hers as he took it. "I don't think you'll find anything on it. Haley had it in her mouth."

"You never know. They might find something. I'd better get back to Warsaw. There's a pile of paperwork to finish, and I'm supposed be off in an hour."

"All right. Thanks for filling me in, although I was hoping we could talk about the hit-and-run car and that license plate."

"Sorry, not today. How about Tuesday? I'm off then, and I can do a little more digging beforehand."

"That should work. How about going down to Letchworth for a picnic?" Gracie was shocked at her sudden forwardness.

He grinned and rubbed his face. "Good idea. Where do you want to meet?"

They decided on Inspiration Point. It was one of her favorite places—a great view of the Genesee River gorge, and the arched stone bridge over the little stream made it a touch romantic. Gracie would bring the sides, and Marc would bring steaks to grill.

Gracie's head still ached, emotions churning. The idea of Uncle Stan being killed in his own home by men trying to rob him made her sick. It was even worse if there was a connection back to her. At least he hadn't had a dog at Milky Way. It wasn't any consolation though. She began dialing Jim's cell number.

Chapter 26

The news of Joe's arrest and the possible connection to Stan's death was all over town like a spring grassfire. Gracie wanted to take a permanent vacation to some remote tropical island. But after an executive session, Jim and Gracie decided to stay high profile, talking about the kennel working with the sheriff's department to steer the gossip in their favor if they could.

Theresa's early morning phone call to her daughter informed Gracie that Isabelle and Tim were unhappy about the ticket stub find. It might tarnish the family reputation. Why her mother had thought it necessary to mention that to them was beyond her. She really didn't want to tell Investigator Hotchkiss that she'd made that other visit inside her uncle's house. There would be way too many questions if that came up.

Jim came back from Midge's to report that he was still doing some damage control for the kennel. Most were sympathetic, but none had left their dogs at Milky Way either. He'd also spent time at the feed store and hardware, hoping that he could work on PR. Only time would tell if it had done any good. It was Gracie's turn to go to town in the afternoon. The post office, Midge's, and the bank were her targets. She cheerfully spoke to everyone and managed to let the post mistress and about a half dozen people picking up their mail know that the kennel had helped identify the robbery ring, and they were cooperating fully to bring all of the men to justice.

When Gracie entered the bank, she noticed Tim at his desk in the back corner, talking with a customer. Deciding to take the high road, she raised a hand in greeting while she stood in the business teller's line to make the deposit. Tim half-heartedly mirrored her greeting, quickly averting his eyes to continue his conversation. Isabelle swept into the bank as the teller began counting the cash and Gracie waited for the receipt. Tim immediately stood, shook hands with the customer, and walked to the board room with Isabelle.

"She's been here a lot lately," the young teller, Felicity, said conspiratorially as she banded the last of the bills. Gracie guessed that Felicity was in her early 20s and spent her salary on salon appointments and wardrobe.

"Is that unusual?"

"Sort of. She always shows up for lunch on Wednesdays and sometimes drops by other times, but she's been here almost every day. Hey, I love that pink in your hair."

"Great, thanks." Gracie was grateful for the stripe that distracted the teller's need for information. But she started in again as she totaled the checks.

"Mr. Baker has been kind of a grouch lately." There was a slight pout in Felicity's lower lip.

"Understandable with all that's been going on."

It was obvious that the teller wanted some inside family information, but Gracie wasn't going to bite. It went against her grain to defend Isabelle or Tim, but she thought of Greg and Anna. They didn't deserve to have more dirt shoveled on them. Her whole family had enough to deal with right now.

Isabelle came out of the board room door, her mouth set in a grim line. Her eyes looked a little red to Gracie. Tim watched his wife stalk through the row of desks to the bank entrance. He straightened his blue striped tie, smoothed his mustache, and went back to large cherry desk.

"Doesn't look like that went well." Felicity's eyes shone with curiosity.

"No, but then my cousin just lost both her parents. It's been pretty rough. Thanks for your help." Gracie reached for the receipt and effectively dismissed the disappointed teller. A phone call to her mother might shed a little light on the home front with Isabelle and Tim.

Midge's was busy; the tables were all filled. Gracie quickly grabbed her favorite stool at the counter when it was vacated by a slick-looking guy in a pin-striped suit. He had to be a salesman or a businessman traveling through by the looks of him. Midge was at the cash register, and she took Gracie's order after ringing up the stranger's bill.

"The usual?"

"Please."

Midge yelled to the kitchen for a chicken finger salad. She filled a tall red pebble-textured plastic glass with lemonade and set it in front of Gracie, along with a napkin and a fork.

"What did you do to your hair?" Midge looked over her glasses at the pink stripe.

"Don't ask. It has something to do with a skunk and my mother."

"I won't ask, but I hear you've had a lot of excitement out your way again." Midge was chewing her gum thoughtfully.

"You're right. I think the sheriff's department has a handle on the robberies now. I think they'll be able to track down the two guys that were messing with Joe."

"That's good. Too bad about Joe, though. His grandmother is pretty broken up about it."

"Yeah, I know, but he's cooperating fully with the police. They may cut him some slack."

Gracie wasn't too sure that would happen, and she wasn't quite sure she really wanted it to happen for Joe. This was the end of his second chances, as far as she was concerned. She and Jim had already had that discussion.

"Heard that they might have something to do with your Uncle Stan's accident, too." Midge arched an eyebrow and looked over her reading glasses.

"Well, there's some talk about it, but they're still investigating that." Warning lights came on in Gracie's head about going too far with Midge.

"Seems like it could be what happened. Don't you think it's pretty strange that your cousin Charlotte and your uncle would have weird accidents? Oh, hi, Howie."

Howard Stroud eased himself onto a stool two down from Gracie and smoothed his Buffalo Bills tie over an expansive belly. He pushed his glasses up onto his broad forehead.

"Hey, ladies." He grunted as he adjusted his position on the stool.

"What'll it be today?" Midge had her pencil and pad ready.

"A cheeseburger all the way and a side salad, no dressing."

"You're kidding, what's going on?" Midge demanded.

"Ah, my doctor is after me to lose some weight. Gotta start somewhere, I guess."

"All right, but didn't you do that last summer?"

"Yeah, but he told me if I don't lose 25 pounds and start exercising, I'll end up having a bypass or worse."

"Well, good for you, Howard. Men always lose weight easier than women." Gracie smiled encouragingly.

"We'll see. It's no fun, though. Polly is all over me at home. At least I can have some red meat in peace here." Howard looked dismal.

"Gracie was telling me about the big robbery investigation." Midge ripped off Howard's order from her pad and walked toward the kitchen. A waitress came through the swinging doors with Gracie's salad. Midge grabbed the salad and handed the order to the waitress.

"I hear that Joe Youngers got arrested." Howard took a sip of the ice tea that Midge managed to hand him, while giving Gracie her salad.

"Unfortunately, yes, but he's cooperating fully with the sheriff's department." Gracie felt like a broken record.

"I was just telling Gracie that it's pretty strange that her uncle and cousin would have weird accidents."

"What cousin? Did something happen to Isabelle?"

"No, no, Charlotte, Isabelle's sister. You remember that hit-and-run," Midge called from the coffeemaker as she dumped out grounds, put in a fresh coffee, and poured water into the Bunn.

"Oh, yeah. That was a long time ago." Howard looked quizzically at Gracie as she stabbed the salad methodically with her fork.

Gracie was frantically thinking of something to steer the conversation away from her family.

"I think the sheriff's department will get it figured out soon. Hey, you know we're busy getting ready for a dog match at the kennel. We've only got a few weeks to get an agility course put together."

"Dog match? What's that?" Midge was now distracted, and Gracie gratefully capitalized on it in excruciating detail.

Howard inhaled his lunch, looking eager to escape. It wasn't lost on Gracie, but an idea had popped into her head, and she needed to see him alone. Midge rang up their bills, and they both stepped out onto the sidewalk into the bright afternoon.

"Howard, do you have a couple of minutes? I've got a harebrained thought to run past you."

"Sure, I'm walking these days for exercise, so just follow me back to the office." He pulled a toothpick out of his shirt pocket and started picking at his front teeth, dislodging a small piece of lettuce.

"Great. I need the exercise myself."

The office was just two blocks down Main Street. A group of kids played tag in a front yard next to Midge's, as they strolled under the maples.

"I've been doing a little family history lately, especially about Charlotte."

"Really? Genealogy stuff?" He flicked the toothpick into the street.

"Kind of, but actually about her accident. There seems to be some information missing about the car that hit her." She hoped her voice was nonchalant and steady.

"Well, it was a hit-and-run. They never did get a good ID on the car or the driver."

"I know, but they had a partial license plate number."

They had reached the insurance office, a converted Victorian house complete with perfect gingerbread. The house was painted in blue, gray, and white. "Stroud Insurance Agency" was hand-lettered in gold across the large bay window in the front.

"I guess it didn't do them any good, though." Howard pulled the office key from the pocket of his brown polyester pants and stuck it in the old-fashioned brass lock.

"Right, but I think my Aunt Shirley kind of shut down the investigation for some reason, so I'm wondering if you have records on vehicles you insured from back then."

"How many years ago was that?"

"About twenty years, 1992."

"I don't throw out much. I keep a lot of old records in the storage room down in the cellar. It's not the driest down there, and I'm not sure how far they go back."

"Would Polly know?" Gracie's pulse quickened, and her mouth was dry.

"Probably. But, Gracie, I can't let you just go through those records, if that's what your next question is going be. It's confidential insurance information."

"I know, but if the police made an inquiry, you'd let them look, wouldn't you?" There had to be a way into Howard's cellar full of paper.

"Well, I guess. I'd have to. I'd need a subpoena duces tecum, you know, a subpoena for records. I don't know why you're so focused on this. Seems like you have enough of your own troubles without borrowing from others." He gave her a reproving look.

"I know, but Charlotte's been on my mind since..." She felt tears pricking and blinked to gain control.

"Hey, I understand. I think. Gracie, let's get the lawsuit handled with the kennel first."

"Right, but I try not to think about that too much. I'm just trying to keep the kennel solvent until all this bad publicity goes away."

"Goes away? Remember where you live, honey. This is the best scandal around, right now." Howard's face crumpled into a broad smile.

He pulled a white handkerchief from his pocket and mopped his forehead. He turned the floor fan to "high." The air-conditioning must be out of commission, thought Gracie. The office was stuffy and very warm.

"Yes, I remember. But I'm stubborn, and Jim's an optimist about the kennel. I hope we can contain the robbery damage and get the lawsuit settled soon. I'm not going to allow this business go down in flames."

"I'm doing my part. The insurance company is sending an investigator to check out Beth's story. I think there's something fishy going on with it, but for the life of me, I don't know what. Beth's been brought up right. Frank and Evie are good folks. Maybe a stranger can discover the information we can't."

"Thanks, Howard. I really appreciate all the work you're doing on this. Jim and I will see Nathan this week. He needs our signatures on some paperwork, so we'll see what he says about it."

"It'll get resolved, and with a little luck, we'll have it settled in six months."

"Six months? I hope it's sooner than that." Gracie wanted this whole thing well behind her before winter.

"Six months is fast, Gracie. Patience is a virtue, you know." Howard looked properly cherubic as he settled himself into the large, creaking swivel desk chair.

"So my mother tells me, Howie." She gave him a good-natured glare and turned toward the door.

It was obvious that she should go, but Gracie couldn't resist one more stab at the agency's old records.

"So, is there any chance Polly could do a little research for me on that license plate? You know, check on who might have had a plate close to that number?"

"Ah, well, I guess I wouldn't have a problem with my lovely spouse looking through the records, but you'd have to talk her into it. I'm not going to get in the middle of that. She's pretty busy off hours playing tennis and biking this summer. She's trying to set a good example for me." He grimaced and patted his stomach.

"Great, then. I'll give her a call and see if we can come to an agreement. Thanks a lot." Gracie was out the door in a flash, the little bell on the door jingling happily as it closed.

Although kennel reservations were down, Marian was doing a brisk business on the grooming side. There were two Golden Retrievers, each waiting for a summer haircut when Gracie returned to Milky Way. Marian was finishing up a Dalmatian that had clogged anal glands. The putrid smell hit Gracie as she went by the grooming room.

"Better you than me today," Gracie cheerfully called out.

"Thanks. You get the next dog that needs this done," Marian retorted.

Cheryl was manning the reception area, and Jim was working on the fence for the agility course.

"Seems like all is well today," Gracie said as she took a look at the messages waiting for her. There was nothing from Marc, but James Johnson, an insurance investigator, had called. She'd need to call him back soon.

"Pretty quiet, but the work is steady," Cheryl answered. "Jim and I got the runs done in short order this morning, and poor Marian has been busier than a one-armed paperhanger with grooming appointments. After these two hairy beasts, there are three more coming in."

"Good, at least we're bringing in some money. Did you get a chance to print off those coupons?"

"Got 'em right here." Cheryl handed her a sheet with the current special of twenty percent off a week's stay.

"They look good. Make sure everybody gets a couple when they come in."

"Right. Oh, Stinky went home about a half hour ago. The owner's sister picked him up."

"Good. Did you let her know about the medication they need to pick up at the clinic?"

"Sure did. And I gave her the two pills the vet gave us. Looks like everything is OK with them. No blame, and she actually said to thank you for taking Stinky to the vet so early today."

"I hope we get some good PR out of that. He's such a good little dog. The medication should keep the seizures under control."

"He was perky and full of it when he left, so the sister could tell he got good care while he was here." Cheryl hesitated and cleared her throat. "Uh, Gracie, before you start returning calls, could I talk to you about an idea that might help the kennel?" Cheryl was chewing the end of a pencil and looked anxious.

"Sure. I'm open to any advice right now. What's the idea?"

"I was thinking that if we had a line of dog treats—you know, gourmet stuff—it might bring in a little more money."

Gracie swallowed the negative answer that jumped to her lips. "I don't know, Cheryl. I considered a line of designer treats before. Those products are expensive to begin with. We can't mark them up enough to make anything. I'm not sure our customers would bite, so to speak."

"No, don't buy them from a supplier. I can make and package them. I have a friend in Buffalo who has a little pet bakery. She's willing to give me a few recipes and get me started."

"I'm not really..." Gracie saw more expenses mounting and unsold goods sitting on a shelf.

"Just let me try for a month or two. With the match coming up, we might do pretty well selling gourmet training treats. We could give away little treat boxes for winning dogs."

"Well, that might be a good place to start." Gracie was starting to catch a little of Cheryl's enthusiasm. "OK, make up some samples, and we'll test them on our own dogs to see what they like best.

"Perfect. I'll start tonight."

"And we'll have to figure out how to pay you for them. You'll have expenses, and the kennel will need to purchase them, or we can work out a percentage of sales. Do you know how to do a cost analysis?"

"I'm not worried about that right now. I just think it would be an easy way to help make some more income and help you and Jim out."

"OK. We'll work out payment details if this flies."

Gracie didn't want to be a wet blanket, but gourmet treats in a farming community might not be as a big a hit as the leftover bone from the Sunday roast. But then again, she had some customers who were pretty particular about what their dogs ate. She knew there were a few who insisted on supplying their own organic food, even though Milky Way fed high-quality kibble. Cheryl's face shone with excitement, so it was worth giving in, even if it didn't make sense to Gracie. She also didn't want to discourage a valuable employee. Owning your own business wasn't always what it was cracked up to be.

Gracie thumbed through the pile of messages and found one from Dr. Kelly Standish. She was available Wednesday to get together. Gracie called the vet clinic number back quickly and left a message that supper would be at seven on Wednesday. She could hardly wait to find out what Kelly knew about Charlotte's pregnancy, and if she knew who the father was. It was also a chance to find out more about the mysterious English teacher. Maybe she should start searching for him online.

She fingered the message slip from the insurance investigator as she left a voicemail for him. She and Jim could give their account of the dog bite incident to Mr. Johnson tomorrow morning as was requested. Then, with some hesitation, she punched in the number for Investigator Hotchkiss. Before the phone rang twice, the investigator picked up. Without wasting pleasantries, she let Gracie know that Joe's cohorts had been picked up in Kenmore, a Buffalo suburb, along with a couple of other guys who had recently violated their parole. Gracie's laptop was part of the recovered loot, and she'd be able to get it back soon. The prison pals were all on a robbery spree throughout Western New York. However, Joe's buddies adamantly denied any robbery at her Uncle Stan's. They also insisted that straight up robbery was the objective, not murder. The felons' alibi was being checked out and there would be more information soon.

Relief trickled through her that these men were sitting in jail, but if they were telling the truth, it still meant Uncle Stan's "accident" was unsolved. She shivered. It wasn't over yet.

Chapter 27

The interview with the insurance guy went smoothly enough. He toured the kennel and took a few pictures of the place where the incident had occurred. He was interviewing Beth and her parents in the afternoon. Then he was talking to poor Barney's owner. Frank and Evie had demanded he be put down, but Barney had gotten a reprieve, at least until the suit was determined. Gracie and Jim sat looking at each other in the quiet office, after James Johnson had left.

"Well, I guess I'll get back to that fence." Jim stood and put his Yankees cap on his head. "One of the Kennel Club members is hauling over the agility course stuff this afternoon. They want to start practicing with their dogs this weekend."

"OK. I'll get the deposit together." Gracie double-clicked the QuickBooks icon on the screen to enter the deposit information.

They were both avoiding any comments about the lawsuit. It seemed like a threatening presence in the room, and the uncertain outcome meant either disaster or survival by the skin of their teeth. They were both weary of thinking about it, and Gracie wished desperately she'd called her doctor to refill the anxiety meds. Her resolve about medication was shaky at the moment. Sweating palms and racing heart gave her second thoughts. Sleep had been elusive the last couple of nights, and she was bone-tired. Cheryl knocked on the open door and stuck her head in.

"Sorry to interrupt, but I've got those samples. My dog loves them all. Do you want me to see what Haley thinks?"

Gracie smiled, "Sure, although Labs aren't known for their discriminating tastes. She likes varmints, you know."

"Haley may think she's a hunting dog, but when she gets a whiff of these, she'll give up her redneck ways."

Cheryl opened a brown paper lunch bag for Gracie's inspection. There were biscuits in several shapes—bones, fire hydrants, cats, and squares.

"There are peanut butter, liver, chicken, and veggie treats. I'm sure they'll be a hit." Cheryl's confidence obviously knew no bounds.

"They look and smell good." Jim reached in the bag and pulled out a fire hydrant.

"That's the peanut butter one." Cheryl smiled.

Jim crunched down on the biscuit.

"Tastes good to me."

Gracie's eyebrows rose, and she shook her head. "OK. Wonderful. We'll market them as treats for dogs *and* their owners then." Gracie dutifully sniffed and examined the bagful of canine goodies.

"Give me a handful, and I'll have Jack test them at home." Jim's old collie was about 12 years old and had some of his teeth.

"Are you sure Jack can handle the crunch?" Gracie had her doubts.

"Here, take some of the liver ones. They're soft training treats." Cheryl scooped out several dark brown cubes.

"Thanks. I'll let you know what Jack thinks." Jim shoved them in the pocket of his jeans and whistled his way out the back. It sounded like Chicago's "Saturday in the Park."

"Aghh, the park. I was supposed to cook. I promised to make some homemade something or other for a picnic at Letchworth tonight."

"Anyone we know?" Marian came into the office and stood by the doorway with clippers in her hand.

"Well, yes, but it's not for public consumption. Deputy Stevens and I are doing some more research on Charlotte's death."

"Research. Right. Keep thinking that way, Gracie. Good for you." Marian winked and turned toward the grooming room. "Lots of customers today, so I'd better get going."

"That's great Gracie. I hope you have a good time." Cheryl closed up the paper bag and headed to the reception area. Customers were arriving; the bell on the front door jingled, and dogs were barking excitedly.

Gracie decided to cruise around town after making the deposit. The Minders were doing yard work. The Reverend was mowing, and the Mrs. Reverend was weeding the front flowerbeds. Her flowerbeds were casual, lots of daisies, sweet peas, and hollyhocks. Midge's looked busy as usual, and the Village Park had a few mothers and kids on the playground. She also saw Isabelle playing tennis with the mayor's wife. Gracie quickly made a U-turn back to the park entrance. Avoiding Isabelle was a priority at the moment. Pulling out onto Main Street, she recognized Polly Stroud's red Camaro in the insurance agency's parking area. Sliding into the adjacent parking space, Gracie hurried to the door. Polly was at the big desk, and Howard was nowhere in sight.

"Hey, Polly, is Howard sick or something?"

"No. He had a conference in Rochester today, and I promised to cover while he was out."

Polly's brown-gray hair was swept up into a loose bun, two pencils suspended in its thick mass. Her reading glasses were on a blue beaded chain, which rested above her ample bosom. Even in the summer, Polly wore a navy blue suit and a no-nonsense white blouse. Her face sported a healthy tan, and she looked trimmer than the last time Gracie had seen her. Howard was probably having a heck of a time keeping up with his health-conscious wife.

"Can I help you with something?" Polly asked.

"Actually, yes. Howard said to talk to you about going through some old car insurance records that might be in the basement."

"Oh, he mentioned that. His records go back forever. I can't get him to throw anything out. But I'm not sure what you're looking for."

Gracie needed to spill her story to someone, and it was Polly's lucky day. After swearing Polly to silence, she shared her suspicions of a Deer Creek resident running Charlotte down. Tears suddenly came out of nowhere, and Gracie impatiently brushed them away.

"Honey, don't get upset. I understand. You and your family have been through some rough things. If we can help, we will." She pulled one of the pencils from her bun and chewed the eraser thoughtfully. "You know, we used to get reports from the insurance company of all the motor vehicles we insured every quarter. I think license plate numbers were included with the other information. Hang on a minute, and let me see if I can grab one of those for you to take. It's old information now, and there's no reason you couldn't have it. Howard's a dope. I'll be back."

Polly swept through a curtained doorway at the rear of the office area, and Gracie could hear the click of her high heels on the stairway to the basement. Gracie paced around Howard's big desk and the two black leather wingback chairs that faced it. Main Street had a steady stream of cars, trucks, and tractors with wagons loaded with hay. One with a manure spreader chugged by and layered the air with a bovine piquant. Then she saw Isabelle driving by in her Lexus, probably headed for the bank or Midge's. Isabelle looked her way, and Gracie slid into one of the chairs to avoid detection. She heard Polly's heels once again on the stairs.

"I've got it, Gracie. It's for the quarter ending September 30, 1992. It does have the plate numbers. No social security numbers or driver's license info, so here you go."

The old printout was faded, but still readable. The musty, green-barred, pin-fed paper draped over Polly's arm. Her hair had traces of cobwebs, and there was dust on her lapel.

"Thanks, Polly. You don't know how much I appreciate this. I'll bring it back as soon as I can." Gracie's fingers itched to start turning the pages, but she quickly tucked the report under her arm and headed out the door. She knew exactly the name she'd start with.

Chapter 28

G racie was an hour early getting to Inspiration Point. She chalked it up to a case of nerves. She'd run out of time to make anything homemade, so a quick drive-by to her parents, who were still knee deep in bereavement food, produced large containers of potato salad, baked beans, and a fresh blackberry pie. When she'd answered her mother's question about who was joining her on the picnic, surprisingly, there was no comment. She wasn't sure if that was good or bad.

The information gathered from the insurance report, along with her notes from Charlotte's diary and a list of suspicions about Uncle Stan's death, were piled on the front seat. Hauling the red and white cooler from the back, she carried it to the shady picnic area. There were several cars in the parking lot, but no one seemed to be around. Grunting, she hefted the cooler onto a wooden bench and pulled out the tablecloth. The worn oilcloth in blue plaid shook out easily over the weathered picnic table. In the lower branches of a sweeping elm, a pair of robins fed squawking babies that fluttered in a nest. Satisfied the tablecloth would stake a claim on the table, she strolled to the bridge toward the panoramic view over the stone walls.

A walk through the woods would steady her nerves and collect her thoughts. She didn't want to come across as a half-crazed woman, accusing a family member of manslaughter or maybe even murder. Gracie shuddered. She turned to the view spread over the Genesee River.

Inspiration Point was beautiful anytime of the year, but especially so in the summer. A stone bridge arched gracefully over the small brook that ran into the deep gorge.

The observation telescope was being used by a young couple who were obviously honeymooning. Gracie caught a glimpse of an extravagant diamond and shiny wedding band on the bride's left ring finger. Her husband was "showing" her how to use the telescopic viewer. His hands, however, weren't on the viewer. She gave the couple a polite berth and took the upper path.

The river wound through the gorge, running deep and fast after generous summer rains. In dry years, it could be just a trickle. From her vantage point, she could see that the Middle Falls had plenty of water tumbling over them, making a great show for the carloads of summer visitors. With three sets of falls, Letchworth, "The Grand Canyon of the East," was breathtaking. It was such a perfect day; she was surprised that she hadn't seen much activity on her way in through the Castile entrance to Letchworth Park. Maybe most people were enjoying the pool at the south end of the park or dining at the Glen Iris Inn.

The couple continued their visit by sitting on the bridge and watching the water bubbling over the moss-covered stones. They didn't even acknowledge her presence. Gracie decided she'd take the trail through the pines toward the Lower Falls while she waited for Marc. He'd see her vehicle and know she was around. She felt like a teenager again with a fluttery stomach, waiting for Michael to pick her up for a date. The picnic was just a research session, she reminded herself. She wasn't ready for anything else, but then again, maybe she was. It was too confusing to contemplate.

The shade from the evergreens was thick and cool. Gracie always imagined Seneca hunting parties or Mary Jemison, called "The White Woman of the Genesee," traveling through these woods. The broad trunks would have provided cover for hunters, but now they housed a large community of gray squirrels that chattered at her intrusion. Her sneakers were cushioned in the deep pine needles that covered parts of the trail. Two does browsed in a patch of grass in a small clearing. The broad walking trail meandered by the stone walls guarding the edge of the dangerous, sheer limestone gorge that plunged to the river. Gracie remembered her father's stern admonishments to stay off the walls when she and Tom were kids. In fact, the park signs gave the same warning. The gorge was deep— 500 feet plus in some areas. Stone steps led her further toward the Lower Falls picnic area. She stopped and looked at her watch. Marc should be along anytime, so she should start back. Two whitetail deer in the clearing suddenly bolted, and there was a snap of a twig to her right. Gracie turned toward the sound, but couldn't see anything. It was probably a squirrel or raccoon. Hopefully, it wasn't a skunk.

Dark clouds were mounting overhead, blocking the sun, and the trees creaked in the wind that had suddenly come up. There was a smell of rain in the air. It looked like the picnic might be turned into dinner eaten in her SUV.

A feeling that she was being watched crept over her. She looked around uneasily, but saw no one. Gracie decided to keep nearer the wall to catch more light to see her way. The clouds were definitely thickening, and the wind was stronger. A rumble of thunder sounded from the west. She picked up her pace and stumbled over a gnarled tree root. She felt her left ankle twist as she went down. Pain shot up to her knee. Gingerly, she stood and tested the foot. It wasn't too bad; maybe it was a little strain. She brushed the dirt and leaves from her white shorts—always a mistake to wear white, especially to a picnic.

The pain grew as she began walking again. She hobbled to the wall to get a better look at her ankle. She perched on the fieldstone wall, both legs stretched out on the uneven surface. The left ankle was definitely swelling. The gorge now had an eerie purplish light, with the thunderclouds spilling in. She'd better hurry and get back to the parking lot. A walking stick would help, but of course, there were none on the path. Spotting one just on the other side of the wall, Gracie swung her legs over the forbidden side.

A pair of hands pushed her hard in the middle of her back, knocking the air from her lungs. Totally off balance, Gracie fell headfirst over the ledge, the terrain scraping her hands and face, as she desperately grabbed for anything that would stop her fall. Rocks and dirt cascaded down the gorge ahead of her. There was no way to get a foothold, and the jagged stone face tore her light tank top. She couldn't even scream for help. Her breath came in short gasps.

The branch of a scrubby maple tree hit her outstretched right hand, and Gracie grabbed it with all her strength. She dangled in mid-air over the darkening river gorge, scrambling to find some leverage in the crumbly limestone. The tree sagged and groaned under her weight. It had to hold. She finally found a narrow foothold. Carefully, she redistributed her weight from the tree to her right foot and inched her hands toward a thicker portion of the trunk.

"Help, I'm down here. Help me. Somebody, help." Her voice echoed hollowly.

More rocks slid past her, and the tree pulled slightly from the unstable earth. She gripped the trunk tighter with both hands. Turkey buzzards circled the gorge, as if watching her dilemma and waiting.

"Anybody, help, I'm... just help me, please." Her voice cracked.

She lost her footing and fought to find the small toehold again. Her left foot found a tree root, and pain shot through her leg as she shifted her weight to balance. Climbing wasn't an option. There wasn't enough leverage to work with, and the swollen ankle wasn't cooperating. Her arms felt like they were being wrenched from their sockets. A few drops of rain stung her face, and lightning shattered the sky. She shifted her weight from one toehold to another, leaning into the rock for more support.

"Help me, somebody, please help me." Her throat was gravelly. She couldn't hold on much longer. She squeezed her eyes shut, blocking out the fast running river far below. It was probably a good time to pray. No words but "help" came to mind.

"Gracie!" It was Marc calling.

"Help me. I'm down here."

"Dear Lord in heaven, let him hear me," she prayed.

"Gracie! Where are you?" Marc's voice shouted above the storm.

"Over the wall, Marc. Help me—I can't hold on."

Gravel and rocks skidded past her, and the thud of boots above her brought some hope.

"Hang on, Gracie. I'll get you. Don't let go."

"I'm trying. I can't feel my hands anymore." Every muscle in her body burned, but she gripped the tree tighter. She didn't dare look up or down, pressing her face instead into the rocky soil.

"Gracie, I'm going to lower my belt to you. Put your arms through the loop, and let me pull you. Just relax and put your arms through the loop." Marc's voice was even and calm.

"I don't think I can." She couldn't bear to think of releasing the tree trunk.

"You can, and you will. I'm on a ledge above you, and I can pull you up."

"I don't know, Marc. I can't..." The pain was disappearing; she felt as if she could almost fall asleep.

"Gracie, listen to me. Take the loop, and I'll pull you up." His sharp instructions snapped her back to reality.

"All right."

The loop was just out of her reach.

"I can't reach it. It has to come lower." Gracie was almost past caring. She was soaked through and starting to shiver.

She heard Marc talking to someone, but she couldn't tell who. Maybe he was on his cell. He called to her again.

"I'll lower it a little more. You're going to have to really stretch this time."

The loop came toward her, and she stiffly pulled her left hand from the tree and finally felt the soft leather. Small waterfalls of rain ran off the rock face, slickening the surface. A T-shirt was knotted onto the belt. Would it really hold her weight? She wasn't sure.

"Gracie, put your other hand through the loop."

"It's not going to work."

"It *will* work, and you *can* put your other arm through the loop." Marc's voice was still even and patient.

"Hey, we've got our rescue team here. Let's get her."

Gracie forced herself to look up and saw three green uniformed men coming over the wall with ropes and a harness. She shut her eyes and clung to the tree and the belt. Suddenly there was a young and very muscular man, with dark curly hair, holding a harness by her side. She was strapped in and hoisted into air before she could say "thanks."

Marc sat in the Emergency Room at Wyoming County Community Hospital, waiting for Gracie to be examined. She had forbidden him to call her parents. He leaned forward and held his head in his hands. The curtain in the exam room had been drawn for a long time, and he wished the nurse would pull it back. Gracie was cut up and bruised, but the EMT was pretty sure she didn't have any broken bones or a concussion. There seemed to be a lot of drama every time he had contact with this woman, but for some reason, she intrigued him like nobody he'd met in a long time. She was determined and had a temper, but that red hair drove him crazy. He didn't dare ask about the pink stripe. That was new, but women did strange things with their hair sometimes.

"Deputy Stevens?" A doctor in green scrubs slid the curtain back from the exam room.

"Right here, doctor." Marc stood and shook the doctor's outstretched hand.

"Your girlfriend's one lucky lady."

"Uh, she's not..."

"Nothing broken, no concussion, but she's got a good crop of bruises and some cuts. And she's going to be hurting for a few days. I've given her a couple of prescriptions to fill. You can take her home."

"Home? Are you sure?"

"She won't stay here, so take her home and make sure she gets some rest. She shouldn't be working for two or three days either. Watching TV reruns and reading should be her most strenuous activities."

"All right then. Thanks, doctor. I'll get her home."

The ride back home was filled with long silences, and Gracie tried to find a position that didn't hurt. The pain medication was beginning to make her drowsy, but she needed to tell Marc the whole story. Gracie wasn't sure how much sense she'd made when they'd finally gotten her to safety.

"I need to make a report, Gracie. Somebody tried to kill you."

"I know, but I'm not sure I can do it tonight. My head is really getting fuzzy." Gracie's mouth was dry as cotton, and she could hardly keep her eyes open.

"We'll do it first thing in the morning. I'll make some arrangements to get your vehicle back. The park police are going to keep an eye on it."

"OK. I guess I need to call my parents and Jim. What time is it anyway?"

"It's after ten. You'd better call." He handed his cell phone to her.

Everyone would meet them at the house. She dozed off only to awaken as they turned into the driveway and barking began.

Gracie was almost comfortably sitting in the recliner with a cup of hot tea in her hands, when Investigator Hotchkiss appeared at her door. The questions were brief, and Gracie's mother hovered to make sure she was all right. Jim, Marc, and Gracie's dad stood out on the patio talking quietly. Reality was soft and fuzzy for Gracie, and before she knew it, her mother had her in bed. Her parents were in the guest room for the night. Haley slept close to Gracie. Thunder rumbled in the distance; another storm was coming in.

Chapter 29

Investigator Hotchkiss was back at nine o'clock, along with Marc. Gracie could hardly move, but she forced herself to make coffee. Her stomach rumbled, but she had no appetite. She'd sent her parents home with the promise they could come back and fix lunch. They were only slightly appeased, but Gracie didn't want them to hear the whole story just yet.

Marc and Jim had retrieved her SUV from the park. They'd piled the documents from the front seat on the dining room table.

"All right, Mrs. Andersen, you need to tell us exactly what you've been researching about your cousin's death." Investigator Hotchkiss had her pad ready.

Gracie looked at Marc, then back to the investigator. Clearing her throat she began. "I believe my Uncle Stan wanted me to look into Charlotte's death, and that's why he gave me her diary, the death certificate, and the police report. He suspected it wasn't an accident."

"How so?" Marc spoke quietly and sipped the strong black coffee.

"My cousin was pregnant when she died. My Aunt Shirley was rabid over family honor and appearances. In fact, even my parents didn't know she was pregnant, until I told them. Isabelle is just like her mother. Charlotte was pretty clear in her diary that she was terrified to tell her mother. She did tell her dad, my Uncle Stan. He most likely told my Aunt Shirley."

"Lots of girls get pregnant in high school. It doesn't have to be the end of the world. She could have gotten an abortion, couldn't she?" The woman's face was impassive.

"I think the father of the baby wanted her to, but Charlotte refused, according to her diary and cheerleading coach. My aunt would have told her the same thing. But Charlotte didn't want to have one." She sipped at the cooling coffee and adjusted her position. Setting the mug on the table, she pushed the copied documents to the policewoman. "Here are the pages from her diary that talk about telling her parents. You can tell she was afraid of her mother."

"Where'd you get these? I thought you returned the diary to your cousin Isabelle."

"Well, I made copies before I gave it back. I had an obligation to my uncle." Gracie felt a small surge of temper that she had to explain herself to the investigator yet again.

"It's not uncommon for a teenage girl to be afraid to tell her parents she's pregnant. Why do you think this has anything to do with Charlotte's death or your Uncle's?"

"You didn't know my Aunt Shirley. Charlotte's 'condition' would ruin the family's reputation. Her indiscretion would bring down the perfect world Aunt Shirley lived in. She would have been desperate. Maybe desperate enough to do something about the problem." Gracie flexed her scraped and bruised fingers tentatively.

"What are you saying?" Marc's jaw tightened, and his eyes were dark.

"I'm saying that I wouldn't be surprised if she had something to do with it."

"What proof do you have?"

"None, really. But somebody doesn't want me around." Gracie's voice cracked with tension. Tears threatened, but she blinked them back.

"Obviously the attacker wasn't your aunt." The woman stood and paced to the front window. She turned to face Gracie. "All right, I guess you'd better lay out the rest of your suspicions and let us handle it from here, Mrs.

Andersen." Investigator Hotchkiss returned to her seat at the dining room table.

Just then, Cheryl opened the kitchen's screen door.

"Sorry to interrupt, but I baked a couple blueberry buckles this morning, and I thought you might like some." She carried a cake pan, and the aroma of warm blueberries filled the kitchen and dining room. Her face blanched when she saw Gracie.

"Oh, Gracie, are you OK? Jim didn't tell me you were so..."

"So scary? Really, I'll be fine, but I guess I don't look the greatest and won't for awhile." Gracie had only glanced at her bruised and cut face this morning in the mirror. The cuts were pretty superficial, but the bruising would probably take two or three weeks to disappear.

"Thanks for the cake, Cheryl. It really smells good."

"Uh, right. Well, I'll leave it here on the counter. Or do you want me dish it up?"

"Just leave it on the counter. We'll get it. Tell Marian I'll be fine. I'll be out this afternoon."

Cheryl turned and quickly left for the kennel. The screen door closed with a click.

"Let's get back to your suspicions, Mrs. Andersen." Investigator Hotchkiss seemed anxious to wrap up the interview.

"It's clear to me that Isabelle is involved in all of it. She's the perfect daughter, and she was her mother's favorite. Isabelle would do anything to please her mother. It's always been that way. Isabelle despised her father. He was an embarrassment because of his drinking, and he gave *me* Charlotte's papers. He really didn't want Isabelle to know about it, but she found out. If Isabelle had something to do with Charlotte's death, then her father was a liability and so am I."

"Anything else?" The investigator was scribbling furiously on her pad. Marc had gone to the kitchen and brought the cake to the table.

"Plates are in the cupboard to the right of the sink, and forks are in the drawer below." Gracie directed him. "The other information I have is the partial license plate that Matthew Minders gave the sheriff's department the night Charlotte was killed. I was able to get some old insurance reports from the Stroud Insurance Agency. My aunt's license plate number from that time is pretty close to the one that Matthew gave. I think that Isabelle saw a chance to help her mother out and..."

"That's a pretty serious accusation, Mrs. Andersen. A sister killing her sibling because she's pregnant? To please her mother? It's a little hard to believe." The investigator frowned as she looked up from her notes to Gracie.

"Look at the insurance report for yourself. The plate number is very close to the partial that was reported. The car belonged to Shirley Browne. My cousin could have easily used that car when she was home from college, and she was home the weekend Charlotte was killed. Why did my aunt close down the investigation? I think she knew what Isabelle had done and didn't want it to go any further. It could only lead back to her door and more embarrassment." Anger rose in Gracie's voice.

"I suppose that could be the case, but what about the father of Charlotte's baby? Where does he fit into the picture?" Marc took a generous bite of the warm blueberry cake.

"I don't know who the father was, deputy, but Charlotte was seeing a couple of guys during that time period. The people I've talked with don't know anything about the father. She kept that detail to herself and didn't put it in the diary either. I did make contact with one of Charlotte's close friends. She may know, or at least, have a better idea."

"What about your Uncle Stan? Do you think that Isabelle killed her own father too?" Marc questioned her.

"It's possible. He left the message for me the night he was killed. Isabelle could have easily pushed him down the stairs. He wasn't very well, and he wouldn't have suspected Isabelle would actually harm him. Unless it was Joe's buddies. Did you find out about them?" Her head was aching along with her body. She needed to get up and move. Her body screamed in the simple motion of standing, and she grabbed the table to steady herself.

"Hey, Gracie, you really need to be lying down on the couch at least. The doctor was pretty serious about that." Marc was quick to gently guide her toward the couch. He smelled of woodsy cologne that was clean and comforting.

"I know, and I think I'm going to take his advice." She eased herself onto the deep sofa and lay down.

"Joe's buddies' alibi checked out. They *were* at a bar that night and it's on video. The bartender also remembered them. They were there the whole night, until closing time, past the time your uncle was killed," the investigator answered, shutting her notebook.

"Then you really need to get Isabelle to talk. I don't think I'm going to be safe until we find out how Charlotte really died."

"Mrs. Andersen, we're going to reopen your cousin's case, but I'm going to need your notes and these other documents. Do you mind?" Investigator Hotchkiss pointed to the pile of paper on the table.

"Please take them. Find out who killed Charlotte and my uncle. I think I know whose house you'll end up at." Gracie grimaced to find a more comfortable position.

"We'll do our best to get to the bottom of it. Thanks for your time." The investigator left with her arms full of paper. Marc waited until she was walking down the steps.

"Gracie, we *will* find out who did this to you. I promise." He bent over and lightly kissed her forehead. The brush of his lips gave her a peaceful feeling as she drifted into sleep.

The next couple of days were a blur to Gracie. People came and went. Reluctantly, she took the pain medication and made herself walk around the yard to stretch her stiff and aching muscles. The bruises turned colors, and the cuts scabbed over. She didn't look good, but she was alive. Her mother's stylist had come over on the second day and repaired the pink stripe in her hair. At least something was going right. Jim had the agility course put together, and she'd even watched several Border Collies zip through it with their owners.

Even though Marc assured her that everyone was working overtime on her attack, she wanted to bypass law enforcement and confront Isabelle. Gracie was tired of tiptoeing around. Cabin fever was pushing her to take a drive into town, but Jim had taken her keys, so she was effectively under house arrest. He knew her all too well. Her parents were sleeping in the guest bedroom, and the sheriff's department had a very visible presence day and night. Marc stopped off Thursday morning with a half dozen of Midge's sweet rolls, and the church ladies came by with soup and homemade bread.

On Thursday afternoon, Jim strode through the screen door without knocking. The door slammed, waking Gracie.

"Are you decent?"

Still foggy, Gracie mumbled, "I guess."

"Look what I found in the kibble bin today." He held a rectangular black remote control with two stubby prongs.

"What's that?" Gracie tried to focus on what Jim wanted her to see.

"You know what this is. It's a cattle prod."

"How'd that get in the kibble bin?" Rising from the sofa, she grabbed the device from his hand. "We don't have any cattle prods."

"I think we need to ask our former employee, Beth, about that." Jim's jaw was clenched, his eyes uncharacteristically angry.

The cobwebs were clearing as she realized what Jim was telling her.

"No wonder Barney bit her, if she used that on him. I don't have a doubt Frank would have at least couple of these." Frank and Evie Simmons raised beef cattle as their main source of income. The prod was a useful tool when they were penning and loading the cattle on trailers for the weekly livestock auction. "Beth was pretty intimidated by bigger dogs. I don't want to believe she'd use that on sweet Barney." Now fully awake, Gracie was outraged that a dog in her care had been hurt intentionally.

"I'm going to talk to Frank." Jim left before Gracie could get another word out. She had a feeling Jim would get to the bottom of their lawsuit problem very quickly. Within two hours, Nathan Cooke, Esquire called to inform his clients that the Simmons family was dropping the suit. There were some details to work out, but he'd have the necessary paperwork within a few days. Good job, Jim. Gracie was suddenly feeling much better.

By Friday, Gracie had had enough of incarceration. She'd sent her parents home, and hauled her bruised carcass back to the kennel. Marc called her to let her know there were a couple of real developments in her attack, and he was on his way to talk to her about it. He couldn't get there soon enough. The phone rang seconds after she'd hung up with Marc.

It was Kelly Standish. Since their mid-week dinner plans had been postponed, Gracie was anxious to pick Kelly's brain.

"I hope you're feeling better." Kelly's tone was concerned.

"I am, but the bruises have started to turn colors now. I'll be pretty strange looking for a while longer." Gracie looked down at her arms, which were yellowy and purplish, mixed in with her generous sprinkling of freckles.

"How are the police doing on finding the person who attacked you?"

"No word yet, although they think they have made some progress. You know, I wanted to talk a little bit more about Charlotte. Do you have a few minutes?"

"Sure, I'm on a short break right now."

Gracie was itching to ask if Kelly knew the father of Charlotte's baby. Although Matthew Minders denied even getting a date with Charlotte, he seemed to be a close friend. Maybe a friend with benefits. And then there was Galahad, the English teacher. Was it possible he was the father?

"Do you remember Matthew Minders or any other guys hanging out with Charlotte that summer through October?"

"Well, Matt was around a lot. He was like a puppy dog following Char. Nice guy, but a little too tame for her, I think. He took her home almost every day. There were guys from our class who were interested, but I don't think she was." Kelly paused, "You know, Char did talk about a guy, but she never said his name. She called him Lancelot or maybe it was Galahad, but she wouldn't tell me his real name. She had a pretty big crush on him when cheerleading practice started, but by the beginning of October, she didn't talk about him at all. Char told me she was pregnant about a week before she was killed. She hadn't been herself, and she was sitting the bench with a sprained ankle or something. I remember her sister coming to practice, and they got into a big scene."

"What were they fighting about?"

"I don't know, but Char's sister said something about doing the right thing for the family, and Char said, well, something not so complimentary about the family."

"Did you ever talk to her about that 'discussion' with her sister?"

"Never got the chance. That was the night she was killed."

"Oh." Gracie swallowed hard. "Do you know who Charlotte went home with that night?"

"It was Matt. Charlotte left the locker room without talking to anybody. I ran after her to see if she was OK, but Matt was walking her to his car. He had his arm around her, and I could tell she was crying."

Why hadn't Matthew mentioned that to Gracie? Maybe he knew a few more details, and he wasn't telling for some reason. He found Charlotte. He saw the license plate. Just maybe the preacher's son didn't want her to find out all the details. The trail to Charlotte's killer was taking a new path for her. A rap on the office doorframe startled her and she looked up to see Marc.

"Hey, Kelly, a deputy is here, and I need to go. I'd like to talk with you some more if you have time."

"Sure, Gracie. Give me a call tonight."

Gracie motioned for Marc to come in as she hung up the phone.

Chapter 30

Marc's "developments" were unsatisfactory to Gracie. The sheriff's department believed Gracie was most likely attacked by a man and not a woman. There had been a report of an attempted rape at the Lower Falls cabin area the previous weekend and a peeping Tom report at another area campsite. Their theory was the unknown male attacker and/or peeper was still lurking in the park. Isabelle's alibi of taking her children to the airport for out-of-state camps had checked out. Greg was in Massachusetts at a football camp, and Anna was in Virginia attending an exclusive D.A.R. History camp. Poor Anna. It was unlikely Isabelle had time to get back from the airport and find Gracie in the park to try and kill her. Apparently, they didn't know her cousin like she did.

"How would Isabelle know where you were anyway?" Marc was obviously irritated that Gracie wasn't joyful about the possibility of her cousin's innocence.

"Most likely, my mother. My parents live just down the street from Isabelle, and they talk all the time. Plus, keeping a secret in Deer Creek is like collecting rainwater in a sieve. No one's life is all that private." Gracie got up from her chair and paced the living room.

"Apparently, there are some secrets in this place." Marc's face was unreadable as he stood to leave.

"Sorry if I'm not more excited about what you've found out. I know that I was attacked because of Charlotte. It has everything to do with that and not with some would-be rapist in the park."

"We haven't found that connection yet, but like I said, we're still working on a few other pieces of information. The insurance report and—"

Gracie cut him off.

"I appreciate that, but I think you should talk to Dr. Kelly Standish at the vet clinic. She told me some things today that could help you."

Gracie wasn't ready to name any more names. She wanted to see for herself if Matthew Minders was still in town, and if no one was taking her seriously, then she'd do her own investigating. She also needed to try and find Bryan Murdock. What if Matthew was Galahad or even Lancelot? What had her cousin been doing with all these guys? If Marc talked to Kelly, then maybe he'd start connecting the dots, as she had.

"OK then. How do I get in touch with her?"

Gracie quickly scribbled the clinic's number on the message pad by the phone.

"Here's the number. I just talked to her a few minutes ago."

"All right. I'll call her. And by the way, you *are* looking better, even if you are multi-colored." He grinned and swept up his hat from the dining room table, placing it on his head.

"Thanks, I think. And thanks for the report. I do appreciate what you're doing." Gracie grinned back.

It still hurt to smile. There was a moment when she wished he would grab her and kiss her hard, but then she winced inwardly, deciding it would probably be painful. That would have to wait for another day. Now she wanted to get to town and do a drive-by of the parsonage.

When she saw Marc's cruiser disappear over the small knoll on Simmons Road, she grabbed the keys to the SUV. Haley was already at the door, panting and wagging.

"All right, I'll take you. I probably need the protection, although I don't think killing raccoons qualifies you."

Gracie drove slowly from the yard, hoping the dogs wouldn't alarm significantly to get Jim's attention. She really didn't need a chaperone or any more safety speeches for single women. Looking in the rearview mirror, she determined that she'd made a clean getaway.

Main Street was quiet for a Friday afternoon. It was right before the bank and the other scattered businesses would be closing for the weekend. Midge's only had a few cars, but within an hour, there would be a line out the door. Haley was already sleeping on the back seat. Not a sign of a great guard dog. Labs weren't known as reliable protection anyway. They're just not built that way. Gracie drove toward the Village Park, taking Maple to swing around the block, rather than turning off Main onto Park. That way, she could cruise a little less conspicuously past the parsonage.

She struggled with the thought of Matthew stalking Charlotte and possibly fathering her baby. It wasn't the Matthew she'd known growing up. But then she didn't think he'd withhold information about Charlotte after all these years either. How could he live with himself? He had a family. He was the minister's son, but maybe he had gone off the deep end for some reason. Had he been tired of rejection? Had Charlotte pushed him, or was there another trigger?

Gracie drove slowly down Park Street. Matthew's minivan was parked next to his parents' sedan. She could see two children playing in the shady backyard of the parsonage. The old rusty swing set she remembered playing on as a kid, with its red and white striped poles, was still in use. Matthew hadn't left town after all. Her stomach felt queasy. Why was he still here?

Gracie's cell phone began ringing. While she dug in her tote bag to find the phone, she made a quick U-turn and parked around the corner on Maple, out of sight of the parsonage. It was Marc.

"Gracie, where are you? I've been trying to call your house."

"I got a little cabin fever, so I'm just driving around."

"Gracie, you really need to go home. I'll meet you there." His voice was tense and humorless.

"All right. All right. Is this about my cousin? Do you finally have something on her?" Gracie was actually hoping that it was about Isabelle and not Matthew.

"It's not what you think. Just go.... now." Marc's voice faded, and the connection ended.

"Figures, the call would drop." She threw the cell phone back into the bag and pulled out into the street. Haley sat up on the backseat and pressed her nose against the closed window. She panted in Gracie's ear as the SUV headed for home.

The kennel was already closed when Gracie pulled into the driveway. With no pickups this afternoon, Jim had given the dogs their supper early and sent Marian and Cheryl home. He had an important date with Laney. They were going to Rochester for a fancy dinner and then to a concert. Jim must be truly smitten to get dressed up and actually get out of Deer Creek.

The house was quiet as Gracie dropped her keys on the kitchen counter. Now she'd have to wait for Marc. This had better be good. Haley bounded to the patio door, begging to be let out.

"Hang on, girl. I'll let you out in just a second."

She opened the door, and Haley ran onto the lawn, stopping to roll on the grass before heading toward the hydrangeas. Before Gracie could close the door, a strong hand covered her mouth and dragged her backward into the living room. She twisted and tried to swing around to see her attacker, but the other arm caught her by the throat and pulled her away from the door. Gracie's body was in overload with pain and fear as she struggled to pull the arm away from her throat. She tried to get a deep breath, but it was impossible. With a violent jerk, she lunged, put her chin down, and bit the strangling arm.

"Ahh, you stupid…"

The adrenaline rush helped her momentarily forget the throbbing pain coursing through her arms as she grunted and broke free. Tim Baker faced her, panting and rubbing his bleeding arm. He lunged and grabbed her long hair, slamming her to the floor. Gracie felt disoriented staring into Tim's dark, enraged eyes. He was a man who'd lost control. She didn't know this Tim Baker. His breath was heavy with liquor as he glowered over her. She noticed a V-shaped gash on his right cheek. Blood was smeared toward his hairline. His hands were pressed on her windpipe, and she felt herself slipping into unconsciousness. Gracie knew she didn't have the strength to fight back. It was useless. She heard Haley growl, and the pressure on her throat suddenly lessened. Tim struggled to get off Gracie. Haley had nailed the seat of his pants. Tim pushed away from Gracie, kicking and cursing Haley, who yelped and jumped away as Tim's foot landed on her flank. Gracie rolled toward the coffee table, frantically looking for any kind of weapon while Tim was distracted with the dog, who nipped at his leg. He punched Haley's chest, knocking the dog's front legs out from under her. The big dog dropped to the floor like a sack of potatoes.

"Get up, Tim." Isabelle's voice was measured and calm.

Gracie got up on all fours to see her cousin standing over Tim, holding a pistol at his head.

"I said, get up." Isabelle's face was cold, and her eyes glittered with anger. Every blond hair was in place, and the expensive, hand-embroidered blue shorts outfit looked freshly pressed.

"Isabelle, you don't want to do this." Tim's voice was suddenly penitent as he sat rubbing his right leg, examining the tears in his pants.

"I'm doing something I should have done long ago. You seduced my sister, got her pregnant, and then killed her. I'm tired of your threats, and I'm tired of keeping promises to my mother. You killed my father, coerced me into covering for you, and now you're trying to kill my cousin. You're not going to get away with anymore. I don't care what I have to do."

Gracie gulped for air, horrified at the scene unfolding in her living room. She could only croak weakly for Haley. The dog was breathing, but not getting back up. Tim's arm suddenly struck like a snake and grabbed his wife's well-tanned leg, pulling her off balance. Isabelle squealed in surprise and tumbled backward to the carpeted floor, the gun falling from her hand. Tim stood, a frightening smile smeared across his face.

"Your mother thought she was protecting you, not me all these years. You're the one who had an 'accident' the night Charlotte died," Tim gloated. "I set her straight the day she died. She was pretty upset."

He picked up the gun and shoved it into his pants. His left foot was pressed against Isabelle's throat. Isabelle grabbed Tim's left leg with both hands. He shook her off, and then with a flourish, pulled her up.

"Stand up, my dear. There are a lot of things you don't know, and now you and your sweet cousin will leave this world without finding out. What a shame. If Gracie had minded her own business, we'd still be living the good life, so you can blame her."

Tim pulled the gun out of his pants and pointed the barrel at Isabelle. He motioned to Gracie to join her cousin on the sofa.

"Put the gun down, Mr. Baker."

Marc was somehow standing in the living room, his Glock aimed at Tim. Gracie hadn't heard even the squeak of the screen door.

"Well, ladies, I guess the cavalry has arrived." Tim laughed and swung the pistol toward the deputy.

Chapter 31

Gracie spread a red-checkered tablecloth over the rough-hewn picnic table and looked toward the Middle Falls, spilling in beautiful ferocity down into the Genesee River. A perfect day, and from all appearances, a normal one too. Families played Frisbee, and kids chased each other on the broad lawns of the Middle Falls picnic area in Letchworth Park. Haley slept soundly on her back under the shade of the picnic table. The sturdy Lab had recovered from her nasty encounter with Tim. She had a deep chest bruise, but otherwise seemed to be fine. Haley sported a new shiny tag on her collar that read "World's Greatest Dog."

A small caravan of vehicles pulled into the parking lot— her parents, Jim, and then Marc. They were lined up in a neat row next to Gracie's RAV4.

Laney stepped out of Jim's pickup. She was carrying a large foil-covered dish, and Jim was lugging a cooler. She had long black hair that swung easily at her waist. Tanned and graceful, she had an easy smile and exuded confidence.

Marc and her father hauled two more coolers to the table. Her mother toted her classic harvest-gold Tupperware cake carrier. Serious picnicking was about to begin.

After the past week, normalcy seemed abnormal and numbing. Tim had died a day after surgery with a gunshot wound to the chest. His funeral had been a private family affair. Isabelle said she'd only gone for Greg and Anna's sake. Tim's parents and two brothers and their families had barely spoken after the short service performed by Rev. Minders. How do you bury a murderer? Gracie had a new respect for her longtime pastor. He had done it with a grace and simplicity that even brought a measure of comfort to Gracie.

The last week had also given Gracie some real time to sort out a lot of emotions and baggage she'd carried since Michael had died and she had lost their baby. She still ached for them, but she'd finally begun the process of forgiving herself—for finding Michael too late to help him, and for the fall that caused the miscarriage when she was scrambling up the steep bank to get her cell phone from the SUV. After two attempts on her life, Gracie also had come to grips with the reality that her life meant something, and just maybe, she needed to get on with living.

She watched Laney and Jim and saw a comfortable relationship, one reminiscent of her own with Michael. Jim and Marc pulled out gloves from a beat up duffle bag, along with a softball. Laney laughed and talked with Theresa as they laid out plates and silverware. Her father was cleaning the grill and making sure the fire was just right to grill the burgers.

Marc looked relaxed in khaki Bermudas and a blue T-shirt. He threw the softball with a practiced arm. He was on mandatory administrative leave for another week while the details of Tim's death were officially determined. There was no question he'd be cleared of any wrongdoing. Besides Isabelle and Gracie, Investigator Hotchkiss and another deputy were present when Marc pulled the trigger. Tim had decided in a split second on his own fate—suicide by cop. From his twisted viewpoint, he was tying up the messy story into a neat package for his family. There was too much he didn't want to face.

Gracie shook her head at the rampant mis-communications and sorry concept of right and wrong that some of her family members had. Tim, the handsome and charming college man, had seduced a willing Charlotte, promising that he loved her and not Isabelle. When she turned up pregnant, Tim was livid, accusing her of trying to trap him into marriage. All the power had suddenly shifted to Charlotte and it was unacceptable. His fling had gone seriously awry. He demanded that Charlotte get an abortion, which she refused to do. He then threatened her with harm if she told anyone who the father was. Charlotte had already told her father about the pregnancy, and Tim was afraid that she'd told him the whole story. Tim had gotten Isabelle to come home with him that awful weekend on the pretense that he wanted to ask for her hand in marriage. He decided to take one more crack at Charlotte over that Friday night. He waited for her to leave the babysitting job and followed Charlotte up the street. He tried to get her in the car, but she ran away from him. When she crossed Main Street, he saw his opportunity and hit the accelerator—hard.

Isabelle had been out visiting friends that same night and had hit a deer on her way home. The front end of the car was a mess, but the deer had managed to get away. Isabelle had come home hysterical after her accident. Then they had received the phone call about Charlotte. Shirley and Stan had labored under the misconception that Isabelle must have accidently killed her own sister. In an attempt to hush up the pregnancy and the possibility of Isabelle receiving jail time, they had effectively discouraged the investigation, pleading emotional distress. If Isabelle had accidently killed her sister, they didn't want the police to find out and run the risk of losing both daughters. It was something Shirley and Stan couldn't contemplate.

Gracie's instinct about the license plate proved correct. Although she intended to implicate her aunt or cousin, Investigator Hotchkiss discovered Tim's car had a similar vanity plate at the time. A little further investigation into the insurance records showed that Tim's car had been in a "deer accident" the same night. A collision shop in Buffalo had made repairs a week after Charlotte's funeral.

Isabelle hadn't really understood her parents' suspicions over the years. It was only when her father had given Gracie all of Charlotte's papers, and Tim became increasingly agitated, that she began her own investigation. When she found her mother's diaries full of fears and suspicions in Tim's desk, Isabelle was desperate at first to preserve her lifestyle. She eagerly gave Investigator Hotchkiss information about Gracie's temper to keep her cousin in the hot seat.

Tim had confessed to Stan's murder and the attack on Gracie at Inspiration Point as he lay in the hospital bed. He was actually proud of his prowess as a killer and the ease in taking his father-in-law's life. He'd walked in on Stan as he was leaving the message on Gracie's machine. Stan had tried to get upstairs to his bedroom to lock Tim out, but it only took seconds to choke Stan and throw him down the stairs for good measure.

After the porno ticket was found, Tim knew it was only a matter of time. Isabelle knew about Tim's little diversion and the trips he took on Friday afternoons. His debit card also showed he bought gas in Geneseo, just minutes before the matinee. She had painstakingly gathered the online banking records and turned that piece of information over to the sheriff's department. Expecting her husband's arrest, she'd sent Greg and Anna out of town. Tim had become increasingly abusive, and Isabelle was afraid for her own safety.

Everything had blown up Friday afternoon. Isabelle called 9-1-1 after Tim had attacked her while she was working in her flower gardens. She'd hit him with a trowel, and he'd taken off. Isabelle guessed where he was headed and followed her husband to Gracie's before the police could get to Milky Way.

Gracie rubbed the bruises on her arm. They were finally disappearing. Life just might finally settle down. Marc came up and put his arm around her. His touch was light and comforting.

"Feeling any better?"

"I think so, but it all still makes my head spin."

"It probably will for years to come," her father said as he put thick burgers on the grill. "It's not easy for any of us to understand. If only Shirley and Stan had confided in us. We could have helped."

"I don't know about that. It was hard for Aunt Shirley to ever be wrong. I still can't believe Isabelle actually came to my rescue."

"Blood is thicker than water," Theresa piped up.

"Yeah, but I've never been sure that we were actually related."

"When the cards are down, family comes through." Theresa's eyes were bright with emotion.

"All right, but what will she do now? What will those poor kids do?" Gracie already felt Greg and Anna's pain of returning to high school and trying to explain about their father, the crazed murderer.

"I think she's going on an extended cruise with them," her mother said as she placed a large bowl of tossed salad on the table.

"A cruise? With Isabelle? I'm not sure that would be my idea—"

"And what would your idea of a good time be?" Jim shot back before Theresa could say the same to her daughter.

"A week off, sleeping in every day, and having someone wait on me hand and foot."

"That's a cruise, Gracie, and just so you can make plans now, your mother and I have booked one for you in September. When Jim gets back from his fishing trip, you can go." Her father was smiling, but his tone was reminiscent of one of her many childhood scoldings.

"By myself?"

"Take a friend, or you can take me, if you want," Theresa's eyes twinkled.

"I'll think about it. Who knows what'll happen by September? We have to get through the church's chicken barbecue next week, Deer Creek Fun Days, Pike Fair, the dog match, and—" Gracie's mind whirled at the thought of her upcoming schedule.

"I think it's a great idea, Gracie." Laney released Jim's hand and walked toward her. "It's relaxing and a lot of fun."

"I agree, but there's way too much to do at the kennel."

"It can be handled, Gracie," Jim quickly jumped into the conversation.

"The trip is five weeks away. That's plenty of notice for you." Her father turned the burgers on the grill. "Plus when you get back, Tom should be home. They're kicking him out of Afghanistan." Bob grinned broadly.

"Tom? He's coming home?" Gracie's heart suddenly felt pounds lighter. Her brother was finally coming home, and it was two months earlier than expected.

"His email came today, and he'll be home mid-September. He says he's bringing home a surprise." Her father flipped the burgers with a flourish onto the waiting buns his wife held out to him on a large white platter.

"A surprise, as in presents, or something else?" Gracie's curiosity was piqued now.

"We can talk about this later. We're ready to eat." Theresa said firmly.

ৡৡৡৡৡ

The church was filled close to capacity, but this time, it was for Sunday morning worship and not a funeral. Rev. Minders peered over his reading glasses in surprise at the large congregation. He hadn't seen a Sunday morning like this in ages. His wife looked at him from her front pew with the same bewilderment. He hoped he'd prepared the right sermon for this crowd, and he prayed that someone else hadn't died. These last three weeks had been the most exhausting of his 40 years in the pastorate. No wonder he'd had an angina attack right after Tim Baker went on his rampage. He was thankful Matthew had been home at the time to help. It was good to have family around.

Wonder of wonders, Jim Taylor was in the back row with a lovely woman on his arm. Midge was there, sitting next to Mrs. Youngers, who sniffed into her tissue and wiped her eyes every few minutes. Midge hadn't darkened the door of the church since her husband had left her, and poor Mrs. Youngers was suffering over her oldest grandson Joe yet again.

Gracie stood with the congregation when the organ trumpeted the opening measures to the *Doxology*. There was a hand on her arm, and Marc slid into the pew beside her. Theresa and Bob smiled brightly at their daughter and then at each other. Gracie joined the voices for the first time in a long time. It was then she decided that a cruise was a great idea.

ACKNOWLEDGMENTS

There's no place like Wyoming County in rural Western New York for its natural beauty, especially the "Grand Canyon of the East," Letchworth State Park. Small town life is the best, where people still check on their neighbors, and show up to help. I'm grateful for being able to grow up in such a community and raise my family there.

Thank you for reading Family Matters. I hope you enjoyed the first mystery in the Gracie Andersen mystery series. If you have a moment, please post a quick review of *Family Matters* online and help other mystery fans discover Gracie too!

–Laurinda Wallace

ABOUT THE AUTHOR

Laurinda Wallace lives in the beautiful high desert of southeast Arizona where the mountains and fabulous night skies inspire risk taking. A native of Western New York, she loves writing about her hometown region including Letchworth State Park. A lifelong bookworm and writer, she made her foray into the publishing world in 2005. She's contributed to a variety of print and online magazines, and along the way created the Gracie Andersen mysteries, and more.

Visit **www.laurindawallace.com** for more information and be sure to sign up for the Mystery Mavens Society. Subscribers receive free short stories and insider book news. Your email is never shared or sold.

Books by Laurinda Wallace

The Gracie Andersen Mysteries

Family Matters

By the Book

Fly By Night

Washed Up

Pins & Needles

The Mistletoe Murders

True-Crime Memoir

Too Close to Home: The Samantha Zaldivar Case

Inspirational

The Time Under Heaven

Gardens of the Heart

Historical Fiction Short Story

The Murder of Alfred Silverheels

Historical Mystery

The Disappearance of Sara Colter

Made in the USA
Monee, IL
01 November 2020